CHILDREN OF EDEN

ALSO BY JOEY GRACEFFA

In Real Life: My Journey to a Pixelated World

CHILDREN OF

EDEN

A NOVEL

JOEY GRACEFFA

New York Times Bestselling Author

WITH LAURA L. SULLIVAN

Keywords
PRESS

ATRIA
New York London Toronto Sydney New Delhi

First published in Great Britain in 2016 by
Keywords Press an imprint Simon & Schuster UK Ltd
A CBS COMPANY
This paperback edition published 2018

First published in the USA in 2016 by Keywords Press an
imprint of Simon & Schuster, Inc.

5 7 9 10 8 6 4

Simon & Schuster UK Ltd
1st Floor, 222 Gray's Inn Road
London WC1X 8HB

www.simonandschuster.co.uk

Simon & Schuster Australia, Sydney
Simon & Schuster India, New Delhi

A CIP catalogue record for this book
is available from the British Library.

HB ISBN 978-1-4711-6050-9
PB ISBN 978-1-4711-7355-4
eBook ISBN 978-1-4711-6051-6

Printed and bound by CPI Group (UK) Ltd, Croydon, CR0 4YY

Dedicated to those whose imagination makes this world a more beautiful place: Never stop dreaming. And to my readers, who turn my dreams into reality.

1

"GIVE ME MORE!" I insist, pounding my fist on the gleaming steel of the outdoor dining table. Above us, the stars glimmer through the nanoparticle haze that keeps us safe from the ruined atmosphere. Across the table from me, my brother Ash's eyes twinkle.

"The priests say our ancestors ruined the planet that way, Rowan. More, more, always more, until the Earth couldn't give any more and she died." He grins. He's teasing me, I know, but I see the secret shudder that always makes his body tremble when he thinks of the Ecofail. He is an avid temple-goer, and spends hours on his knees in penance for the acts of our ancestors. Not that it does much good. The atmosphere is as broken as ever, the world is dead, and only the tender care of the EcoPanopticon keeps us alive now. Praying will never make a tree grow in this world again. The Earth is dead, but we still survive.

Of course, I've never been to temple. Maybe if I had I wouldn't be such a cynic. But then, I haven't been *anywhere* in the last sixteen years. At least, not officially. You see, I don't exist.

I might as well be a figment of my twin brother's imagination. If I were, I think he would have gone inside and fallen asleep long ago. Figments are easier to shake than I am. Ash knows I never give up. Through long habit—and Mom's insistence—he is used to devoting a good chunk of every day to my persistent questions.

For a girl who doesn't exist, I can be a pain in the neck. Or so Ash tells me almost every day.

I smile wickedly at my brother. "More!" I tell him again. When he hesitates, I spring on him, toppling him backward. The chair thuds on the thick carpet of moss that my mother so carefully maintains. Ash tries to roll out of the way, but we're the same height, and much to his embarrassment I'm a little bit stronger than he is. "More!" I shout as I pin him down. "Tell me more!" I begin to tickle him, and he squirms until we are both near hysterical.

"That's enough," comes the gentle voice of our mother from the veranda. "Do you want the neighbors to hear?"

That quiets us quickly. Even though there is almost no chance of our laughter penetrating the high, thick stone walls around my family's compound, it would be a disaster if anyone knew I was here. Oh, Mom could probably pass the girlish laughter off as coming from one of Ash's visiting friends—even though we almost never have visitors. (When we do, I have to run to one of the many hidden nooks and walled-off secret chambers my parents have improvised all through the house.) But there is always the chance some nosy neighbor will check the regional scans and put two and two together. That would be the end of me. Literally.

I help Ash to his feet and sit down across from him. In a more decorous voice I do what I do every day: I beg him to tell me more about the world outside the family compound. I'm not just hungry for all the experiences I'm missing out on. I'm starving. Ravenous.

"What did Lark wear today when she changed out of her

school uniform?" Lark is the girl my brother has a crush on, and I'm fascinated with her. The way he describes her makes her seem so real to me, almost as if she were my friend, too. Almost as if I were a real person. I know that if we ever met, we'd be instantly close.

Every afternoon when Ash comes home I quiz him about every detail of his day. Academics I learn on my own from vids and datablocks. I'm more interested in the people. The tiniest details enrapture me. *Did your Environmental History professor flirt with the headmaster today? Did the autoloop attendant smile when she scanned your eyes on the way to school? Did Brook chew his lavercakes with his mouth open again?* These are the friends I will never have, and I love them all.

Unfortunately, Ash isn't always good at the details I crave. When I ask what Lark wore, he only says, "Er, something yellow."

"Bright yellow? Pale yellow?" I press eagerly. "Lemon or buttercup or sunshine?" Of course, no one has seen lemons or buttercups since before the Ecofail.

"I dunno, just kind of medium yellow, I guess."

"A dress?"

"Er . . ."

I fling myself dramatically back in the chair. "Ugh, you're useless!"

Ash, bless him, can never quite understand how all those things that are so trivial to him can mean the world to me. He does his best, he really does. But it's never good enough. Between the two of us we're trying to build a shadow life for a shadow girl. I have to be ready for the glorious day I will finally emerge into the light. *If* that day ever comes. Mom and Dad always assure me it will, someday. Sixteen years of assurances later, *someday* still hasn't arrived.

I look at my brother as he struggles to recall the details of his day so I can feel like I am a part of the real world. He is my mirror, almost exactly like me. He has the same night-dark hair, the strong chin softened by a dimple, the light bronze skin. He's told me that he doesn't like his face, that his features are too delicate for a boy. Maybe, if I knew more of the world, I'd think my face was too strong for a girl.

Our main difference is in our jaws, I think. In both of us they are sharply angled and strong. But when Ash worries about something, he works his jaw like he's chewing on the problem, like it's a tough nut he's trying to crack. (I learned about nuts in an Environmental History vid. Food, growing on trees—can you imagine?)

Me, when I'm upset my jaw gets tight and still. I just clench my teeth until the muscles in my cheeks ache.

Been clenching my jaw a lot lately.

There are two other obvious differences between us, other than our gender, of course. Ash's eyes are a flat reflective blue-gray, like our mother's. Mine are a strange, shifting color that seems to alternate from green to blue to gold, depending on the light. When I look closely in a mirror, I can see a starburst of amber in the middle of the blue, flecks and streaks like meteors shooting across an azure sky.

My eyes would give me away in a heartbeat, if anyone ever saw them. Soon after birth, children have their eyes corrected with lens implants. This is because human eyes have evolved to withstand exposure to certain wavelengths of light. Now that the atmosphere is damaged, we're exposed to increased low-band ultraviolet radiation, which can harm un-treated eyes. The surgery implants a filter that protects everyone's eyes from the rays. It takes a long time to cause damage, but if someone doesn't get the surgery they will eventually go blind. I haven't noticed any damage yet, but I'm told around thirty my vision will start to dim. The filter is coded to identify every resident of Eden with a quick scan.

Of course, I couldn't have the surgery, so my eyes are still their natural color. Sometimes when Ash looks at me too long I see him blink and shake his head, and I know that they unnerve him. My father, whose own eyes are dead brown like a wall, can hardly look at me.

The other difference between Ash and me wouldn't be apparent to anyone. He's older than me. Only by about ten minutes, but that's enough. It means that he is the official, legal child: the firstborn. I am the shameful second child who never should have come into this world at all.

Ash goes inside to finish his homework. My lessons, assigned by Mom and closely paralleling Ash's, were done hours before he even came home. Now, as the night deepens, I begin to pace restlessly around the courtyard. We live in one of the inner circles, just beyond the Center, because my parents are both in the government. It's a huge house, much bigger than we need. But whenever Dad talks about selling it, or dividing it into parcels to lease, Mom shuts him down. It's *her* house, inherited from her parents. Unlike most buildings in Eden, ours is made of stone. When I put my hands on it, I can almost feel the Earth breathing against me. It's alive, somehow. More alive, anyway, than the metal and concrete and solar cells that comprise the other buildings in Eden. These stones have been in dirt, I think. Real dirt, with worms, and roots, and life. None of us in Eden has experienced such natural circumstances.

The moss that carpets the walled courtyard is alive, but it isn't a real plant. It doesn't need dirt. It doesn't have roots, only threadlike anchors that help it cling to rock. It doesn't take its nutrients from the ground, but from the air. Like everything in Eden, it is separate from the Earth. Still, it is growing, living, and as my feet pace along its carpeted softness a sharp, fresh smell rises to meet my nose. If I close my eyes, I can almost imagine I'm in one of the forests that died almost two hundred years ago.

As chief archivist in the Central Records Division, Mom has access to the oldest records, the ones from before the Ecofail. My datablock lessons only have graphic illustrations of the way things used to be, but Mom told me that in the secret chambers of the archives there are images — ancient and crumbling — of tigers and lambs and palm trees and meadows full of wildflowers. They are so old and precious that they are kept in a static-free room and handled only with gloves.

She gave me one. She could have gotten locked up for doing so, but the photo would probably never be missed, and she thought I deserved something special, for my years in captivity. One day when she was going through the records she found an undocumented image of a night sky over a great chasm. Tucked behind another document, it was labeled with a date immediately before the Ecofail.

The stars don't look like anything I've ever seen. There are thousands of them, swimming in a milky sea, and beneath them I can make out the contours of trees clinging to the rocky ridge. It is a vastness I can scarcely comprehend. Eden is big, but I can bisect the city in an autoloop in half a day.

The ancient, folded image my mother smuggled out for me shows a world. The World, in fact. It is my most precious possession.

Because my mother has seen such things, she cherishes living organisms even more than most. The majority of households, Ash tells me, make do with cheerful, neon-green turf and plasticized trees. But Mom prefers to get as close as possible to the real thing, even if it isn't as pretty. Besides the moss, we have chunks of rock covered in white and pink lichens. A creeping black slime mold coils its way up an abstract sculpture. And at the center of the courtyard is a shallow pool where red and green sheets of algae swirl continuously in an artificial current.

Mine is a luxurious house, large and comfortable. But a large, comfortable prison is still a prison.

I know that I shouldn't think of it that way. Home should be thought of as a sanctuary, and the alternative to having a home is too horrible to even consider. But all the same, I can't shake my sense of entrapment.

With so many lonely hours to fill, I've learned to schedule my days tightly. Empty time leads to daydreaming, and daydreams are dangerous for a person in my position. Schoolwork, art, and exercise are all arranged in regular sequence so I don't have too much time to yearn for what I can't have.

Right now, it's too dark to draw or paint, and I feel as though I've read every book in the database. So I run.

In the dim starlight I can just make out the faint path where I run miles every day. The moss is resilient—that's why it is one of the few kinds of vegetation that survived the Ecofail—but even it loses its spring under the onslaught of my feet.

As I run, the steady hypnotic pounding centers me. I can feel the blood start to move more quickly through my veins. When I push my body I feel alive. Alive, when almost all of the world is dead. But what good is it to be alive when I'm trapped?

Frustrated, I run faster, taking the corners of the courtyard hard enough to kick up bits of moss. Mom will be mad, but I don't care. I am madder. Furious. Just because of some stupid law, I'm hidden away behind walls, a pariah who will be slaughtered or enslaved if I'm ever discovered.

Movement usually makes me feel better, but tonight it is torment. I am so sick of running in this same rectangle, clockwise, then counterclockwise. With a cry of frustration I begin to zigzag, sprinting faster and faster, jumping over the lichen-covered rocks, the chairs, leaping to the tabletop and springing off again.

All at once, I feel like I can't breathe. The high walls seem to close in on me, like a giant mouth about to crush me with stony teeth. I dash one way, then the other, crashing into the walls, pounding them with my fists, almost snarling in bitter frustration. I know I'm spinning out of control, but I can't help myself. Most of the time I'm somber, regulated, content. But sometimes, for reasons I don't quite understand, I become enraged at my situation.

It's the strangest thing, but what bothers me most is that Ash couldn't describe Lark's outfit. It's so stupid, so trivial, but it gnaws at me that, with all his privileges and freedom, he couldn't bother to take note of the one thing that mattered to me. Why does that little detail matter so much? I don't understand it. Ash does the best he can, and it can't be easy having to give up most of his social life so he can regale his secret sister with stories about the outside world. He must resent me sometimes.

Yet tonight, I resent him, and that makes me feel guilty, and even madder. At myself. At the Center and its laws that took everything away from me. Even at the EcoPan that keeps us all alive. I have to get away from these walls. I have to break free!

With an animal gasp of relief I begin to climb a wall, digging my fingers into the handholds I know so well, jamming my toes into crevices where the mortar has crumbled. I climb these walls as part of the physical conditioning my mother insists on. Almost every night I would pull myself up to the top, some thirty feet above the ground, and slyly peer over the edge.

Tonight, that isn't enough. Not nearly enough.

Without so much as a moment's hesitation I fling a leg over the rough stones and sit straddling the wall, one leg imprisoned, the other free. No one will see me; no one will look up. I'm feeling reckless as I gaze out at Eden stretched before me, its concentric circles looking like some strange glyph carved into the land.

Instead of trees, tall spires of algae protein synthesizers jut hundreds of feet above the highest building. The vibrant circles just beyond the Center are lit with bioluminescence that shows off the abundant greenery that carpets the city. Most of the city is equipped with artificial photosynthesis, engineered to act almost as real plants and convert the carbon dioxide we exhale into breathable oxygen. Some of it is like what Mom cultivates in our courtyard—hardy mosses and fungi, decorative algae swirling in liquid mediums. Even in the near-dark it is a green city.

If I didn't know better, I might be fooled into thinking that it is a thriving ecosystem instead of an artificial survival pod. What isn't green, glitters. Unlike our stone house, most buildings are made of polymers and coated in either clear or reflective photovoltaic panels that convert sunlight into energy to power our city. In the daylight, Eden shines like a giant emerald. At night, it looks more like a huge green eye, darkly bright with hidden secrets.

Past the rings of the luxurious inner circles comes the less elegant outer circle. Here in the inner circles, where we live just beyond the Center, the houses are large and fine. Nearer the boundary, though, houses grow smaller, more tightly packed. No one would ever starve in Eden—the EcoPanopticon makes sure of that—but from what Mom and Ash told me, life is not nearly as comfortable near the boundary as it is here, near the Center.

Even at this height I can't begin to see as far as the boundary of Eden, but I know from my lessons what lies there. Desert, burning and merciless. And beyond that, a wasteland far worse.

Compared to my courtyard, Eden is an infinity. It is so big, and I'm so small! The city teems with people. I'm just a particle in that cosmos of humanity. All my life I've only ever met three people. The idea of meeting anyone new frankly terrifies me even more than the very real possibility of being caught. Strangers seem like dangerous animals.

But in a world without life, I would risk being torn and rendered by fearsome fangs just for the chance to see a real live tiger up close. I would give anything, even my own life, to experience what I've been missing out on.

I've thought about going out so many times. There are days when I think of nothing else, when the lure of freedom consumes my thoughts and I can't draw, or study, or run. Now, tonight more than ever before, as I think about that one detail about Lark's outfit and how Ash doesn't know it and I don't know it and I may never know it, Eden seems to call me with its strongest voice yet, and though I'm terrified, I swing my other leg over the edge of the wall—my elation overpowering my terror.

2

AS I POISE on the precipice between safety and freedom, about to descend into the unknown, I hear a small sound: the melodious chime of three notes that announces someone is at our front door. *Bikk!* I curse under my breath. I freeze, and the air around me is suddenly cold. Did someone see me? Is it the Greenshirts coming for me? I try to steady my breathing. It's probably just a delivery, or maybe a messenger from the hospital, come to fetch my father for an emergency surgery.

Then Ash creeps into the courtyard. I see him look around, quickly, then when he doesn't immediately spot me, again more slowly. I whistle softly, a bird call I heard on a vid, and he looks up.

"You have to hide!" he hisses urgently. "He has a Center uniform on!"

My eyes fly open wide, and for a moment I feel like I'm pinned to the wall, immobile and helpless.

"Hurry!" Ash says, and even from up here I can tell he's panicking. It's only because I climb this wall every day that I can make my way down so fast. Even so, I push out and let myself drop the last few feet, landing in a light crouch.

"Who is it?" I ask as we sprint together to the house.

He only shrugs, and I hear a rasping sound as my brother breathes. Nerves and even this small amount of running are making his lungs act up.

"You have to go straight for your inhaler," I insist, suddenly more worried about him than myself.

He slows down, but shakes his head. "Gotta . . . get you safe," he gasps.

"No!" I say too loudly. "I'll be fine. But if you code out I *won't* be fine. Can you make it upstairs by yourself?" His breathing is ragged. These attacks, mostly brought on by stress, come only rarely. But every time it happens I'm sure I'm going to lose my brother. I force my face to stay calm, because I know that any kind of worry will only make him worse at this point.

He nods, not wanting to waste his breath on speaking.

"Okay, then. You go, and I'll use the wall hideout."

There are four hiding places in our large and sprawling house. The best of them, a small cellar, has a trapdoor that has to be closed from above and then concealed under a carpet and heavy chair. Next best is a secret recess in the wall behind a bookcase that looks immovable but can swing out on pneumatic gliders. Unfortunately, that mechanism has a design flaw in that it has to be operated from the outside. So both of those depend on someone outside to seal me in (and release me again).

That means I have to go either up to the attic—which is spacious and comfortable but also one of the first places someone would search—or into an insufferably narrow space between two walls. The gap, no more than a foot and a half wide, used to hold some kind of ventilation system that was modernized and moved at some point in the house's history. Now only the old air vent remains, and serves as an access port to a place that is so uncomfortable it makes torture sound like fun.

Ash is gasping now. I take his arm and guide him to the foot of the stairs that lead to his room. *Our* room, really. I have a bedroom of sorts, but there's nothing of my own in it. It's a guest room, which I make up every morning just as if no one has slept there in weeks. If anyone ever came to inspect the house, they'd find nothing more than a neat, generic bedroom waiting for a visitor.

For everything other than sleeping, Ash and I have more or less shared a room since childhood. Shared *everything*, really. Any personal possessions I have are in Ash's bedroom, hidden among his things. And they all look like things a boy might have. I can't have too many possessions of my own. Imagine if someone came in and found a bedroom with dresses, and holoposters of shirtless pop stars and all the other things other girls probably have in their rooms. Dead giveaway. Ash and I even share most of our clothes.

I don't want to let Ash go. He feels my hold on his arm tighten, sees the fear in my eyes I can't quite hide. I'm hardly even thinking about the unexpected visitor. "You go hide," he says in a raspy whisper. "I can make it."

I'm not sure he's right, but I don't have any more time to spare. I hear the quiet whine of the front door sliding open, and then the murmur of unfamiliar voices. With a final worried glance at Ash hauling himself up the stairs, I whirl and run for the closest sanctuary, hoping I'll be in time.

I have to crawl backwards on my belly through the low ventilation access door into an impossibly cramped space. If I go forward, I won't be able to close the door myself. I have only about an inch of clearance on either side. As I snap the door shut, I remember that I was running on moss, climbing on rocks just a moment before. Did I leave any telltale marks on the floor outside my hiding place? Too late to check now. I slither backwards on my elbows and toes, an inch at a time, for several feet, until I reach the place where the crevice opens up enough for me to stand.

It's a little better here, but not much. Unlike my other hiding spots, this one isn't built for any kind of comfort. It's an emergency bolt-hole. We run periodic drills, Mom timing me, to make sure I can access all four of my hiding places quickly. But I've never had to use this one before. It's the last resort.

I have room to stand, and that's about it. Each time I breathe, my chest and back press against the plaster of the wall. It smells odd in here, stale and close. I've gotten used to having a limited life, but this is a little extreme. My vista ends about three inches away from my eyes.

But I'm safe, hidden away. Just in time. I hear an unfamiliar voice coming nearer. I'm surprised I can hear it so clearly. The walls must be thinner than I thought. For a crazy second I think about knocking on the wall, sending a mysterious message like an unseen spirit. Mom has told me ghost stories, gleaned from records in the archives. In the days of ignorance, people believed in all kinds of things. I don't believe the old tales, though I've always liked hearing them. But if Ash is right, this is a Center official. They're known for having zero patience with superstition or anything to do with the way we lived before the Ecofail. Not to mention, of course, the whole threat-of-death thing if I'm discovered.

So I stand at attention in my narrow sliver of safety, upright and alert like a Greenshirt recruit, and wait for the all clear.

When I hear the distinctive sound of people settling themselves in our living room, I figure the all clear will be a long time coming. I sigh, and my breath bounces against the wall back to me, warming my face.

I don't know exactly what I'm expecting out of the unknown visitor. Probably something terse and official. Most likely, they've come by for some after-hours emergency, or what passes as an emergency. Maybe Mom needs to sign off on the duplication and distribution of some pre-fail artifact, or Dad has to authorize one of the restricted drugs for an upper-level Center official. Usually they message ahead, either calling on the unicom or sending a messagebot to herald their approach, giving me time to hide. What can be so urgent that it has to be a surprise?

Whatever I expect it's certainly not the sound of weeping from my mother. She sounds like she's right on the other side of this wall, and I actually take a step forward, stubbing my toe. Do they hear? No, I don't think so, because the stranger speaks. I hear him clearly through the wall.

"One week," he says. I frown in puzzlement. What is happening in a week to make Mom cry?

"So soon?" Mom asks, despair in her voice.

Dad immediately cuts in. "We've been waiting almost seventeen years," he says gruffly. "Not nearly soon enough if you ask me."

Almost seventeen years? Are they discussing something about me? They must be. Either me or Ash.

"You understand there have been difficulties," the stranger says, placating, though I can tell from his voice he must be a little annoyed, too. "Black market lenses are just the beginning. Half the criminals in Eden can get fake lenses that show another person's identity on a level-one scan. The problem is creating a new identity."

"We paid you enough," Dad snaps. "It should have been done long before now."

"Hush," Mom says to him. She sniffs hard, and I can tell she's trying to pull herself together. "Go on, Mr. Hill. Please tell us the rest."

"I don't care how he did it, as long as it's done," I hear my father say in an undertone. I can picture his face, impatient and peevish as it so often is, his eyes restlessly glancing side-long. "A week, you said? Why not sooner?"

I hear the doorbell chime, and Mom gasp, at exactly the same time, so I can't tell whether she is shocked by that, or by what my father has said.

"Are you expecting anyone?" the stranger asks in evident alarm.

I'm wedged in my tight nook, blind and stifled, but in my mind's eye I can see clear as day the way Mom and Dad exchange a quick look. Their relationship isn't always perfect, I know, but they do have that trick of silent communication. I've often wondered if other couples can do this, hold rapid unspoken conversations with a glance, and reach a conclusion without a word. I wonder now if I'll ever know someone that well.

I hear quick movement through the wall, and a startled sound from the stranger. I realize he's being hustled upstairs to my attic hideaway. Whoever he is, at least he'll be more comfortable than I am.

Mom rushes back a moment later, and when she talks in a hushed, urgent voice I realize Dad hasn't gone to answer the door yet.

"Will they find him?" she asks.

"How should I know?" he snaps. "I don't know who they are or what they want. Probably just someone from work."

Mom sighs in frustration at his optimism. "But why now, of all times? We should get him out of the house."

"He's a Center official," Dad counters. "Why shouldn't he be here? He could be my friend."

"No, they might be watching him. If he's involved in the

black market, we can't afford to be linked to him. Not when we're this close. They'll get suspicious."

"They'll get more suspicious if we don't open the door soon," Dad says, rightly enough.

"Where's Rowan? Did she make it to the basement?"

"I don't know, but she's sensible enough to stay out of sight until one of us comes for her. Go have a drink and join us in a few minutes. If anyone sees your face now, they'll know something's wrong."

I hear the heavy tread of his feet as he goes to the front door. The living room is completely still now, and I can hear the sound of my own breathing again. For a moment I think Mom has left, her lighter step unheard. Then I hear a little scratching on the wall just outside my nook. She knows I'm here. Or she thinks I'm here.

Gingerly, I scratch back, once, twice. I hear a gentle sigh from the other side, and I feel a love so overwhelming I would sit down if I had room. Dad has done whatever is necessary to keep me safe, but it's always been Mom who let me know that everything she did, everything she sacrificed for me, was done out of love, not obligation or fear or necessity.

She walks away with a deliberately heavy step so I will know she's gone. Still, in this moment, because of her love, I don't feel alone. I don't feel trapped. I feel safe.

But it isn't long before my sense of safety evaporates entirely. I hear the clump of multiple pairs of boots, and though I can't be entirely certain, I'd bet anything that they're Greenshirts, the police force of Eden.

Ash always makes a joke of the Greenshirts, telling me how they chase down kids who hijack the public lighting system to spell out rude words like *teezak* and *koh faz*, or break into the lichen gardens after hours with their girlfriends. Maybe the Greenshirts are benign to kids pulling childish pranks. But I know that they are really a deadly civil defense squad whose main purpose is to root out anything that goes against the survival mandates of the EcoPanopticon. And that's pretty much the definition of me.

Greenshirts patrol the streets and investigate any crimes that happen in Eden. They're more heavily concentrated in the outer circles, far from the Center where people are poorer and more desperate. But they're here in the inner circles, too. I've glimpsed them a couple of times from the top of the wall, stomping in black-booted pairs along the avenues. I always duck down quickly, and usually don't risk popping my head up again for a few days after every sighting. I've never been spotted, though, by them or anyone else. No one on the streets ever looks up, and I confine myself to the uncertain light of dusk and dawn.

Now there are almost certainly Greenshirts in my living room. What if they're here for me? Did someone spot my peeking head after all and grow suspicious? Could Ash have been careless and let a word drop into the wrong ears? If they have discovered my existence, I am hopelessly, helplessly trapped. There is only one exit out of this hiding place, and simply squirming out would be a struggle. I wouldn't have a hope of flight. I can picture their black boots waiting outside the grate, almost feel them grabbing me to drag me away to some awful, unknown fate . . .

There's some kind of bot with them, too. I hear the whir and beep of one of the smaller models. Is it a securitybot come to sniff me out? What is it doing here? Bots are nosy; they can be trouble.

Then I hear a silky voice speaking social pleasantries, its unique upper-class Center accent marking the speaker as one of the Eden elite. The voice sounds familiar, but I can't place it until Dad addresses him by his title.

"Please, have a seat, Chancellor," my father says, his voice more polite and deferential than I've ever heard it. As the physician general he is a high-ranking government minister himself, and looks down on most of Eden.

The bot rolls across the floor, coming closer to my hiding spot.

I've heard Chancellor Cornwall's voice on newsfeeds, seen the man himself on vids. I remember that wherever he appears, he has a cohort of Greenshirts standing guard behind him.

What is the head of the government doing in our house?

Part of me is starkly terrified. Another part is almost reassured. A hidden second child might be a serious, even capital offense. But it certainly doesn't warrant a visit from the leader of all Eden. He'd just send in a Greenshirt strike force to capture me. He wouldn't be standing in my living room while Dad ordered a servebot to fetch him a cup of fauxchai, the fragrant drink made of algae that is genetically modified to taste like pre-fail tea. He must be here for something really terrible, or really wonderful.

It turns out to be both, I think.

I listen, amazed, as Chancellor Cornwall tells my father that the current vice chancellor is resigning due to medical reasons.

"I'd be happy to examine him and offer a second opinion," my father ventures, but the chancellor ignores him.

"I believe you would serve Eden well as the next vice chancellor."

There is dead silence in the room. My father, who came from an outer ring of Inner City, has risen high in the government ranks to become physician general. It was mostly by his skill as a surgeon, I always thought. But apparently Dad has been playing a deeper political game than I ever realized. Why else would the chancellor notice him? My father makes occasional pronouncements about health, monitors public policy on mandatory sterility surgeries and vaccinations, and occasionally provides personal treatment to ranking members of the government and their families.

This is a surprise to me. Perhaps it is to Dad, too. He always seems to keep as low a profile as he can, given his position. By "position" I mean me, his shameful secret. He keeps his head down and doesn't socialize or network as much as other people in the government. He can't exactly host cocktail parties with me hiding in the cellar, can he?

But somehow, he's attracted notice.

The silence hangs too long. At last my father says, "I would be honored to serve Eden in any capacity." His voice is tight, and I wonder if it's from humility or nerves.

They speak of this awhile, and I listen, almost forgetting the first visitor, wondering what this will mean for my family. Will Dad have to move to the Center like all the uppermost Center officials? Will we? Impossible. My safety depends entirely on this house.

Then I hear the small bot roll across the room, pausing right near the vent. I hold my breath. Has it spotted something suspicious, some sign of my existence? I don't know what kind of bot it is, but if it is a variety with good visual acuity it might be able to actually see me if it scans directly into the tiny openings in the vent. It inches closer, and beeps. If a bot can sound uncertain, this one does.

Then the chancellor says, "I won't take up any more of your time now. Let me know what you decide by tomorrow morning." The Greenshirt guards wheel in formation. The chancellor snaps his fingers, the bot glides away after him, and the room is quiet. Though my legs are stiffening and the air is growing stale with my breath, I don't dare leave until I receive the all-clear signal. It takes so long I think they've forgotten about me.

When I scramble out, covered in a light dusting of plaster, Mom is waiting for me in the living room. She's alone.

I have so many questions, about the first Center visitor, about the chancellor, that I don't know where to start. But first, most important, is Ash. "He was having an attack. Is he okay?" My jaw is clenched tightly as I wait for the answer. It takes a long time coming. At first that makes me think it is going to be terrible news.

"I just checked on him, and he's resting comfortably," she says. I sigh with relief. Somehow, the rest doesn't seem to matter as much now. That feeling lasts for all of thirty seconds.

Mom looks at me in silence for a long moment.

"What's going to happen?" I finally blurt out. It is an all-encompassing question.

Mom's answer shakes me to my core. It's like all of my dreams and nightmares are coming true at once.

"They've made lenses with a new identity, Rowan." I wait for her to smile. She doesn't, and I tense. Mom pauses again, then says gently, "And they've found a new family for you. You leave in one week."

My legs give out and I sink to the floor, my back pressed against the very wall that hid me just moments before.

3

"NO," I SAY weakly. I've waited for the freedom to move all my life, and now . . . "No!" I cry again, smashing the back of my fist against the wall. Sorrow and anger are building inside me, fighting for control. I decide to let anger win for once.

"I won't do it!" I shout. "You can't make me leave this family. *My* family!" I jump to my feet and don't know whether to hug my mom or punch the wall or run for Ash or collapse again.

It was always a possibility. I've known that for years. But I always believed there would be another way.

I always believed my parents wouldn't let me leave them. Ever.

But there are only two fates for a second child. A life hidden away . . . or a life in a new identity.

Well, there is one more, the usual one. Termination after conception—or after birth. However long after birth the child is discovered.

When the Earth died just a little more than two hundred years ago, humanity was doomed along with every other higher animal on the planet. Everything bigger than a paramecium became extinct—and life probably wasn't all that good for the paramecia, either. Of course, we humans were the only ones who had it coming. It was our fault.

We were the only animals with brains clever enough and fingers agile enough to create nuclear power, to frack the Earth and poison the sea and spew out chemicals that would destroy the atmosphere. We, intelligent humans that we are, fiddled with the DNA of our crops to make a better soybean that could survive anything and feed the world—until that soybean proved so hardy and aggressive it took over the rain forests. We raised living things for food, forcing them to live as prisoners, walking in their own feces. So we dosed them with antibiotics—dosed our children, too—and then we were surprised when bacteria mutated into superbugs.

We killed the world and ourselves at the same time. The planet began to die. The Earth's temperature jumped ten degrees in a decade when greenhouse gases trapped the sun's heat, turning our planet into an oven. A team of scientists had a bright idea to inject a revolutionary new product into the atmosphere to fix it.

Can you guess how that went?

The Earth cooled, all right. But when the sun's radiation reacted with the new man-made atmosphere, it created a cascade reaction that killed nearly every plant and animal on the planet.

Except a few of us. Remember our big clever brains and agile hands? The best thing humans ever did with those assets was to create something smarter—and kinder—than us. When it became obvious that the Earth was going belly-up, a visionary created the EcoPanopticon, the all-seeing guardian of nature.

The EcoPanopticon is god and mother and physician and king to us now. We gave it power over us, because we could no longer be trusted with power ourselves. But we don't mind being ruled, because like a mother, the EcoPan's only goal is to keep us alive.

With our flesh and blood and weak fallible bodies, we didn't stand a chance in this harsh and terrible broken world. But all the things we created went along just fine without us. The man who came up with the idea of the EcoPan, Aaron Al-Baz, created an artificial intelligence that would link into every last bit of electronics and internet and communications that we left behind. It completely co-opted the systems we created—the power plants and reactors and factories that had destroyed the Earth in the first place—and turned them toward saving the planet. The EcoPan directed factories to make robots, every one of which was linked to its all-seeing global eye. The robots in turn created this sanctuary, Eden, for the few human survivors. At the same time, it went to work on repairing the devastation we'd wrought on the planet. Fixing the world to the point where it was safe for us to live in would take hundreds of years, though. In the meantime, we lived in this paradise that the EcoPan had made for us.

Except, as in every paradise, there are a few rules. Break them, and you get tossed out.

Because we are a completely closed system, our resources are severely limited. With no plants or animals left to eat, we subsist on the things that were tough enough to live through the Ecofail, like algae, fungi, and lichens, as well as synthesized proteins. Everything (and I mean everything—think about that) is recycled, reused, re-consumed. We've been in Eden for just shy of two hundred years, and we'll have to be here for at least a thousand more before Earth normalizes. So we have to be careful.

It's funny. Humans were almost wiped out, but too many survived. Too many to keep that kind of population alive in

Eden for a millennium. So EcoPan figured out our ideal sustainable population, the exact number of people that will keep us going until we can leave Eden. Until we reach that, our numbers have to be gradually diminished.

EcoPan, in its wisdom, decreed that there can only be one child born for every two living people of fertile age, until we reach the ideal population. Any more than that, and our resources will give out, and the small remnant that is left of the human race will die out once and for all.

A more practical artificial intelligence might have culled us at the very beginning, creating the perfect population and then regulating it. But EcoPan loves us like a mother. It decided to save us with as much compassion as possible.

And so I, and other second children like me (if there *are* any) really are monsters who would doom the human species if we could, simply by our very existence. I feel guilty when I let myself think about it. The food I eat, the air I breathe, the waste I produce, might be the thin edge of the wedge that makes Eden fail. I am one too many.

But I'm glad to be alive, and I'll hold on to my own life strongly, selfishly, if EcoPan or anyone else tries to take it from me.

Now I start to realize the full implication of my position in this society. Mom takes my hand and pulls me gently to the sofa. Her touch is soothing. I remember when I was much younger, if I ever got sick, it was my father who healed me, but my mother who made me feel better. The touch of her hands, the look of love and kindness in her eyes, is better than any medicine.

Now it just screams at me what I will lose by gaining my freedom. It's not worth the price.

"Every child grows up," she says softly. I can see her lower lip tremble slightly. "Everyone leaves home someday."

"But not like this," I say between clenched teeth. "Not forever."

She sighs. "It's too dangerous for you to stay here."

"Why?" I demand. "If you've gotten the false lenses and a new identity for me, why can't I just be that other person and live here?"

"You've lived a very sheltered life, Rowan," she begins, and I snort. Understatement of the year. "You don't realize how it is out there." She gestures to the vast city, unseen beyond our high walls. "There is *always* someone watching. Greenshirts, Center officials, even the most innocuous little cleanbot scouring the streets for refuse. They're all on the lookout for something just a tiny bit off. With your father in such a high position, and apparently about to rise even higher . . . ," she makes a face I can't quite interpret, ". . . we'll be under tight scrutiny. You'll be taking on the identity of a stranger. It would be almost impossible to concoct a scenario in which a stranger could move in with us. You'd be investigated, and all our hard work over your lifetime would be for nothing."

"But Mom," I begin.

"This is life-and-death, my love," she says, pulling me close. "Death if we fail, if anything goes even a little bit wrong or anyone has even the slightest suspicion. And life for you—a real life, with friends and a job and a family of your own someday—if this works." She's whispering, her cheek pressed against mine. I feel like this is good-bye already.

"I don't want to leave you and Ash," I say miserably. My anger is still dominant, with sadness creeping along slyly at the edges of my fury.

"You deserve to be in the world, your own person," Mom says. And part of me thinks she's right. But I feel like a starving girl offered a bite of poisoned food. I want to snatch what is offered and swallow it down, because I need it with every fiber of my being. And yet . . .

"I don't deserve anything special," I protest.

"But you do," Mom says, pulling away from me. "More than you know."

There's something in her tone that makes me stop. "What do you mean?" I ask cautiously.

She bites her lip. "Never mind."

"Mom." I look at her evenly. "Tell me."

And she does. I wish she hadn't.

My world flips upside-down as she tells the story of my birth.

When my mom found out she was pregnant, she had just been named chief archivist and was in the middle of so many projects that she and my father just decided he would be her attending physician. So for the first few months of gestation, Mom didn't miss any meetings at work, and Dad took care of all her nutritional monitoring and fetal health scans at home. As long as it was an uncomplicated pregnancy, there wouldn't be any problem. They'd transfer care to a specialist when it came closer to her delivery date.

Everything went fine until the third month, when my father heard two heartbeats.

What Mom should have done—what the laws of Eden compelled her to do—was immediately report her condition and leave it to a Center panel to decide the babies' fate. Most of the time, one would be terminated right away. The panel might make the decision about which would live—if one was obviously healthier than the other, or if a girl or boy was necessary to balance that generation's gender ratio. But other times it would be random. One fetus would live, the other would die before it was born.

"We couldn't. We just couldn't," she said, tears in her eyes at the memory. "You were only three inches long, we'd never met you, but we loved you both with all our hearts and we decided then and there to do whatever it took to keep you both."

She says "we" but I know, from the way my dad treats me, from the coldness in his eyes when he looks into mine, that there was no "we." Mom made the decision, and Dad followed for her sake. Because his eyes are never cold when he looks at *her*.

"We hid it, and then when I went into labor we hid that, too. We told everyone it came on quickly, that there was no time to go to the hospital, but actually it lasted more than a day. I gave birth in this house, in secret. When you were born first, Rowan, and I looked into your perfect eyes, I knew it was all worth it. All the secrecy and difficulty that had already happened, and was yet to come . . . all worth it. We would show you to the world, and keep our second born a secret. But we'd treasure you both."

I was a first child! I stare beyond my mother, looking at the past, at a different history in which I am the real child, I am the one out in the world, with school and friends and a room of my own with my own things in it. I am the one who laughs and chats with Lark and the others, while Ash . . .

No. I might wish it had been me, but I can't wish it were me instead of *him*.

"Then Ash was born, small and almost blue. He didn't breathe for the first minute of his life, and when he did, it was obvious that he was in trouble. Your father diagnosed it immediately as a serious chronic lung condition."

Mom nods as she sees I understand.

"We *had* to make him the firstborn, Rowan. We didn't have a choice. Without being in intensive care for the first few months of his life, he wouldn't have survived. There was no way he could have lived if we'd hidden him away."

Unspoken in that moment of silence is the other bitter truth: no matter what our birth order, if it had been up to the Center officials to decide our fate, they would have chosen me to live and terminated Ash even after birth. I was strong and healthy, an asset to Eden. He was not. It's probably only because both of his parents are high officials that he was allowed to live at all. For a poor person on the fringe of Eden, a far-flung outer circle, a sickly first child would be eliminated, the parents encouraged to try again.

My brain is in a tumult. Angry, terrible thoughts seem to attack my head, bitter thoughts that are unworthy of me. Unworthy of the love and protection I've known all of my life. But I can't keep them at bay. *It should have been me.*

I hardly listen while Mom tells me what will be happening next. Soon, I'll go to a secret surgical center and have my lenses implanted permanently. Then I'll be smuggled to my new family. I don't understand exactly how this is possible. If my own family can't fabricate a story to keep me, how can a stranger?

Ash comes downstairs, his hand raised to the wall but not quite touching it as he walks, as if he doesn't trust his legs to hold him up. He gives me a weak smile.

I glance at Mom, and she shakes her head. *Ash doesn't know.*

I want to shout the truth to him. *Go hide in the hole, second child! Let me be free, like I should have been all along.*

I hate myself for thinking this.

I can't be in this house anymore.

4

MOM MUST JUST think I need a minute alone to process everything she's told me, so she doesn't follow me when I run out to the courtyard. Neither does Ash. I think she must be holding him back. Alone? How can they think I want to be alone when my whole life has been essentially alone? My world is three people, and they are gone all day having lives of their own. I exist in a state of loneliness. Alone? Solitude is the very last thing I need.

What I need, I decide suddenly, is everything that has been denied to me. I feel angry, resentful, reckless. For nearly seventeen years I've left my fate up to my parents and whatever machinations and bribes they've been arranging to get rid of me. Now it's time I take matters into my own hands. I may not be a real, official person according to the only humans left alive on Earth, but maybe I can be in charge of my own destiny. For one night at least.

Dimly, miserably, I'm aware that I'll have to conform to whatever my parents arranged for me. I'll have new lens implants that will mark me as a different person, and somehow a new family to fit that identity. But right now I want to take a taste of everything I've been missing all these years. Everything I was entitled to and didn't realize it until a few minutes ago.

I climb once again to the top of the high courtyard wall. Eden glitters around me, a mix of the greenish-blue fairy lights of bioluminescence from the modified microorganisms that permeates the city at night, providing a base light, and the electric glow that lights up wherever a human moves. I can see a living diorama in flashes of light all around me, the people showing up as deeply contrasting shadows. There, just down the block, a neighbor I've never met, and never will, opens his front door and steps into the night. For a fraction of a second the city seems to examine him. Then, as if the very street itself must have decided to accept him, it lights up beneath his feet. He walks on in the direction of the entertainment district, and the light leads him on, following his footsteps just long enough to let him know he's not forsaken. I watch his personal light grow smaller in the distance, a will-o'-the-wisp from Mom's old stories that seems to call me.

From my height I can see the lights of several people from our circle all heading toward another ring, where they'll be going to parties, clubs, restaurants, the theater. If only I had someplace to go, someone who was waiting for me to arrive. I picture myself entering a party, all of my friends calling my name, beckoning me over. Someone hands me a drink, another cracks a joke about something we've all shared. I am welcome. I am accepted.

Again, I swing one leg over the outer edge of the wall, but this time, I start to climb down.

Mom sometimes uses an expression: *I know it like the back of my hand*. As I lower myself in grueling slow motion down the far side of the wall, I realize that defines my entire life until this moment.

In the first few seconds of my first foray away from home, I am overwhelmed with *difference*. Since birth, I've known every detail of my whole world to a hair's breadth. If I lost my sight I would hardly notice—I could navigate my tiny realm without any of my senses. The home side of the wall is a friend, with crevices that reach out to help me like welcoming hands. On this side, the wall almost seems to be trying to throw me off.

I cling, frozen, just a couple of feet down from the ledge. Deliberately I steady myself, trying to feel the memory of the Earth within the stones. This helps a little, and I ease myself down another few inches. As I breathe slowly, the rock seems to breathe with me, pressing rhythmically against my chest. Smiling a little to myself, I descend again.

I make it down two more hand- and footholds before a crevice I thought was stable suddenly collapses under my toe. My hands tense and my foot scrapes against the wall, searching frantically for a hold. I find one—barely. The edge of my shoe is just touching the tiny outcrop. Worse yet, my hands are slipping.

The inside wall has been neglected, giving it character and, more important to me, irregularities and crevices I can use to climb. This outer facade, with its face to the world, has been maintained so that all the plaster between the stones is relatively fresh, the rocks themselves smoother. The holds are so much narrower than I'm used to.

I pick the worst hand grip and let go, to skitter my fingers over the wall like a long-extinct spider, searching. There's one! I shift my weight, trying to remember not to hug the wall too much. If I try to press myself against the stones too hard, I'll actually thrust my body out away from the wall.

I hear voices in the distance, but I have to focus all my attention on not falling. I'm still twenty feet up. The fall would be survivable—probably. At least the effort of climbing has distracted me a little from my anger and resentment and confusion. It's hard to think about emotions when your life, or at least your safety, is on the line.

I have managed to lower myself another few feet, when I notice the voices are coming closer. Careful not to shift my precarious balance, I turn my head and search for the source. *Bikk!* At the very farthest limit of my vision, several blocks away, stands a cluster of Greenshirts on patrol. They are illuminated in a glowing orb of light, and rays of their flashlights extend from that center, making it look like a many-armed underwater creature. The Greenshirts are searching the neighborhood for any signs of suspicious activity.

If they see me, they'll think I'm some outer circle punk high on synthocybe looking for gelt to finance her next fix. What could be more suspicious than a girl scaling a wall in a ritzy inner circle neighborhood?

Well, a second-child girl with no lens implants, of course. I'm not just any common criminal. I can be as law-abiding as I like. My life itself is a violation of the highest order.

Time for this nonexistent, illegal girl to get back home. My urge to see the world suddenly begins to evaporate as the chance of capture looms. They haven't seen me—their lights are focused in the other direction—but they're out, and much too close for comfort.

I lunge for a hold right above my head. As my fingers grip it, though, I have a strange, dizzying, disjointed sensation. The world seems to shiver slightly, and the entire block comes loose in my hand. I'd committed too hard, and with a sickening lurch I fall, my body scraping against the rock wall as I try to slow my descent. After what feels like an eternity—though I've only slid about a foot—my fingers catch and I dangle, swinging by one aching arm, still ten feet above the ground.

The stone has crashed below with a deafening noise, and I expect the Greenshirts to come running. But they don't react. I'm panting now, crying at my own stupidity, wondering how on Earth I was ever so foolish as to try to go out into the world on my own. I'm not equipped for this. Why, I can't even make it safely out of the house! What did I think I was going to do? Go to a party? Make a friend? I probably can't even navigate the streets or figure out how to talk to someone I'm not related to and haven't known my whole life!

Only a moment before, I'd felt in a panic to escape. Now I'm frantic to get back inside, where everything is predictable and safe. I have to leave in three days. I need to cherish what little time I have. Or so I tell myself. Some part of me still yearns to be out in the city, to defy the fate that has kept me a prisoner all my life.

But no matter how I stretch and twist I can't find a single handhold above me. I've slithered into a trap, and there's nowhere to go but down.

I try to picture Mom's face when I ring the chime, and she opens the door to find me, shamefaced, on the wrong side of it. She's going to be so disappointed in me.

It takes me another few minutes to climb low enough that I feel confident to jump without injury. I push away from the wall and drop lightly. Then I freeze in amazement.

My feet are on ground that's not inside my house. For the first time in my life, I'm outside. I look down, rocking back on my heels, lifting my toes to see the novelty beneath my feet. There's nothing special about the ground, really. It's just the smooth, clean, shining photoreceptive surface that lines most walls and floors in this city, gathering solar energy. But it's not like anything I've known before.

It's *outside*! I'm *free*!

It's like the very ground is sending electric sparks into my feet, ordering them to move without my volition. I take a step . . . and it isn't toward the front door. It is *away*. Away

from the familiar. Away from the safe prison. Toward dangerous freedom.

I take another step. My body wants to run, to revel and
leap as I do at my most exuberant moments inside the courtyard. But I can't attract any attention. A third step, and I'm
on the public sidewalk. Between that and the road stand
artificial trees. I know they look exactly like the real, living
trees that once covered the world, thriving even in densely
populated cities, before the Ecofail. But they are as false as my
new identity will be. They're just tree-shaped photosynthesis
factories, making oxygen for everyone in Eden to breathe.

I touch one, and it is cold and dead.

In a daze, almost in a dream, I walk on, down the gently
curving sidewalk of our street. Just three rings outside of the
Center, our street is a relatively small circle. The houses are
low, no more than two or three stories. Eden regulation keeps
the inner buildings low so that the Center will always stand
proud and tall. I glance over my shoulder at that structure, a
huge emerald dome that stands like a giant faceted eye in the
heart of Eden. Although I know it holds offices and high-level
workers like my parents, I sometimes feel as if the Center is almost the eye of the EcoPanopticon itself, watching over Eden.

Tonight, I feel as if it is glaring at me balefully through the
dark.

I turn my back on the Center, square my shoulders, and
walk slowly into Eden.

It's night, but there are a few people outside, talking to
neighbors or coming home from restaurants. I recognize some
of them, though I've only seen them at dusk or dawn when I
peep from my aerie. A gentle glow illuminates them wherever
they linger or walk, lighting up before them, darkening behind them once they pass. But no lights come on for me as I
go. It is as if Eden is shutting its eyes to me, rejecting me.

All my life, I've felt like I'd be pounced on if I ever set foot outside my home. But strangely, the scant handful of people on the streets don't seem to pay the slightest bit of attention to me. I'm relieved, of course, but there's a sting to it, too.

Then, unexpectedly, a man emerges from his door, fumbling with his keycard as he moves. He sees my shadow, cast in the light emanating from his house, and he looks up for a fraction of a second, giving me a quick nod and smile before turning back to secure his lock. I've moved past his threshold before he sets out, and he goes in the opposite direction.

I'm elated and shaking. My first contact!

But if I'm not careful, someone will notice my difference. I pull my cap over my kaleidoscope eyes and wrap my pale gold jacket more snugly around my body, hunching a bit as I walk. Why isn't the ground lighting up for me? They might not look directly in my eyes and see that I lack lenses, but eventually someone will notice I'm the only one moving in darkness. I only have two choices: get to a more populous part of Eden, where my darkness won't be noticed among everyone else's light, or go home.

I know I should go home. Has Mom discovered my absence yet? Maybe she thinks I'm sulking in my bed and decided to leave me to my thoughts. Maybe she knows what I've done, and she's going frantic.

I should go home, but I turn my steps toward the nearest entertainment circle.

The radial streets that branch out from the Center are usually more bustling, largely business rather than residential. The one I'm walking along is pedestrian only at this point, with a canal running down the center and walking paths on the side. Many of the shops here—mostly clothes, jewelry, and home décor—are closed now, but a boatman poles a cuddling couple along the center of the canal. The waterway in front of the boat looks like mercury, silver and still, until the prow pushes through it. Then it dances like skipping minnows, and leaves an undulating snake-like wake.

Even though the businesses are closed, there are more people out and about than on my street. The traffic all moves in one direction—toward the entertainment circle. Here near the Center, where the rings are smaller, the entire street will be devoted to restaurants, clubs, bars, theaters, and the like. Farther out, in the outer circles, there are no dedicated entertainment circles. By that point, the rings are too huge. The poorer residents out there don't have the resources to go to the theater or out to eat very often. Still, I've heard Mom say that there are plenty of bars out there.

I merge into the crowd, using their light so no one can see I have none of my own. I realize I'm grinning like an idiot, from excitement and from nerves. But still no one notices me. They assume I'm like them, on my way to my own fun, my own friends.

All around me, I see things I've only glimpsed from a distance, atop my wall. To my left is one of the towering cultivation spires. It rises high above the tallest buildings in Eden to catch the sun. Inside, I know, a liquid slurry of genetically modified algae moves through sinuous tubes, harvesting sunlight and growing into a substance that fills all of a human's nutritional needs. It is then shunted to the factories where it is turned into synthetic food that (so I'm told) looks and tastes exactly like the real dirt-grown fruits and vegetables humans used to consume pre-fail. I have eaten strawberries, more or less, though the last true strawberry withered two hundred years ago.

The cultivation spire may be functional, but tonight it is beautiful. The twisting semi-helix of the tubes looks like a sculpture, made only to please the eye. I stop abruptly, looking up in wonder at the massive structure, and someone bumps me from behind.

"Oh, hey," a boy about Ash's age says, and I think I see quick recognition in his eyes. I lower my own and turn away. Peripherally I see him shrug and move on.

The brief encounter frightens me. I don't know if I can do this. A stranger says "hey" and I feel like running away, or taking a swing at him, or curling up in a ball. What's the right response? I feel my heart fluttering in my chest, and my breath is fast and shallow. The crowd is getting thicker as I near the entertainment circle. *Please*, I silently beg the mob. *Don't look at me. Just let me watch you, pretend I'm part of the crowd*. I feel like if anyone else tries to talk to me I'll break down completely.

But despite my growing anxiety, my feet keep propelling me forward.

The lights in my home circle are subtle and beautiful at night, pale green and mercury-colored, gently swirling to maintain an air of calmness and safety in the elite residential district. Here, though, light is ornament, statement, and above all, glaring, vibrant color.

I've seen animated Eco-history vids of fields of brilliant wildflowers, of forests painted red and gold in the autumn, of bright blue oceans capped with foamy white waves. The color of Eden's most snazzy entertainment circle eclipses them all. The city designers have created a panorama of hues that are dizzying to my eyes. I wonder if they have the same effect on everyone else. Maybe they're used to them. Maybe they don't really see them anymore.

It's beautiful, but a cold kind of beauty. I think of the natural splendors the lights remind me of, the things none of us will ever see. I guess this is the wild landscape of Eden, the human environment until the world heals.

I'm in the thick of it all now. There's a club on my right. Strange, exciting music comes from inside, and pulsing strobes in a rainbow of colors. I move past it, slyly peeking in to see people gyrating, their arms raised above their heads as they dance. The next place is a more sedate theater with a marquee promising a sophisticated comedy. I flinch when I see the uniformed usher at the door. But no, his uniform is kelly-green with brass buttons, only superficially like a Greenshirt uniform.

I hear raised voices and for a second I almost break into a run. But it is just a crowd of young people arguing happily about something. They're shouting, but smiling, and I just stare at them. Until I remember my odd eyes. Then I turn away.

I need a break, just a short respite from all this stimulation. Is there a place where I can see without being seen?

I spy a narrow alleyway between buildings. I know from Ash that these are conduits for cleanbots and ferrybots, the ubiquitous metal robots that zip through Eden. I can see a cleanbot out on the street now, a squat rolling chunk of metal that's vacuuming up everything from garbage to strands of hair and shed skin cells. It will all be taken to a reclamation center and reused in some way. A sleeker silver ferrybot toots to warn pedestrians of its passing as it scoots along with a delivery box from New Leaf Savory Chapati, which Ash tells me is the most popular takeout restaurant. But so far none of them have ducked down my alley, and I'm safe in the shadows. For the moment.

Eden is all so big, so overwhelming! Here in my nook, though, I can experience it in a sliver, which makes it easier. People walk past, and for a fraction of a second I spy on their lives. It's just enough, a taste.

There's a couple arm in arm, their heads bent close. He's

whispering something to her, and as they wink out of sight I hear her laugh. Next comes a larger group, men in identical jerseys, members of some kind of team. I get a whiff of the strange masculine scent of their bodies, and it makes me take a half step forward before sinking back against the wall. Behind them is a giggling gaggle of girls. I hear them commenting on the men in front of them. "Nice *teezak*," one says with a leer. Another whistles, low and appreciative.

None of them so much as glance my way, which makes me both grateful and sad.

5

WHAT'S THE USE of being out here, I berate myself, if you're hiding in an alley the whole time? Go out into the light and color. Are you really risking your security, maybe your very life, on this adventure, only to spend it skulking in the shadows?

Maybe, I answer myself. I feel pulled in two directions, timid and bold at the same time. I want, desperately, to interact with people. At the same time, I'm nervous and tongue-tied and certain that I'll make a fool of myself.

What's wrong with me that I worry marginally more about social humiliation than about being caught by the authorities?

But anger trumps fear—always. I'm still fuming with the injustice of actually being a first child and still being condemned. Just go out there, I order myself. Take what is yours.

I step around the corner . . . and bump hard into the broad chest of a Greenshirt.

I know, even as I react, that I'm doing the wrong thing. Act normal. But I don't know what normal is. I look up at him, gasping, terrified, my wide eyes staring directly into his, giving me away at a glance.

He's a new recruit, I think, because for a long moment he

just stares back. He's a lot bigger and wider than me, but he looks awfully young, not much past twenty, with fair, fine hair in a short fringe on his forehead peeking out beneath his helmet. His name is embroidered on his chest: Rook. He takes a deep breath, and his mouth works as if he's about to speak. I can tell he doesn't believe his own eyes as they look into mine. He has trained for this, I can practically hear him thinking. But he never thought he'd actually come across a second child.

His hand twitches toward the radio mic clipped to his shoulder, but he doesn't press the button to call his backup. Instead he says to me, "Don't move." His voice is very low.

Like hell I won't move! Anger is still foremost in the confusing mix of emotions, and I look at him in disbelief. "Really?" I ask. "Is *that* what I should do?"

Then—I can't believe myself—I shove him as hard as I can with both of my hands, sending him staggering backward. I whirl to run . . . and find myself face-to-face with a security-bot.

Unlike the small, innocuous helper robots like clean-bots and ferrybots, the securitybots are tall, jointed, angular, slightly primate in their movements and stance. They don't look like humans—they're metal and circuits, without skin or expression. But still, there's a sinister humanity to them. As if a machine tried to make a human and it all went horribly wrong.

These are the bots that cruise Eden diligently, searching out any kind of violation of the EcoPan directives. Most of the time they police things like waste, or vices that might corrupt the gene pool, or destruction of public property. But they're also on the lookout for more serious threats, such as members of criminal gangs, or the rumored heretical sects that believe an ancient folklore stating that humans should have dominion over the creatures of the Earth.

And, I'm sure, for second children.

This time I act more sensibly. I duck sharply to the side as the securitybot begins its scan of me. Maybe I was fast enough that it didn't get a thorough scan. It might not have seen my face. But the young Greenshirt certainly did.

"Stop!" he shouts, and launches into a tackle that misses as I twist away. He catches the securitybot instead and they go down in a tangle of metal and flesh. I don't pause to thank my lucky stars, but dash off into the crowd. A nearby concert has just ended, and I quickly lose myself in the masses spilling out of the theater.

I've been prey all my life, but I've never been hunted. Without the practice or natural instinct, I have to think through my evasion. At first it's easy, and I slip through the crowds that part indulgently before me. Everyone is yielding and polite, because so far they think I'm one of them. I see smiles, and one older woman calls out after me, "Take it easy, kiddo—the party will wait for you!"

But any moment the Greenshirt will have scrambled to his feet to pursue me, and the securitybot will have flashed whatever data he grabbed from me and sent it throughout all Eden. The hunt will be on. And then, every resident will be my enemy.

I think I've gotten far enough away that I can slow a little bit. Running is attracting too much attention. My best bet is probably to just blend in with the crowd. Half of the people are about my age, teens or in their early twenties, and a lot of them are dressed more or less like me, in the student uniforms that are the hallmark of every young person whether they're in or out of class. Each school has its own color, and the outfits—baggy pants, a sleek, tight, stretchy shirt, and in tonight's chilly weather, a wide-shouldered jacket—mark a young person's neighborhood and friends instantly. Now they school like garishly colored fish. Ash's uniform (which I'm wearing now) is subtle and beautiful, the shimmering gold of desert sand to match his school's name: Kalahari. But the Macaws are scarlet, the students at Iris wear a vibrant blue-purple, and the Cherry Blossoms are a strong, sweet pink. I'm glad Ash's uniform is among the more quiet . . . but I'm glad I'm dressed to fit in.

Cautiously, I sneak a backward glance. To my surprise, I see nothing out of the ordinary. No signs of pursuit, no commotion. There's no shouting, no flashing lights. Surely the young Greenshirt has alerted his comrades by now.

I keep walking, briskly but steadily, along the entertainment circle. I probably should leave this neighborhood, slipping down one of the radial streets to a new ring. But it feels too dangerous to head directly home. Without a lens implant to scan, they can't know who I am, who my family is. I don't dare take the chance of leading the authorities directly to my home.

Or I could branch outward, away from the Center, toward the outer rings. I've studied maps of Eden, and I'm pretty confident that I could navigate through the rings and radii that make up this huge city. But simply being in this crowd is incredibly nerve-racking—and these are highly civilized inner circle people who are well educated, wealthy, and polite. As you get farther from the Center, though, the well-maintained single-family homes and brightly lit shops gradually turn to crowded high-rises where the middle class live, and crowded sidewalks where the pedestrians will trample you to get to their offices on time. Or so I've heard from Ash, who has only rarely been more than a few circles away from home.

Beyond that, in the farthest-flung outer circles near the desert wasteland, I would not dare to go.

So I stick to this entertainment circle, walking around its periphery, attaching myself unobtrusively first to one group of people, then another, trying to look like I'm a natural part of it all. Could it be possible that there is no pursuit? Maybe I flinched fast enough that the securitybot didn't get a clean scan, or it was damaged when the clumsy Greenshirt knocked it down. Maybe the Greenshirt hit his head and couldn't set off the alarm.

I'm tired, from my earlier run, from stress, and mostly, I think, from anger. Fury, I've just discovered, is incredibly draining.

Along the edge of the gently curving walkway there's a bench for two molded in the shape of a tiger, fashioned so the beautiful orange-and-black animal seems to curl its long striped body protectively around the sitters. I perch on one side, thinking about the empty seat beside me. I try to look like I'm just waiting for someone, like I'm not completely alone in this sea of people. The smile I'm attempting feels tight, but I scan the crowd as if I'm searching for my own particular friend. What if someone meets my eye and smiles back? What if they break from their own group—because everyone seems to be traveling in a pack—and join me? They might sit, and say hello, and look into my eyes . . .

I blink and turn my head down, looking at my hands clenched tightly in my own lap. Tonight is not the time for finding a friend.

Because I'm looking down, I miss danger approaching. Which is probably just as well. If I'd seen it coming, I would have panicked and bolted. This way, though, they're practically on top of me before I notice them, and there's nothing I can do but stay still and innocuous.

Two Greenshirts are walking slowly along the sidewalk right toward me. I look down again quickly, but not before I make fleeting eye contact with one of the Greenshirts. It's the same one from before. My heart races, and I can't move.

I know what's coming next. He'll shout out a warning and they'll both pile on me, drag me to the Center, and then . . .

But nothing happens.

They keep walking slowly toward me.

I sneak another glance. The young Greenshirt with the pale fringe of hair is looking away from me now. He *has* to have seen me! What's going on?

"Did that bot signal turn out to be anything, Rook?" the other man asks, pausing right in front of me. He's older, and has gold stripes on his sleeves.

"No, sir," the younger one says. "I was standing right next to it and didn't see anything out of the ordinary."

I can't believe it. Why is this Greenshirt lying? Why doesn't he say what he saw?

"Must have just been a glitch then," the sergeant says. "There's no record that it actually scanned anyone. Probably nothing, but stay alert anyway. Look at everyone closely. Don't let the smallest detail slip by." He starts deliberately scanning the crowd. They're so close that if I wanted to, I could reach out and touch their gear. Since lethal guns have been outlawed since the founding of Eden, they carry nonlethal weapons that shoot charged plasma, with a current strong enough to bring a human target to their knees.

The younger man's eyes seem to flick my way swiftly, but I can't be sure. I feel like I'm going to pass out. The sergeant begins to turn toward me.

"Huh," Rook suddenly says as a thought seems to strike him. "A glitch, did you say? EcoPan controls the security-bots. Didn't think the EcoPan ever had glitches."

I gasp as his commanding officer hits him, a hard punch to the solar plexus that makes him double over. "If I ever hear that kind of filth coming out of your mouth again, you'll be off the force." Then he makes a sign I've seen in my lessons on Civics vids: a closed fist rising up the center line of his body, spreading to an open hand, palm inward, when he reaches his face. It is a symbol of a seed burgeoning into life. The sergeant bows his head briefly as he makes it.

"Forgive me, sir," the young Greenshirt mumbles, and the pair moves on.

My heart seems to drop into my stomach, and I think I'm going to be sick. What on Earth just happened? Why didn't that Greenshirt Rook report me? Greenshirts are the first—and most vicious—line of defense against any threat to Eden. He should have pounced on me the second he saw me, beat me to the ground, taken me into custody . . .

And when his sergeant was about to look right at me, he deliberately blasphemed against the EcoPan, earning his commander's wrath, and immediately distracting him so he wouldn't turn in my direction.

I sit frozen for a minute more, because I don't think my legs will work right now. I watch the people walk by, flights of birds in bright feathers. None of them knows what I am. But none of them knows *who* I am, either. I'm safe but alone. And I'll always be alone—until I have my new identity and I'm no longer *me*.

A sudden *whir* comes from my left, and I turn to see the flash of a metal bot streaking toward me. They're coming for me after all! I jump to my feet to run, but sure enough, my legs are shaky, and before I can even begin to stagger away the bot crashes into my shin. I cry out, first in pain, then in relief. Oh, sweet Earth! It's not a securitybot, just a ferrybot delivering more takeout. It beeps irritably and zooms around me on its mission.

Bots are known for their fast reaction. In fact, I read in one of Ash's Civics books that bots are designed to be as un-obtrusive as possible, zipping through the city autonomously, serving humans without ever causing them inconvenience. I remember one section noting that however fast a bot moves, it never collides with a human. Ever.

But that ferrybot crashed right into me as if it didn't see me.

I think about how the city lights illuminate around everyone else as they stand in their doorways or walk along the city streets, lighting up just for them, turning off immediately behind to save precious energy. The world didn't light up for me. My way was dark.

Can it be possible? Can the city not see me?

The thought makes my stomach knot. I always knew I was secret. But invisible? It is as if I don't matter at all. Sure, it's lucky for me. Still, it hurts somehow. I have a mad desire to scream, "Look at me!"

A few people have noticed the bot accident, and several curious pairs of eyes regard me. An elderly woman says, "Are you all right, young man?" I want to look at her, the first person in the real world to show me a scrap of kindness. But even as I raise my head, I lower my lashes. If she sees my freakish kaleidoscope eyes, she'll know I never received the eye implants. She'll know I'm a second child.

Instead I pull my light gold scholar cap low over my face and mutter something she can't possibly hear.

"I'm not surprised," another voice says with disdain. "Kalahari *teezaks* can never hold their *akvavit*." I've never even tasted *akvavit*, the potent, sharply spiced liquor.

I haul myself up to my feet and sneak a sideways glance. It's the gang of young men in sports jerseys, evidently a team from a rival school of Kalahari, where Ash goes.

"Don't be such a prune," another tells him. "Hey kid, if you're looking for the Kalahari party, it's at the Rain Forest Club, on the next street."

I remember now that Ash had mentioned that party.

Nearly everyone in his grade was going to be there, celebrating the end of midyear exams. Everyone except him. Part of the reason is that our family needs to keep a low profile. Ash isn't the type to get arrested, but if he was ever with the wrong crowd and any little thing brought attention to our family, or a search of the house, it would be a disaster. So he almost always skips the parties.

I think maybe he does it for me, too. He thinks I'd be jealous of him out having all that fun while I'm stuck at home. He doesn't realize how the very idea of a party terrifies me. A huge crowd of people, all looking at me, talking to me . . .

But now I have no choice. The pedestrians are beginning to lose interest in the momentary interruption of their nightlife, but those who are watching think I go to Kalahari, think I'm headed to the party. So the only thing I can do is walk away with my head down. I'll head toward the Rain Forest Club until I'm out of sight, then make my way home. It's the best way not to attract unwanted attention.

As I walk away unmolested, I think about what the elderly lady called me: young man. In my baggy pants and boxy jacket, with my hair up under a scholar cap, I must look like a boy. In fact, I must look exactly like my twin, Ash. That thought gives me a measure of confidence. I might not be at home in this world, but he is. If I pretend to be him, I'll feel bolder, more sure.

Still, I'm in danger. Not just my eyes, but the smallest thing could mark me as a second child. I try to attach myself to other walkers so no one notices how the streets don't light up for me. For the most part, though, I look like any of the students out that night, in my slightly shimmering, gold-colored school uniform. I'm at the Rain Forest Club in just a few minutes. It's hard to even walk by the door. The music pulses, and inside I can see bodies writhing in dance, hear voices shouting to be heard above the music. It's not a place for me. I bite my lip and turn away . . .

Only to see a Greenshirt rounding the corner at the end of the block. *Bikk!* Without thinking, I dart into the Rain Forest Club and I'm immediately engulfed in brilliant light and sound, in the crush of bodies. The place is decorated to look like one of the long-dead rain forests, but the trees are all synthetic, the birds and frogs and ocelots robotic. There are shrill, discordant sounds piercing the music, and I think they must be the sounds of artificial insects singing in the make-believe canopy.

My breath comes fast. I close my eyes almost all the way, focusing on a narrow sliver of floor, and start to walk toward the back, doing my best to shut out the confusion that attacks all of my senses. I'm overwhelmed.

I bump into someone—most of my social contact so far seems to be from accidental collisions—and sneak a peek at them. What I see is alarming: a man, I think, but not a man. At least not quite anymore. At first I think his skin has simply been painted, but when I look closer I see that it is sculpted, with some kind of implant beneath the skin to give it an odd texture. Tattooed color enhances the effect, making all of his exposed skin look like intricately patterned snake scales. Shocked, I make the mistake of looking at his eyes, and find that they are gold with narrow vertical black slits for pupils. They make my own eyes look normal! They must be contacts. He catches me looking—my own eyes are shadowed by my scholar cap—and flicks out his tongue at me. It is forked, like the snakes I've seen animated in Eco-history vids. Then he slips sinuously through the crowds.

I've heard that a few fanatics take their connection to the Earth's lost animals so seriously that they feel like they have to actually become one of those animals. Ash hasn't talked about them much. It isn't common in any of the inner circles. Farther from the Center, though, I've heard people spend fortunes on changing their appearance to mimic animals. Some, Ash says, feel that they were born in the wrong bodies, that they should have been born an animal instead of a human. They call themselves Bestials.

I never dreamed I'd see one. It's almost like seeing a living snake. I watch him dance, his arms above his head, his slim, supple hips twisting.

The room is full of such strangeness. Many of the young people are wearing their vibrant single-color school uniforms. Many are the light shimmering gold of Ash's school, Kalahari. Some of the slightly older ones, those beyond their student years, are dressed in homage to extinct animals. One woman is covered in plastic feathers, though she resembles no bird I've even seen in Eco-history vids. Another has painted herself in spots and teased her short hair up to look a bit like cat ears. They look artificial compared to the snake man, though. At the end of the night they'll pluck their feathers or scrub off their spots and be human again. Then the next night they'll be a fish, or a wolf.

Finally I reach the back of the dance hall. There's a dark hallway branching out in two directions—one to the kitchen, I can tell by the savory aroma, the other to the restrooms. I choose that way, thinking I'll attract less attention, hoping there's a back door.

There is! I surge toward it. I've pushed it halfway open, and can just see the blessed quiet solitude of a back street outside when I hear a voice behind me.

"Ash? Is that you?"

I turn, and there in the shadows is Lark. Ash has shown me pictures of her so many times I know her face by heart.

Her dress is the yellow-green of new leaves in springtime.

6

FOR ME, IT'S as if the clouds that were darkening the sky of my life suddenly parted and the sun shone a glorious beam directly on me. As I stare at Lark, a strange longing fills me. I don't understand half the things I feel. It's as if I've known her my entire life, and we're already in perfect harmony. It's as if I've been running a seemingly endless race, and she's the finish line finally in sight.

"Ash, what's wrong?" she asks, her voice like honey from a long-extinct bee. I've never heard such sweetness.

The corridor is dim, and I realize she can't see me well enough to notice my strange eyes. In this light there is nothing to distinguish me from my twin. My hair is tucked up under my scholar cap, and the jacket probably disguises my curves. Though not exactly identical, our features are so similar that in the school uniform she'd naturally assume I'm Ash.

Until I speak.

I don't want to break the illusion, so I just shake my head to tell her nothing is wrong. She takes a step closer.

I should leave. Just stalk away without a backward glance. If she takes just one more step she'll see my unfixed eyes. If I open my mouth she'll surely know I'm not Ash.

"Are you having an attack?" she presses, leaning toward

me. I can smell a pleasant fragrance wafting from her. Not sweet, exactly, more spicy and earthy, like when rain hits the moss in my courtyard. "I have a spare inhaler for you if you've forgotten yours." They're that close, I think, that she not only knows about his condition, but carries his medicine with her.

I can't walk away from her. Lark's hair is lilac-colored, her eyes gray and luminous, huge as they shower me with concern and friendship. Seeing her is like . . . like seeing one of the extinct animals I've learned about in Eco-history videos. A bird of paradise. A jaguar. For all my life, someone like her has been just as rare, just as impossible to ever experience firsthand. I know it's an illusion, just as the images of long-gone animals in my vids are illusions. If she finds out what I am, she'll scream for the authorities. She's Ash's friend, not mine.

But right now, for just a brief moment in time, I can pretend.

I try to memorize every aspect of the encounter so I can savor it later. The way her flower-colored hair seems to glow in the dim light, the long, soft curls a bit wild. The way she stands poised, about to move nearer to me, her weight just about to shift to her front foot to take a step, but hesitating for some reason.

Right now, in this magical moment, I have a friend.

It is wonderful.

It is torture, because any moment the spell will break.

"Ash?" she asks again, uncertain.

"I'm fine," I say, trying to deepen my voice. It sounds strange to me. It must to her, too, because she frowns slightly, two fine lines appearing between her eyebrows. Her head cocks to one side, like a bird's.

Then, suddenly, she sits down on a low bench along the edge of the corridor. Tentatively, I lower myself to the one on my side. We've established territories, with a boundary of hallway between us. She's not coming closer. Maybe I can snatch a few more moments of this delicious heaven.

"You seem . . . different tonight, Ash," she says, and I can't help but laugh. "Oh, there you are!" she says, her brow clearing like breaking dawn. Ash and I have exactly the same laugh, a low, throaty chuckle. "I didn't think you'd be able to come to the party."

I take a deep, steadying breath before I venture any words. "I had to get out tonight," I say, my voice odd and gravelly. "I had to . . ." I gulp. "I had to see you."

Even in the darkness I can see her flush. This hallway is undecorated, bland compared to the gaudy rain forest motif of the main rooms. But Lark lights it up like a thousand lanterns.

"Are you serious?" she asks.

"Completely," I say. "I feel like I've waited all my life for this night."

Lark is silent for a moment. All the time, she searches my face. I want to look away, but I can't. I just pray to the good Earth that it isn't light enough for her to distinguish the strangeness of my eyes. If it meant my death, I swear I couldn't look away.

At last she says, "There's something new in your eyes." Immediately, I bow my head. "No, not in your eyes. Your eyes are in shadow." With relief I turn toward her again. "It's in your expression, though. What is it?" She stares at me awhile longer. "I know. You're not anxious," she says with a sigh. "You're happy for a change." She smiles, and the radiance engulfs me. I smile back.

"I am," I say breathlessly, thinking that I shouldn't be. My life is in danger, and even if I get home safely my life is about to be so uprooted it might as well be destroyed. But at this moment I'm completely, blissfully happy.

"You've been my friend since we moved to this circle, Ash. Sometimes I think you're my best friend. But there's always been a distance between us that I never understood. You always held something back. And it bothered me. I never pried, you know. I let you keep that part of you walled off."

I have no idea what Ash is like away from home. I only know what he tells me about his life outside. I'm always jealous of everything he does that I can never do (though I rarely let it show). But it never occurred to me that he carried his burden of secrecy out into the public realm. I thought I was the only one who had to bear the weight. But now I can guess that it affected him, too, strongly enough for Lark to notice.

"And you don't have to tell me now," Lark goes on. "I'm just happy to see you looking out at the world as if it just might be a wonderful place after all."

Then she stands, crosses the scant distance between us, and bends awkwardly to hug me. I stiffen, then relax as the warmth of her hands seeps through my clothes. Then her face is near mine, her lips near mine . . . and suddenly her eyes widen, and she pulls back a little bit. But she doesn't let go of my shoulders. If anything she holds them tighter.

"Oh," she breathes, looking into my kaleidoscope eyes. "I understand now."

I think she'll scream for help, run away, say something cruel. But she slides to my side, one arm still around my shoulders, the other fumbling for my hand. "A second child," she says softly. "A twin. I didn't know." She gives a little laugh that sounds like music. "Of *course* I didn't know. But that explains a lot. What's your name?"

I just breathe, terrified and elated that my secret is finally in public, and that I'm not instantly condemned. And with Lark of all people, the friend I've dreamed about for years!

I try to speak, but I'm so cold with nerves that my teeth are starting to chatter. My fingers are icy in her hand, and she rubs my knuckles with her thumb.

"It's okay," she says soothingly. "If you belong to Ash, you belong to me, too. I'll keep you safe. I promise."

"Rowan," I say in my own voice. "My name is Rowan."

She smiles at me, and I feel like I'm being seen for the very first time.

We talk as though we've known each other forever. In a way we have. I've been hearing stories of Lark for so long that she is a part of me. And she probably sees so much of Ash in me that she thinks she knows me, too. As we talk, she keeps looking at me with her head cocked like the small bird that is her namesake, sometimes frowning when some preconception of me isn't fulfilled, or smiling with sudden brightness when some expression or nuance pleases her, conforms to her idea of what I am, or should be. I think I am both familiar and mysterious.

I tell her about my life, about the endless years of solitude with only Ash, Mom, and Dad for company. About running in circles to nowhere, about climbing the wall around our courtyard to the top every single day, but never daring to go over until this night. I tell her about the loneliness, the yearning, the constant low-grade fever of anxiety that runs through me like a subtle sickness. And through it all she nods, sometimes holding my hand or stroking my arm. She is on my side, completely, I'm sure.

Still, even as I revel in finally having someone to share with, I can almost hear my mother's voice in my head. *Don't trust*, she whispers to me. *You're a secret, a dangerous secret that needs to be kept at all costs.*

I ignore the imagined voice as Lark tells me about herself, her beliefs. She talks about Eden in ways I've never considered before. To her, the city is as much of a prison as my house is to me.

"Are we really all that's left?" she asks. I can only tell her what I've heard in History vids. Our ancestors were the lucky few who survived two hundred years ago. There are no people outside of Eden. No animals, either, just a few lichens, algae, bacteria, and the like.

"But I've studied Ecology and Eco-history," she says, her voice passionate. "Life is enduring, adaptable. I know that humans are terrible, destructive, but the Earth is strong. I can't see how we could do anything to it that would destroy it completely. Ecological collapse, sure. Mass extinction, broken food chain. But I can't believe that *everything* is gone."

Again, I can only reply with what I've been taught: that beyond Eden, the world is a wasteland, dead and barren.

But it is the one-child policy that seems to particularly bother her. "Humans are part of nature," she tells me. "We're animals, just like all the other animals that used to live on Earth. Animals are meant to propagate, to expand, to grow."

"But Eden can't survive if the population grows," I protest, even though I'm arguing for my own doom.

"I don't know," she says, pressing her lips together contemplatively. "There's something that doesn't add up. The vids at school say that the original settlers in Eden were chosen. That means that someone—maybe Aaron Al-Baz himself, creator of the EcoPan—decided on a number of people. Why pick so many only to reduce their numbers later?"

"Maybe it was just compassion," I offer. "He wanted to save as many as possible, and then later generations could deal with the overpopulation."

She shakes her head. "He was a scientist, a computer programmer, a practical, pragmatic man. I think he would have chosen the right number of people from the start. But listen to this." Though we're already close, shoulder to shoulder, she leans in closer so her lilac hair brushes my cheek. I shiver.

"My mom works in allocation. Once when she had to work on a weekend I went in with her and hung out in the records office all day while she was busy. I wasn't supposed to be there, and that was the only place I'd be out of the way. No one cared about old receipts and supply lists. But you know me, I can't *not* read."

She catches what she just said with a low chuckle, and we exchange a knowing look. I *do* know her. I knew this fact about her years before we met. She reads the way other people breathe, incessantly, of deep need.

"I started thumbing through old records printed out on plastic paper. Not important stuff like they'd keep in the archives where your mom works. Just old receipts for food distribution and the algae farms and water circulation volume. Things no one cared about. Most of it was just shoved in any old how. Boring, I thought . . . then suddenly it got interesting."

She tells me how this jumble of printed records went back at least a hundred years, maybe more.

"And what I found, after I'd gone through enough mind-numbingly boring lists and receipts, is that the amount of resources hasn't declined over the years."

I have to think about this for a long moment.

"You mean," I say slowly, "we're not running out of food and water and energy?" But that's supposed to be the justification for the one-child policy. The population has to be reduced or all of Eden will run out of resources and perish.

"Not only that," Lark whispers in close conspiracy. "From what I could see, in this district at least, the resources are actually increasing."

7

AN HOUR LATER I make my way home in a dream. Well, a dream that is part nightmare. So far in my life my strongest emotions have been limited to such things as boredom, loneliness, and occasional hope. Now I've not only learned an entirely new range of feelings, but I've discovered that even seemingly contradictory ones can exist side by side. As I creep home with Lark, I'm both giddy and afraid. Both emotions have the same symptoms: pounding heart, shaking knees, anxious darting eyes.

As we start out, I realize I have no idea where I am. The map I thought I'd had in my head is gone. It should be obvious, and it would be if I was calmer. Eden is laid out in concentric rings with connecting spokes, so all I really have to do is mark the huge emerald eye of the Center and head inward until I find my own circle. But I'm so shaken by everything that has happened this night that suddenly I feel lost.

"This way," Lark says gently, and leads me through a bot access passage.

I turn, pulling against her guiding hand. "Are you sure?" I can see the shining green dome in the other direction. "I thought . . ."

"I see a few Greenshirts on patrol tonight. More than they

usually have in this circle. Are you sure no one spotted you earlier?"

"I think . . . no," I say, not wanting to worry her about my mysterious encounter with the young Greenshirt.

"Still, something's up tonight to have increased security. We should go the long way around. If we cut out to the next ring and then take another spoke back inward, we'll attract less attention."

I'm nervous, but I trust her. "You sound like you've done this before."

She gives me a smile of mischief. "I've snuck out to a meeting or two," she admits. I question her with raised eyebrows and she elaborates a bit. "People who think like me. People who aren't so certain that all is well in Eden. Naturally, the less attention I get the better. And some of the meetings are in outer circles, so it's safest to be sneaky."

I know she means not just safe from the focus of authorities, but from the seedier element that lives in the outer circles. Ash never mentioned any of this. I guess Lark has a secret life, too.

I hardly even see the gaudy lights, the extravagant costumes of the passersby. We've reached the next ring, and though it is visibly less clean and chic than the entertainment circle closest to my house, it is still hopping with activity and crazy with color and decoration, on both the people and the buildings.

"Look out!" I whisper when I see a Greenshirt up ahead. But Lark takes my hand and pulls me so that I veer away from him. He hadn't noticed us before, but the sudden movement makes his head swivel toward us. I tense, ready to run, but Lark laughs and leans toward me as if whispering some secret. What she really says is "Smile! He has no idea who we are. Just girls out for a night of fun together." I stretch my tense face into a smile, and the Greenshirt turns away. We clearly aren't a threat.

Bit by bit, I start to relax. With Lark to guide me I feel . . . not safe, exactly, but as if I'm in good hands. The music, the crowds no longer intimidate me. I feel like I'm a part of it all now. I have a connection. I have a friend.

"Do you have any idea where you'll be living when you go with your new foster family?" Lark asks. I shake my head. I left before I could learn any details of my future. "I hope it's close," Lark goes on, "but if not, there's always the autoloop. You can get anywhere in Eden in a few hours now that they've upped the rail speed."

There's so much swirling around in my head. Just a couple of hours ago I was told I'm about to leave my home, my family. Who knows when I'll see them again? I'll be living with strangers. I'm torn up about that, and yet . . . Somehow, there's an edge of happiness. When I ran away from my home into the night I felt like my whole world had broken. Now I begin to think that I can put the pieces back together. Not in exactly the same way, of course. But maybe, just maybe, even better.

Is it Lark that makes me feel that everything isn't as grim as it first seemed? Now that I've met a friend, shared my secret, anything seems possible.

Not that I don't have enough problems of my own to worry about, but somehow I keep thinking back to everything Lark told me about the supplies, the one-child policy, her vague theories about something being wrong with Eden. But what does that matter? The world is what it is—dead outside, alive in here—and I have to make the best life for myself given what I have. Whatever is going on in the government and supplies, or in the electronic heart of the EcoPanopticon, that's not my problem.

My heart slows to the point that I can have a real look

around me. We're walking briskly through the next entertainment ring. While the one nearest my house—the entertainment district closest to the Center—seemed loud and boisterous at the time, I can see now that by comparison with this ring it was quiet, civilized, and staid. There, people walked slowly, in orderly fashion, politely making way for one another. Here, they jostle and shove. There seem to be many more people. More security, too. Did Lark make a mistake going this way?

"They have other things to worry about," she says when I express my concern. "Look over there."

I see a man standing on a small folding stool, head and shoulders above the crowd. Fragments of his impassioned speech reach me. "Dominion over land and sea, over the beasts of the Earth and the fish of the sea . . ." Few people seem to be paying him any attention. Most just walk by, but every once in a while someone stops to shout a curse, and once someone hurls soggy scraps of a sandwich at him. He keeps on declaiming with the burning eyes of a fanatic.

"Idiot," Lark says, scowling in his direction. "That's the kind of thinking that got us here in the first place."

"What is the Dominion, exactly?" I ask. I've heard the term occasionally, but I only have the vaguest idea what it's all about.

"It's a cult, or a political movement, depending on who you talk to," Lark said. "They believe that humans were meant to rule the Earth, and that destroying it was just part of the master plan."

"Whose master plan?" I ask.

She shrugs. "They talk about a book written thousands of years ago that gives them permission to kill and destroy and conquer whatever they like. Far as I know, no one has ever seen or read this book, though. Now they mostly just spout off about how when the Earth is finally healed then people can reclaim their rightful place at the top of the food chain, slaughtering animals and laying waste to the land."

I shudder. How could anyone actually think like that? I remember reading in Eco-history how in our distant past huge animals like cows and sheep were raised only to be killed and eaten. If a cow walked through Eden right now, every citizen would fall on their knees in amazement.

Except for the Dominion members. They'd probably start slicing steaks.

"But the Dominion does have one thing right," Lark said.

"What's that?" I ask nervously. I know that mere association with the Dominion carries a mandatory prison sentence.

"Humans belong out in the world, not trapped in a prison city."

"But Eden is the only reason we survive!" I say. "How could we live out there?" I gesture in the direction of the far edge of the city.

Lark shrugs. "I didn't say it was possible," she says. "Only that's where we belong. We're part of nature, not this artificial paradise."

I look back at the proselytizer. "Why don't they arrest him?"

"Oh, they will once someone starts listening to him, agreeing with him. He's safe until he has an audience. As long as he has no support he's just an advertisement for the movement's foolishness. He'll be in prison soon enough."

I shudder again. That's my fate—at the very least—if I get caught.

Lark notices. "Don't worry," she says. "As long as you're with me you're safe. I know these streets like the back of my hand." That phrase makes me think of Mom, and calms me. Lark seems so fearless, so confident, that it's rubbing off on me. I feel safe with her at my side.

It's a long, circuitous walk back to my house. We even pass her house, though she doesn't point it out until we've walked beyond it. I crane my neck and see the soft warm glow in one of the windows.

Lark is chatty, which is a novelty to me. Ash tells me all about his day as soon as he gets home, and no matter how tired Mom is after work she always makes a point of sitting down with me for a while before I go to sleep. But so many of my hours have been spent in silence. Just hearing Lark's patter is so interesting that sometimes I lose the train of her conversation and just listen to the flow of her voice, marveling that it is directed at me. Soon all of my life will be like this, with friends and conversation. But Lark will always be the first.

I'm lucky, too, that she takes the burden of conversation on herself. Most of the time I really don't know what to say, how to respond. But she seems to understand, and barrels through any of my awkward pauses with a steady flow of words. She makes all this new socializing almost easy for me.

When we reach our home circle Lark suddenly stops, gripping my hand tightly.

"What is it?" I ask in alarm. She seems frozen. A few seconds later, though, she relaxes, though she doesn't let go of my hand.

"I thought . . . never mind."

"No, tell me," I say.

She sighs, then smiles. "After what you've shared with me, I guess I don't have the right to hide anything from you. I have seizures."

She explains how a quirk in her brain makes her have seizures. "It's kind of like a lightning storm in my brain. The neurons go crazy. The episodes usually aren't too bad, and I can almost always feel them coming on. The world goes kinda . . . different. Floaty. I get a little dizzy. That's why I thought I was going to have a seizure just now. The ground seemed to shift and I felt off-balance. Did you feel it?"

I shake my head. I think my heart is pounding too fast, too loud in my chest for me to notice any other sensation.

She smiles at me, and we walk on, still hand in hand.

When we finally reach my house, I almost don't recognize it. I've always seen it from the inside. My only glimpse from the outside was when I was fleeing it, and I didn't look back. It seems strangely staid after the opulence of the rest of the city. The gray stones look . . . natural.

The rest of the city is all artifice. Beautiful, bright, but not natural.

The sight of home, with its interlocked pattern of real stones, its muted mossy gray color, makes me homesick in anticipation. This is where I belong, I think. I can't leave home! I can't . . .

Lark lays a hand on my shoulder, distracting me. "You are so lucky to live here," she says.

I know I am, but I ask, "Why?" expecting a conventional answer.

She surprises me. "I can't imagine what a thrill it must be to live in the home of Aaron Al-Baz. Always wondered why there isn't a plaque on the wall, commemorating it."

I look at her blankly. "The creator of EcoPan lived here?"

"You didn't know?"

I shake my head.

"My dad told me. He was the only one in Eden allowed to have a real stone house. Everything else is synthetic, but he insisted on keeping a connection to the Earth. Stones aren't alive, people said, but he told them that stones are the Earth's bones."

I process for a moment, then say, "So I'm living inside a skeleton?"

She tilts her head and laughs. "An ossuary—a bone house!"

"Why don't I know this?" I ask.

She shrugs. "We all have our secrets," she says, and winks at me. "Are you going to be in trouble when you go in?"

I honestly have no idea what awaits me.

"Thanks for getting me back safely," I tell her, thinking I should make some formal gesture: a bow, a handshake. "I really like you . . . I mean, meeting you . . ." I stammer.

"Can you sneak out tomorrow?" she blurts out.

"Of course," I say without thinking. Will it be possible? After tonight's escapade I doubt I can elude my parents again. Would I be brave enough? I look into Lark's earnest eyes. Yes, I think I will be.

"Good," Lark says. "I'll meet you here tomorrow. Just after dark. Don't worry, I won't tell Ash what you've been up to." I asked her not to earlier. I'm still undecided about whether I want to tell Ash about sneaking out and meeting Lark. On balance, I don't think I will. At least, not yet. I want this to stay mine. I don't want to share.

She tilts her head to peer up at the wall around my courtyard. Her wisps of lilac hair fall away from her face. "Can you really climb that?" she asks, amazed.

Remembering how I had to fall the last few feet, I have my doubts. Nervously, I find a tiny handhold and grip, tensing my muscles to pull myself up.

"Hold on, silly," Lark says as she catches my shoulder and gently wheels me around. "Aren't you even going to say good-bye?"

Just say the word, I tell myself. But I can't. She's looking at me with a quirky smile, curled up at one side, down at the other. Good-bye feels tragic.

"Until tomorrow," I say instead, and she laughs and hugs me.

"Until tomorrow," she repeats, as if it is a magic spell.

Suddenly I want to impress Lark. She's been the strong one, guiding me through the city, soothing my worries. Now I want to look strong and capable. While she's watching, I leap onto the wall and with nothing but instinct find the perfect holds. Though they're hardly more than hairline cracks, my fingertips and toes seem glued to the wall. Smoothly, hiding the effort under a veneer of pure grace, I ascend halfway up, then throw my head back to look down at her. It's a reckless move, almost pitching me off balance . . . but isn't that what this night is about? Throwing caution to the wind?

I'm gratified to see her look at me in open-mouthed amazement. Her lilac hair is almost glowing, a bright spot against the gray of my house. "Rowan, you're . . . quite a surprise," she says, almost too softly for me to hear.

Elated, I scale the rest of the wall without a single mishap. At the top I pause and look at her for a long moment. Then I swing my legs over the wall to continue the last few days of my prison sentence.

I'm prepared for anything. Mom weeping. Dad shouting. Everyone gone, searching for me. But to my surprise the house is quiet and dark. I creep inside, slip off my shoes, and pad silently to Mom and Dad's bedroom. The door is slightly ajar. Peeking in, I can see their shapes as they sleep: Dad on his back on one side of the bed, Mom curled away from him at the far corner. Did they really not know I left, or did they just give up?

Mom, always sensitive, surely decided I needed time alone and left me in the courtyard, apparently mulling over my fate. I close their bedroom door and head to my tiny bedroom.

I pass by Ash's bedroom and pause by the door.

He's sleeping, too, his breath steady but slightly raspy. For a long moment I look at his face. *My* face, almost. The resentment surges again. Why does he get everything, while I—a healthier version of him, rightfully first—get nothing.

Then his breath catches and stops for a long moment. This happens a lot when he sleeps. I can't tell you how many times I've waited, my own breath held, for his breathing to start up again. So far it always has. Someday, I fear, it won't.

I count, seven . . . eight . . . nine . . . Finally he sucks in a ragged breath, and begins to snore gently. On one hand the sound is annoying, but on the other it is reassuring. The snores are a constant gentle reminder that he's still breathing, still alive.

I creep closer and look at his face, calm and restful in sleep. He looks young, much younger than I myself feel tonight. But then, I remember wryly, I'm technically older than him.

How could I have harbored a jealous thought about him? Suddenly I understand why Mom had to strip me of my first child privilege and let the world believe Ash is the one and only. She must have known even then that I could endure whatever suffering came my way. Ash—sick, sensitive—never could have.

I look back at the endless weeks, months, years of solitude, hidden away in this house. Somehow, I managed to find a measure of happiness for myself all that time. Or if not happiness, contentment. Sure, sometimes I cried. Other times I raged. But I got through it. And as ripped apart as I might be about having to leave home now, a part of me knows that I can deal with it. It will be hard, but I can do it.

A sense of peace washes over me. My anger is gone. Did meeting Lark do all that? Or did it just come from inside, the same acceptance that helped me get through all these years?

I'm so tired. So tired and so happy. Mom's right—every child leaves home. I'm just doing it a little earlier than most, and under stranger conditions. But whoever's identity I assume, I'll still get to see my family, I'm sure of that. Mom wouldn't allow it to be any other way. And now I have Lark. Wherever I am in Eden, I'll have Lark.

I'm almost to my room when I hear Ash stir behind me. "Rowan?" he asks. I know he's only half-awake, that I could make it to my room and be alone with my thoughts of freedom and Lark and friendship if only I keep going. But I turn and sit at his bedside.

His eyes open a bit when he feels the compression of the bed. "Where were you?" he asks sleepily.

"In the courtyard," I reply.

"No you weren't."

"I . . . I was. You just didn't see me. Or maybe I was inside when you were looking for me."

He smiles, then the grin breaks in a yawn. "It's a big house, but it's not *that* big. Where did you go? I checked all your hiding spots."

I don't say anything.

"You went out, didn't you." It's a statement, not a question.

My chin juts out defiantly. "Maybe."

He covers his eyes with his hand, rubbing them hard. "What were you thinking, Rowan? You could have gotten caught, or killed!"

I feel an urge to say I'm sorry. But I'm not, not at all. "I was just fine," I say instead. "W—" I catch myself. I almost said *we*, but I've decided not to tell Ash about Lark. Not yet. Sometimes a thing is too precious to bring out into the light. Somehow, talking about it might make the magic of the night evaporate. "I didn't have any problems. No one looked at me twice."

He's still angry, or scared. "How could you do something so stupid?" he asks. "Never mind what would happen to our family if you got caught." I flush and hang my head. I've hardly thought about that possible consequence of my adventure. "You know what the authorities would do to you if they found out you existed."

I don't, not really. I've never been told exactly, but the consequences hinted at ranged from torture to prison to slavery to death. But oh, great Earth, it was worth it just to escape for one night! I try to explain this to Ash, telling him about the joy—and fear—of seeing the people, the lights, hearing the blare of music and the babble of hundreds of people at once.

He nods, understanding the depth of my loneliness, my need for more. In a conciliatory voice he says, "Mom said you're going to get your lenses soon."

The way he says this makes me think Mom hasn't told him I only have a few days left with my family.

"I'm so happy for you!" He puts a hand over mine. "Are you scared?" Before I can answer he adds, "Of course you're not. You're not scared of anything."

I give a small, rueful laugh. "There's not much to be afraid of when you never leave the house."

"No, that's not true," he says. There's a new depth to him, and he seems to be looking inside himself as he talks to me. "Just being alive can make people afraid. To have something so precious as life, that can be taken away at any moment . . ." He swallows hard and licks his dry lips. "Not you, though. I've never seen you afraid."

I make a small confession. "I was afraid when I was outside the house tonight. For a while, anyway."

Ash shakes his head slowly. "Nah, I don't believe you. Nerves, maybe. Anxiety, uncertainty. But never fear. I know you, Rowan. You're completely brave. Even if all you've ever had to face is boredom and loneliness, you've always faced them bravely. I know exactly how you'll be when you get out into the world at last. You'll eclipse me entirely." He sighs. "Every time I fail, I think of you, what you would do in my place. When I turn away from a group of people laughing and think they're laughing at me. When I try to tell Lark how I feel . . ."

I remember when Lark thought I was Ash, with some subtle difference. When her lips came near to mine. I flush in the darkness, and say nothing.

"I'm basically a coward, Rowan," my brother confesses. Then he adds something that brings tears to my eyes. "You should have been the firstborn. You would have been a benefit to Eden. More than me, anyway."

What can I say? I reassure him that he is a wonderful person, an asset to the community, that he has no failings, only quirks, that he is loved.

That I, in particular, love him, my other self.

I wonder what I'll do without him.

I wonder what he'll do without me.

"Go back to sleep, Ash. We can talk more in the morning."

There is a melancholy edge to my thoughts, like the grim desert wasteland around Eden. But like the city itself, the center of my thoughts is bright as I drift off to sleep.

I sleep late in my tiny bare chamber. When I wake, Ash is at school and Mom is at work. I feel a twinge of resentment. Shouldn't they be home with me for my last few days in the family? Who knows when I'll be able to see them again. I might even live in an entirely different circle, and just be able to see them once a month for fauxchai and chapatis in public.

I hear a noise in the kitchen. My dad is home. I feel my jaw tighten right away, but make myself go in to say good morning. He's making an algae smoothie—straight algae and water, no synth flavors. Ew.

He doesn't hear me while the blender's whirring, but after he pours his green concoction into a tall frosted glass he turns and flinches slightly upon seeing me. As if I shouldn't be there.

A dribble of viscous green slush runs over the edge of his glass, pooling in the webbing between his thumb and forefinger.

"You're up," he says. I don't know enough about people to determine if this stating of the obvious is a common conversational opener, but my dad does it all the time.

I grab a sweet roll from a basket and take a big bite. "Congratulations on your appointment as vice chancellor," I say.

"It isn't official yet."

"Don't worry," I say wryly, unable to resist the jibe. "I won't tell anyone." Who could I tell, for the next few days anyway? Except Lark. I decide to tell her tonight, an act of defiance.

"I need to have you squared away before anything is publicly announced." He wipes the green drips with a pristine white cloth, then tosses the cloth into the reclamation chute.

"Squared away? Is that all I am to you? An issue to be dealt with, a mess to be made neat?" Does my father hate me? I wonder. It's a question I've been shaping in my mind ever since I was old enough to pay attention to the world around me.

"It's not as simple as that, Rowan," he says. "You create—difficulties—by your very existence."

I feel my lip twitch. I want to delve into it more, but I only say bitterly, "You'll be rid of me in a little while. That will be a relief, I guess."

He takes another sip of his drink, scowling a bit as if he just realized how disgusting it is. "In a way," he says evasively.

I look at him evenly. My feelings are mixed, but as before, anger trumps sadness. It's starting to be a trend with me, I think. "And you and Mom can move on with the perfect life I interrupted sixteen years ago. Pretty soon it will be like I never even existed at all."

He doesn't answer, only downs the remainder of his drink and heads out the door.

8

IT IS A day like any other—*almost*. Like every day for the past sixteen years of my life, I spend a good portion of the daylight home alone. I have my routines to keep me sane: studying, drawing, running, and exercising until my body is exhausted and my mind is calm.

But today there is a lilac tinge on everything I do.

When I draw, I find myself sketching Lark's face.

When I run, it's her I'm running to.

When I pull out my datablocks and vids to study, I turn immediately to all of the things Lark and I talked about. I search for information on the Dominion, but there is precious little. That makes sense, I think, with a new touch of cynicism painted onto my personality by Lark. The people in charge don't want people to know about that evil cult, even disparaging things. *Any* information might lure new converts.

So I search for other topics, expanding my knowledge so I'll have more to talk about with Lark. The thing that interests me most is the earliest days of Eden. I want to find out more concerning what Lark said about the original population of Eden. How were the first residents chosen? Were they just the last straggling survivors of humanity, or were they specially selected? I need a clue about why our population started out so large, only to be trimmed down now. As one of the trimmed, I take it personally.

But there's almost nothing beyond what I already know. In fact, every source says almost exactly the same thing, in almost identical words, like a mantra or a prayer. *The remnants of the human species gathered in Eden, to wait until the Earth was renewed.* That's all, as if people were some migrating animals who coalesced by instinct, going into hibernation to wait out a long winter. I never noticed before how few details there are on our own history. I didn't question very much until now. I just swallowed down whatever I was fed.

I turn instead to our founding father, Aaron Al-Baz. There's a ton of information on him, all of it laudatory. It reads more like a legend than pure history. Like every child in Eden I learned this all before, but now that I know I'm living in the great man's house, it seems closer, more vital.

I read how Al-Baz was mocked as a young man for his radical beliefs in the coming end of the world. Still he attracted many followers, even as others condemned him and found fault in his science. He suffered deep humiliation as he was ostracized from the scientific community, his theories about man's doomed interaction with the Earth torn to shreds.

Breathless, I read about his self-imposed exile as he heroically dedicated his life to saving the planet. He was so secretive during that time that there are few facts, only anecdotes. He was trying to stop world governments from approving policies that were killing the environment—and from what I can gather, his methods were not 100 percent above the law. When the heads of nations wouldn't listen, he forced them to listen. In that newly burgeoning digital age when everything on the planet was already well on its way to being linked, a skilled computer scientist could force governments to pay attention.

They called his methods hacking, techno-terrorism,

cyber-guerrilla warfare. But he never harmed a soul, not a person or beast or plant. Unlike the world governments and the destructive weapons and technology they controlled. Al-Baz only took over systems to prove his point, to make people see that they were on a path to destruction—and offer them an alternative. For his pains, he was questioned multiple times and placed under house arrest, his assets frozen.

Somehow he escaped prison for many years. Then came the Ecofail.

According to the history I am reading, the world governments were about to launch their mission to alter the atmosphere to fight global warming. A laudable ambition, though Al-Baz told them it wouldn't work. He tried to stop them, attacking the system that would launch the particles into the atmosphere. But he failed, and was thrown in prison, and while he was captive the Earth died. By the time his followers broke him out, there was barely time to implement his long-term plan, the work of his lifetime: Eden. He activated the program that turned all of the world's technology toward two linked goals—reviving the planet and saving mankind.

In an act of great nobility he saved the people who betrayed him and the Earth—or as many as he could. He preserved the humans who had been unable to care for their own planet. Al-Baz gave us all a second chance, an opportunity to do penance for our selfishness, our stupidity.

And I've lived in his house all my life, and never knew it.

As soon as Mom comes home—before either Ash or Dad—I pounce with questions. "How did we end up living in Aaron Al-Baz's house?"

"Can we talk about it later?" she asks. There are dark circles under her eyes, and her hair is uncharacteristically messy, with strands flying crazily out of her usually tight twist. "We have a lot of other things to discuss."

"No, this is important," I say. "How could I not know?"

She shrugs. "It isn't a big deal. We're distant relations, through his sister, I think. But it was a long time ago. How did you find out?"

I didn't quite think that one through, but she doesn't seem to notice the long pause before I say, "I came across a mention in an old history of Eden. Is there anything here that belonged to him?"

"Oh, no," she says quickly. "It was so long ago."

"Not really. Two hundred years isn't that many generations."

She won't tell me any more, and immediately changes the subject.

"Your lenses are ready to be implanted."

I hurl myself into her arms. She's a little taken aback, and I realize she's expecting me to still be upset at leaving home. I am, of course, but to my chagrin the first thing I think of is that I'll be more easily able to walk the streets safely when I sneak out tonight to see Lark. With my eyes looking flat like everyone else's, and what's more keyed to someone else's identity, I can walk past any Greenshirt without a qualm.

"When do we leave?" I ask.

"Oh, they're ready, but your surgery won't be for a little while. Another couple of days at least."

"And with them I can pass as an official citizen, a first-born?"

She nods. "These will be a huge step up from the black market lenses criminals use. They can't access all of the technology. Some things, like the filter for the altered sun rays, and the identity chip, work okay on the cheap, removable lenses. But there are deeper layers that no one has been able to suss out . . . until we found someone brilliant. Normally, the lenses are manufactured in a factory, and then sent to the Center for further modification by EcoPan. The cybersurgeon we found managed to hack into the Center to get the exact specifications. You don't have to worry. They'll work perfectly. Lots of other second children aren't as lucky as you."

"Lots?" I repeat. This is the first I've ever heard of other second children. What a day for revelations.

"A few, yes, but others use the cheap, removable lenses too. My sources don't talk much, as you might imagine. But from what I gather there are criminals using lower-quality fake lenses, rebels, cheating husbands and wives . . ."

So I'm in great company. But back to the second children. "How many of us are there?" I ask.

She presses her lips together briefly. "Not many. According to my source, perhaps twenty still walking the streets."

"Oh, that's . . . Wait, what do you mean *still*?"

"Oh, honey, you'll be just fine. We found a real genius to make your lens implants, bought the most secure identity, bribed all the right people . . ."

"What are you saying?"

She bites her lip. "My source told me that the survival rate for second children trying to integrate into society . . . isn't as high as we'd like."

"You mean, we die?"

"No, no," she hastily begins, then amends it to "Well . . . a few are captured. But there are a lot who simply . . . disappear."

A chill tickles my spine.

"Don't worry, honey, it won't happen to you. We've taken every precaution." She shakes her head as if tossing away the unpleasant thoughts.

I'm haunted by the image of second children disappearing. The way Mom said it, it sounded like they just evaporate, turn into mist and drift away. It must be the Center, though, capturing second children. They must be dragged away into the night and fog, and no one ever knows what happened to them.

Mom won't talk about it anymore, no matter how much I press. Not long afterward Ash comes home, and with a quick mutual glance Mom and I agree not to discuss anything serious or worrying in front of him. Stress aggravates his condition. I also want to ask where I'll be going. Will it be to a childless couple? Will I be posing as an orphan, adopted by a kind relative? I might even have a brother or sister. Will I like them?

My new family *must* be kind, though, if they're taking the risk of welcoming in a secret second child. They'll be generous and loving and patient and caring, and they'll help ease my way into the world. I know they will, because only that sort of person would defy all Eden to help a child.

How can I worry too much when I have Lark's company to look forward to? Dinner passes insufferably slowly. I know I should be savoring every moment with my family before it all changes, but my thoughts keep straying to tonight.

Before I go to bed, I look at my strange, multicolored eyes. What will I feel like when my eyes are flat and dull like everyone else's? I won't be me anymore.

Even though everyone I've really seen in my life (all four of them, aside from passersby last night) has these flat lifeless eyes, it shocks me to imagine seeing them staring blankly out of my face. Those flat eyes are unnatural, wrong, in a way I never appreciated before, until it became personal. All the light and variation of my irises will be crushed. They'll be a dull gray-blue. I'll look like a blind girl, though my vision will be unchanged.

Mom ducks her head into the bathroom, and I blink to hide the moisture gathering in my eyes. "Your dad and I are taking the day off of work tomorrow to be with you, and Ash is staying home. We'll have a real family party then. All your favorite foods. And we'll have a chance to talk about . . . ," she breaks off, "some important things you need to know."

Whatever they are, why did she wait until my final days to tell me?

Soon afterward, everyone is in bed. I pretend to sleep, too, but under my bed is a bag containing the clothes I plan to wear. I breathe slowly, quietly, listening to the sounds of the house: Ash turning in his sleep, the soft settling sound the walls make when the temperature drops at night. When I'm sure everyone is deeply asleep, I grab my bag and slip out to the courtyard.

Right on the other side is the world. And Lark. My fingers tremble as I strip off my nightclothes and stand almost naked in the dark. Above me the stars twinkle dimly, and I tilt my head back to let their muted light fall on me. I know almost nothing about the stars, not their names or the science behind them. But I love looking at their glowing patterns because they remind me that there's a world outside of my courtyard, outside of Eden even. And they make me think of my most treasured possession: the ancient, faded, crumbling photo from before the Ecofail that Mom smuggled out of the archives. I've brought it to share with Lark. She can keep secrets.

I thought more about what to wear than I did about leaving home. The fact embarrasses me, but I know that if I didn't have the distraction of Lark and sneaking out, I'd be going crazy with what's happening in the rest of my life.

After long consideration and much pawing through my meager wardrobe (mostly made up of duplicates of Ash's school uniforms and casual clothes), I settled on one of my few feminine pieces: a deep red skirt that flares to my mid-thigh.

The material is imbued with subtle sparkles that flash when the light hits them just so.

For the rest I chose black, partly from limited choice, partly from an instinct that tells me I may need to blend into the night if anything goes wrong. I tuck my black leggings into my soft ankle boots, and adjust the shoulders of a snug synthwool sweater knitted in an open weave. I know I'll look dull alongside the lurid magenta and ultramarine and canary colors favored by the residents of Eden. But the shock of red at my hips is a rare treat for me. I hope Lark likes it.

I don't want to risk triggering the alarm on the front door, so I scale the wall—now I remember why I rarely wear skirts—and sit at the top, hunkered low to reduce my profile, looking for Lark. For one terrible moment I don't see her. Then she emerges from the shadows, starlight on lilac, and the entire world seems to settle into place.

I remember most of the tricky holds for the way down, and scale the wall easily, leaping down the last four feet just to show off.

"You're amazing!" Lark cries as she runs up to me. "How do you do that? When you climb you look like a squirrel, or . . . a gecko!"

"And you look like a flower," I blurt out before I can stop myself.

She lowers her head for a second, but when she raises it her eyes are shining.

"Here," she says, and hands me a pair of glasses. I unfold them, and see that the lenses are in a faceted kaleidoscope of pink and sky blue and lilac. Lark slips on a pair of her own. "Dragonfly glasses," she tells me. "Aren't they beautiful? Lots of people are wearing them, even at night, so no one will even think about your eyes."

I put them on. Despite the facets on the lenses, when I look through them my vision isn't fractured. The only difference is that a pink-purple glow is cast over the world. Eden has gone rosy tonight.

Lark takes my hand. "Come on! I want to run!" And then we're off, down the road, our linked arms swinging, laughing, careless of who might hear us. We're just two girls enjoying life. Why would anyone look twice?

It isn't long before she's panting, though I'm only just warming up. I feel like I could run forever.

"I can't run like you," she gasps out. "How did you get so fast and so strong?"

"There's not much else for me to do, except run and climb and stretch and exercise," I explain.

She regards me in what I think is admiration. "You're so . . ." She breaks off, shaking her head. "Do you know what you could do with speed like that? No one could ever catch you. The Greenshirts are soft compared to you. Why, I bet you could even outrun a securitybot. And climbing could be pretty useful to someone who . . ." She stops herself again. "But we shouldn't talk about that now. Not until we get there."

"Where's there?" I ask.

She gives me her quirky up-and-down smile. "That's for me to know . . . and you to find out." She crooks her elbow in mine and we head to the nearest autoloop station.

9

PANIC HITS ME as soon as we slide through the turnstile. Walking through a crowd on a public street where everyone goes about their own business is one thing. But here there is an actual checkpoint of sorts, where passengers have to pay for their ticket. I try to back up, but my thighs hit the turnstile's padded bar.

"One way," Lark says, catching my arm. More loudly she adds for the benefit of those behind us annoyed at the holdup, "Don't worry, the bathroom is over this way."

"What if they . . . ," I begin, but she shushes me with a squeeze.

"You'll be fine. I'll put the fare on my chip. Just act normal."

Bikk! Money! I hadn't even thought about that. There are so many little things that could catch me out. I don't have any funds, of course, nor do I know how to use them or what anything costs.

Lark goes first to show me how it's done. It's simple. There's what looks like a mirror at the entrance to the autoloop platform. She lifts her glasses and smiles into it, adjusting her flower-colored hair coquettishly, and says brightly, "Two please!" The mirror quickly dims and brightens again as it reads her eye implants. Her currency has been transferred, and two small chits roll out from a slot under the mirror. She heads through the corridor leading to the station platform. There are people in uniform everywhere. Only one is a Greenshirt, lounging against the wall at the far end of the station, chewing at a hangnail. But even the station attendants alarm me in their crisp, official-looking costumes. They have the bull's-eye insignia of the Center on their lapels, and even if they're low-level functionaries, they still represent the establishment that is my natural enemy . . . whose lair I'm attempting to infiltrate.

Ash was wrong about me. I *am* afraid.

But I hold myself steady, and even force a playful sidelong smile for the ticket-taker. A smile that pretends to openness, but actually hides my eyes just in case he can glimpse anything from the side of the glasses. He takes my ticket and lets me pass.

I feel elated with that simple success! I was afraid, but I did it anyway. Maybe, I think, that's what it means to be brave. Maybe Ash was right about me after all.

Holding my head as high as any firstborn, I follow Lark onto the platform. Within a few minutes the autoloop pulls into the station and we step aboard. When the pneumatic doors slide breathily shut, I flinch. I'm trapped! My speed and agility won't do a thing for me if there's trouble in here. But Lark sits on a molded lime-green seat and slouches down so her knees press against the fuchsia seat in front of her. I slide in beside her, mimicking her position as the autoloop lurches forward. It gains speed rapidly, accelerating on a monorail that coils in a spiral around Eden, from the Center to the outer circles.

"Where . . . ?" I try again, but she shushes me.

"Just look around. This is your first view of the rest of Eden. I'm curious to know what you think." She stands and wiggles until we've switched seats and I'm by the window.

And I look, at scenery more vivid than a datablock, streaming past me so fast that it almost blurs. Whenever I catch sight of something interesting—an oddly shaped building, the swirling green inside an algae spire—I have to whip my head around to follow it. Everything slips behind me. My body, and my life, are moving forward faster than I ever dared dream.

The quality of the neighborhoods changes quickly. As I watch the gaudy lights of the inner circles dim to muted pastels, the chic evening clothes turn to darker, perfunctory casual garments, I realize we were on an express route to the outer circles.

After what feels like a long time later, we slow our headlong rush and descend to ground level. Figures become once again people, not blurs.

When I was in my own entertainment circle, people traveled mostly in pairs, sometimes in loose, casual formations. It seemed as if everyone knew one another, like no matter their age they were all basically part of the same crowd. People flowed from one group to another. Without exception they were smiling, laughing—happy.

Here, in this dingy outer circle, people either move through the streets in tight packs or completely alone. The packs look uniform and tough. They don't wear the same clothes, exactly, but each group seems to have a common theme. There is one pack in black, with tight shining clothes and flashes of metal. I can't tell if they are studs or armor or even weapons. Another group seems to be made up of people like the fascinating snake man I saw in the Rain Forest Club. Like some peaceable (and at the same time savage) kingdom, they flock together, birds with cats, wolves with sheep.

Moving among them are people utterly alone. Most are hunched and introverted, eyes on the ground, taking care to avoid contact with anyone else.

But a few are different. Here and there, as the autoloop cruises into the final station, I see solitary men, and one woman, who look as if they'd be a match for even the black-clad group. They are upright, swaggering, arrogant in their bearing. They walk as if they owned the Earth.

The autoloop has almost stopped when I see him, a young man not much older than me, with bright chestnut hair and a face set in hard lines. He isn't as big as some of the other loners, but in a glance I can tell that he doesn't care, that he has absolute confidence that he can handle anything the world might throw at him. For a second his face turns, and I catch sight of a crescent-shaped scar from the corner of his left eye to just below his cheekbone. I pull my head back so he doesn't see me. But he was only glancing at the train. The next second we've pulled into the covered station.

Lark jumps to her feet, looking excited. "Come on!" she says, pulling me after her and lunging for the door. Only a couple of other people rise along with us. Some of the inner circle travelers seem to be tourists. "That's the Deadnight gang, I do believe," one woman says in cultured tones to her chic friend. "And do you see that splendid specimen? That's the Jaguar. They say she once killed five men in one night."

"I heard it was four men, a woman, and a child," her companion says, shivering deliciously. They giggle softly behind their hands.

The boisterously civilized inner rings were one thing, but Lark actually expects me to go out into this maelstrom of danger and strange humanity?

"Do you trust me?" Lark asks when she sees the naked uncertainty on my face.

I only pause for a second. In that instant, an image of Mom flashes through my mind. *Don't trust anyone except family*, she would tell me. *Your very life is at stake.*

"I trust you completely," I say firmly.

Lark smiles, and takes me into the outer circles.

What can I say about that night? To say it was like nothing I'd ever experienced would be pointless. I've never experienced *anything*. Like nothing I'd ever imagined? I didn't even know enough of the world, and people, and pleasure, to begin to imagine anything like it.

"A girl who keeps her wits about her isn't in any danger," Lark tells me as we saunter through the dim streets. "They're not bad people. Just poor, that's all. Most would never dream of hurting anyone. As long as you don't make any mistakes."

Apparently, there are a lot of potential mistakes I might make. One gang, she says, would attack me if I spit within their sight. No worry about that. Even if I wasn't too polite, my mouth is far too dry. Another gang insists that anyone they pass should immediately stop and turn their backs on them. "For them, keeping an eye on them is a sign of mistrust, and a grave insult. If you turn your back, though, you're showing you trust them and so they'll leave you alone."

I would be lost without her. Again.

She takes me to a club, a place both calm and wild at the same time. No one is dancing. There are booths and tables, and recessed nooks hidden by curtains. People drink bitter black coffee (or as near as we can get, synthetic caffeine in a liquid suspension) and listen to someone on stage say perplexing, deep things that sound seditious. I don't quite understand him, but he speaks about freedom and autonomy and endless open spaces in a way that makes my heart soar. We take a booth and listen to the conversations all around us. Everyone has an opinion. Voices rise. The mood turns agitated. Someone throws a chair across the room, shouting, "Better to be killed than lied to!" There is a quick brawl, before large bouncers tattooed all over in fern fronds haul out the offenders, and everyone else goes back to arguing about everything under the sun.

It is wonderful.

My skin is positively tingling with excitement, or maybe caffeine, when Lark pays the tab and leads me out. "But I like it so much here!" I protest. It was just right for me—an exciting spectacle I could enjoy without directly participating in. No one cared that I didn't make eye contact or engage in debate. They were too intent on their own points, too in love with the sound of their own voices, to bother with me. It was like a classroom for me, a lesson in social behavior.

"But there's more, even better. Now that we're properly twitchy we have to work it off."

I don't know what she means, but I soon find out when we enter a warehouse tricked out like a jungle. It is almost entirely unlike the Rain Forest Club. I can see the difference now. That was all about décor and style, about creating an impression. This place is as close to real as our dead planet can get. They seem to have ripped up a chunk of actual primordial forest from before the Ecofail, complete with deep earthy, mossy smells, vines with wicked thorns, and shrieking beasts that swipe at my ankles. It seems thrillingly dangerous, utterly genuine.

It is dark, a simulated moon hanging gibbous in the sky, but I can see people dashing across open spaces, diving for cover.

"What is this place?" I ask.

Lark looks at me with burning eyes. "Primal," she says, and hands me a stylized gun.

For the next hour, we work as a team shooting laser beams at our opponents as we leap like mad monkeys through the underbrush. It's a battle of man against man, but also of man against nature. The jungle doesn't take sides. Simulated serpents strike our ankles, giving us electric shocks and de-activating our weapons for several minutes. Robotic jaguars knock us to the ground just as we're about to score a point.

By the end, Lark is out of the game, and so is almost everyone else. It's just me against a team of three, evidently experienced players in matching uniforms. Without Lark holding me back, I scale a tall tree and annihilate them from thirty feet up in the air.

I'm panting, sweating, exhausted . . . and utterly happy.

"Oh, Lark," I say when I slither down the artificial tree. "This is perfect—just perfect! Thank you!"

She sways toward me for a second, then pulls away. "The night's not over yet," she says with her quirky smile. I can't even imagine what might be in store for me next. Dancing? Racing? Fighting?

It is something completely different. And infinitely better.

An abandoned algae spire.

"It hasn't worked for years," Lark says. "My dad was fix-ing the pumping system, but they canceled the repairs before he could get it operational. I snatched his keycard." The door clicks unlocked, and she pulls it open on creaking hinges.

Inside, it is pitch black. I hang back, but Lark pulls me into the darkness and shuts the door behind us. "The power has been cut," she says, "but I know the way." Her voice is like a beacon in the black. I fumble for her hand but she's suddenly out of reach.

"Where are you?" I call, and her voice answers from too far away.

"Walk forward," she instructs. She sounds farther away now. I have no idea of the size or shape of the room, what might be hiding in it.

"Where are you?" I call again. I feel lost, disoriented. "Wait for me!"

She laughs, low and rich. "You're safe. Just walk."

"But I can't see!" What if there's an obstacle, a chasm, a Greenshirt lurking in the dark. I feel paralyzed.

"Do you trust me?" Lark asks again.

I do trust her. I might not have much experience with people, but I know in my heart that Lark will never do me any harm. I take a deep breath, and step into the obsidian darkness.

My paces are shuffling, tentative, but eventually my outstretched hands meet Lark's fingers. They intertwine like vines. I can't see a thing, but I can almost feel her smiling.

"Now up!" she says, and guides my hands to the rungs of a ladder.

We climb forever, hundreds of feet. The journey is surreal. We don't talk, but I hear her breathing just above me, hear the sounds of her feet hitting each slippery metal rung. Without any visual to orient myself I feel like I'm climbing in a dream. And Lark, above, is leading me deeper, higher, to someplace I never imagined.

Finally, an eternity of climbing later, I hear the scrape of a metal latch and suddenly Lark is illuminated from above by a faint glow of light. She climbs out of the narrow ladder shaft, and when I clamber after her I find myself looking down on all of Eden. The pale green concentric circles stretch out far-ther than I can see, away from the glittering eye of the Center. I feel like the EcoPanopticon itself, looking down on all that remains of mankind.

"How did you even find this place?" I ask her, then before she can answer I add, "and what's an inner circle girl like you doing all the way out here in the boonies anyway?" We're far from our home circle. Though the height and the darkness lend a glamour to the streets directly below us, I can still see the squalor, the run-down buildings, the furtive scurrying of the pedestrians.

"I used to live here."

I gasp. I knew that Lark had relocated from another circle when she was about ten years old. When she came to the Kalahari school, Ash was selected to show her around. He told me about her that night, and every night since. But I'd assumed she'd moved from the next ring out. That, apparently, wasn't too uncommon. Moving so far inward from one of the outer circles was unheard of.

I remember that her arrival in our elite circle caused a bit of a stir. Ash told me that some of her classmates wouldn't invite her to birthday parties, and that her parents were shunned. Even my dad wondered aloud at dinner one evening whether Ash shouldn't curtail his friendship with a girl of low origin, as he put it.

This wasn't quite the outermost circle, but it was close, maybe two rings in from the slums of the farthest outer circle. I couldn't imagine Lark living here.

She told me her story briefly while I tried to hide any trace of surprise or, Earth forbid, disgust, from my face. She came from a diligent, hardworking family who lived in a multistory tenement in this district. They scraped by for a living, and were happy. Sure, there were problems. Sometimes there were blackouts, or the water turned the color of rust. Sometimes Greenshirts hauled a neighbor away. Once she even found a dead body on the front stoop.

"But it wasn't bad. You knew who your friends were. And everyone here could keep a secret."

She told me how her father had discovered something while working on the water conduits deep under the spire. "He was a construction worker, basically, laying pipes and repairing valves. Then one day he . . . he found something."

What? I naturally want to know.

She shrugs. "He wouldn't say. Not even to his boss. But

he managed to find a Center official, and told him what he found, and almost immediately afterward he got a Center job in the city planning division and we moved to the inner circle."

"And you have no idea what he discovered?"

"No. He told us just enough that we'd understand why our fortunes suddenly changed. But he made it clear that his life depended on secrecy. And then . . ." Her brow crinkles. "I mentioned it a couple of years later, and it was like he didn't remember it at all. He said he'd gotten promoted because he invented a new kind of automatic shutoff valve and the people at the Center were so impressed they elevated his status."

"Maybe he was just really committed to the lie," I suggest. "Maybe he was protecting you."

"Maybe," she says, then shakes her head so her lilac hair brushes her cheeks. "But let's not talk about that. I brought you here for the view: Look up."

I've been so focused on looking down at the city I've yearned for all my life that I haven't looked skyward. I follow her gaze up to the heavens and gasp. The tip of the algae tower spirals to a sharp point above us, but beyond that . . . the universe!

My fingertips reach in my pocket to touch the ancient photo I've brought. The stars seem so much clearer here in the outer circle. From my courtyard I can only see the faintest pinpricks of light in the sky. Maybe because the city lights are so bright. The gaudy earthly glare is too much competition for those distant heavenly fires.

"It's amazing," I breathe, transfixed. The stars have patterns that I've never seen. I've read in ancient history lessons about how people have given clusters of stars names: the Bear, the Dragon, the Crab. I almost think I can see shapes in the random twinkling dots.

"That's Orion, the hunter," Lark says, pointing out the line of three bright stars marking his belt, and then showing me his starry sword. "And that's the Big Dipper." She settles on the cool, smooth ground, her hands behind her head as she gazes up. It feels natural to lie beside her, so I do, our flanks touching.

"My dad loves the stars," she says. "He taught me every single one—their names, their patterns, their movements. It was the thing I missed most of all when we moved to the inner circle. I can only see a fraction of these from home. So I come out here whenever I can, to look at the stars, and think, and dream."

"What do you dream about?" I ask. I feel like I'm falling into a trance of happiness. Life couldn't get any more sweet.

"Oh, lots of things. Getting out of Eden. Walking through a real forest. Having a government that doesn't lie all the time . . ."

I turn to look at her, my breath brushing her cheek.

"Oh, forget I said that last one. We can talk about that tomorrow." The word "tomorrow" makes me giddy. I want there to be a thousand tomorrows. Ten thousand tomorrows. "I do a few things, along with a few people in this circle. Things that make it convenient to have a good place like this to hide. But don't worry about that now."

I'm not inclined to worry about anything just now.

"What do *you* dream about?" she asks me.

"Finding someone," I say immediately. "Someone who I can trust, someone who makes me complete." I bite my lip, and my face flushes hot. "That's stupid, I know. It's just that I never had anybody, really. Not someone who I chose, or who chose me."

Lark rolls toward me, propping herself up on her elbow. She looks into my eyes and says solemnly, "*I* chose you."

Then, slowly, she bends until her lips touch mine. Her lilac hair tumbles over us, and through it I can see the stars shining. Oh Earth, they're spinning! They're dancing . . .

———

AT HOME IN bed that night—that morning—I lie awake and confused. I don't know what to feel, and a hundred conflicting thoughts bombard me. I bounce from elation to concern to fear, and back to elation again. Always back to elation. Before we parted, I gave her my prized possession, my ancient image of a starscape over a vast chasm, an image captured just before the Ecofail. When she looked at it, I remember she frowned a bit.

"What is it?" I asked her.

"I don't know. It reminds me of . . . something. I can't quite place it. Let me think, and I'll tell you tomorrow."

Tomorrow.

Finally I fall asleep.

It can't be an hour later when Mom is shaking me awake, hissing into my ear, "Get up! We have to leave. Now!"

10

ADRENALINE SURGING THROUGH me like lightning bolts, I'm on my feet before I'm even aware that I'm not dreaming. "No," I mutter even as I move. Let me get back to my dream of happiness. My first thought—really my only thought in these hazy first moments of waking—is that I can't let anything get in the way of meeting Lark again tonight. I don't know what that kiss meant, to her or to me. I don't know how I feel about it. But I need more time to find out.

It is a while before I realize that this isn't just an acceleration of the plan, a blip that will keep me from Lark for the night, a delay of my hopes. This is the end of everything I've known.

"They've found out about us. About you," Mom tells me as she starts to throw all my clothes into a trash bag.

I sit down hard on my bed. Oddly, the first thing that comes out of my mouth is "Why can't I use a suitcase?"

"We have to burn your clothes. We have to get rid of everything that has anything to do with you. When you're gone, we'll sterilize the room, eliminate any prints, kill any DNA evidence of you . . ."

My brain is still fuzzy with sleep, and with Lark. "But Mom, what will I wear?" It seems like the most important question, somehow, in my sleep-addled confusion. When I fell asleep, I was planning my outfit for tonight with Lark, and now . . .

"It doesn't matter—anything! Just throw something on." She's completely distraught. My clothes are flying, tumbling, balled up as she hurls them into the bags. "Hurry! Get dressed!" She tosses me a belted tunic in rich saffron-orange and a pair of shimmering gold pants from Ash's school uniform.

Slowly, I pull on the pants and turn my back to strip off my nightshirt. The tunic top is made of the supple material that is supposed to mimic the softest doeskin. I haven't worn it before. Mom picked it up only a week ago, and it still has the price tag on it. It cost an exorbitant fee.

I stand there, shirt poised to slip over my head, an idea almost clicking . . . but not quite.

"Hurry!" Mom barks again, and I realize she's terrified. Whatever I was almost thinking is lost. I belt the tunic and turn, kneeling down beside her as she throws away my entire life.

"Mom, stop a second and tell me what's happening." I try to sound calm, soothing, but her naked fear is contagious. She takes a deep breath, then another, looking like she's considering how much I should be allowed to know. "Tell me everything," I insist.

"Our friend in the Center just tipped me off that they know about a second child. He didn't have many details, so I don't have any idea how they could possibly know, but now we're all in terrible danger."

Oh, great Earth! I've been so selfish! All this time I was only thinking of myself, of taking my life into my own hands and freeing myself from my captivity, of exploring the world, of making a friend for the first time in my life. I took pains not to be caught, but I was thinking only of *me* not being caught. It was a risk I was willing to take—for myself—and I trusted first in my own abilities, then in Lark, to keep me safe.

I never really thought about what it would do to my family if anyone found out about me. It was in the back of my mind, but only as a logical thread, not as a real conscious fear.

Now, looking into my mother's frantic eyes, I realize what I might have done. To her, to Ash, to my father.

But how could they know about me? If a scanner or bot had detected me, I would have been swarmed with Greenshirts right away. They wouldn't have given me a chance to go home. If I had been spotted and marked, I would have known. The reaction would have been immediate, and brutal.

Unless someone had turned me in. Someone who I'd shared my secret with. Someone I trusted.

I shake my head. No, not Lark. It can't have been Lark. She would never do that. I think of the passion in her eyes when she talks about the problems of Eden, the inequality, the injustice. I remember the way she looks at me, soft and curious.

I won't let myself think that, I decide. But I'd be a fool not to.

Right now, though, I need to calm Mom down and figure out more clearly exactly what is going on. "Do we really have to leave now?" I ask, my hand reassuringly on her arm. "Are they coming right this second?"

She takes a deep, shuddering breath. "No. Maybe. He just said that there's a report of a second child who has been spotted in this circle." She claps her fingers over my caressing hand. "You've been careful, haven't you? I know you sometimes go to the top of the wall and peek out."

I bow my head, ashamed. *Oh Mom*, I long to say, *I've done so much more than that.*

"I've thought about telling you not to do it," Mom continues. "But I know how hard it's been for you all these years. I didn't want to begrudge you that little bit of freedom and exploration. It's so inadequate compared to what you deserve."

"I'm sorry, Mom. I . . . I don't think anyone spotted me." Just a Greenshirt, and Lark, and maybe even other people, too. Oh, how could I have been so stupid, so selfish?

"I don't think it was anything you did. It might not even be you. There are other second children in Eden. He didn't think they'd zeroed in, but he knows that they're tracking a second child in our circle. It's only a matter of time before they figure it all out. When they come, every trace of you has to be gone. *You* have to be gone."

I nod, understanding. It's a shock, and I know that wherever I go I'll have to lay low for a while, but when the hunt dies down, when they don't find me, I'll be able to see my family again. See Lark again. (Unless she . . . No, I can't go down that road.)

"I'm sorry this is all so abrupt. I thought we'd have more time. There are things . . . But I'll save that for later. I'm taking you to get your implants now, and then you're going directly to your new foster home. Oh, there's so much I have to tell you!" She throws her arms around me and for a second I feel like a little kid again, small and utterly safe in her embrace.

"It's okay," I reassure her. "I know it might be a while, but when I come back, you can . . ."

Her look stops me, chilled. "Rowan, you can *never* come back."

I feel as if I'm dangling from the top of a wall high as a mountain, clinging by a single hold that's starting to slip. I grasp at anything. "You mean, not until it's safe?"

"Oh my love, never. You can never come home. You can never see any of us again."

My hand slips and I tumble into the abyss.

She tells me how long they've been working to arrange this foster family for me, a chance at a completely new life where I can be real, accepted, walk the streets of Eden as a free individual. I listen numbly as she explains how I can have a new family, which baffled me before. I thought someone would take me in for love, for commitment to a cause, for belief that all people deserve to live. But no, it turns out someone is just doing it for the money.

Just like the way my family hid me—the extra, living child—some families with an eye to profit hide the fact that their one legitimate child dies. Instead of reporting it to the Center, they do whatever possible to make it look like the child is still thriving. Maybe they say she moved to another circle to help her grandmother. Maybe she supposedly developed an illness and rarely leaves the house. They hold the spot of the missing child, and all the while work with black marketers to find some second child to replace the dead one. Of course the family is paid an exorbitant fee for taking the child. It's enough to set up someone in a whole new circle, if they're clever enough to hide the source of their windfall.

Needless to say, it's mostly people in the outer circles who hide a child's death and hope to profit from it. Mom tells me that the family I'll be going with lives in the next-but-one outermost ring. The slums, even more decrepit than Lark's old circle.

I feel sick. I've become a financial transaction.

"Mom, they don't know for sure who I am or where I live. Can't I get the surgery and . . ." I was going to say hide out with a friend, but I can't tell her about Lark. Mom would be so disappointed in me if she knew what I've done. And she'd believe that Lark betrayed me. Betrayed all of us. I wouldn't be able to stand hearing her say that.

I can fight the truth in my own head, but if it comes from my mom's mouth it will seem real. I don't want to believe it. I can't.

"I can hide out, just ride the autoloop for a few days, find a place in the outer circles to hole up. And then after a few days, a week, if no one has been here to investigate . . ."

Mom shakes her head sorrowfully. "It has to be now, and it has to be for good." She seems to harden herself, standing and turning her back on me to resume throwing my every possession into the trash. I'm hurt, until I realize that she's just trying to carry on, to protect me as always. If she gives in to emotion she'll collapse and she won't be able to protect me.

Protect me by giving me away to money-hungry strangers.

I grit my teeth. This is *my* life! Two nights in the city were enough to fill me with a sense of my own purpose and strength. I decide here and now that even though I have no choice but to go along with Mom's plans, there's no way in hell I'm going to stick with them for the rest of my life. I'll get the eye implants so I can fit in with the rest of Eden. I'll go live with the mercenary family that wants my family's money more than they want me. But it won't be for good. There will come a time when I can be with my family again. When I can be with Lark. When I can stand proudly and be myself, and be with whoever I want, even if I am a second child.

I can't fight this now. But I see a battle coming. Resolutely, I pick up my favorite stuffed animal—a ragged chimpanzee I've cuddled with since I was a baby—and shove it into one of the garbage bags.

At that moment, Ash comes in, rubbing the sleep from his eyes. Mom, with her back turned to him, flashes me an urgent, adamant look and shakes her head almost imperceptibly. I immediately understand: don't tell Ash too much. But is that fair to him? To me?

"What's going on?" he asks. "Why are you throwing away all of Rowan's stuff?"

Mom composes her face carefully. "I'm not throwing it away, silly," she lies with an ease that astounds me. "There's been a change in plans, and the doctor who will perform her surgery is being reassigned tomorrow, so we have to go tonight, right now, to get her implants. We decided it's best if she moves to her new house right away. Since we're moving fast, we don't have time to pack up neatly." She turns to me. "But you don't mind, do you Rowan?"

I gulp, but manage to say, "No, of course not. Who cares about a few wrinkles? I'll iron once I get there."

She's really not going to tell him that someone is actively hunting for me? That I'm never supposed to come back? I open my mouth to tell him myself, then snap it shut. I'm a coward. I don't want to see that look of despair in his eyes. Selfishly, I leave it to Mom to tell him, to bear the brunt of his sorrow. I wonder if he'll forgive me, once he knows. But I just want this last moment with him that isn't marred with too much grief. I will hold it for both of us. What he knows is sad enough.

He's taking it pretty well, though. Mom excuses herself (I hear the hiccup of a sob as she departs), and Ash dumps out a trash bag and starts methodically folding the clothes Mom shoved inside. The repetitive, precise action seems to give him focus, and he talks fairly calmly as he folds. But he doesn't talk about what's happening. He tells me about yesterday at school, how he missed a question on his Eco-history test, how the latest fashion calls for tiny iridescent robotic butterflies in the hair, how Lark seemed strangely tired but happy all day . . .

I understand. He desperately wants everything to be normal. He doesn't want the patterns of the last sixteen years to change.

"I don't know what I'm going to do without you!" I blurt

out suddenly. The shirt he is folding drops into his lap in a messy heap.

He gives a little laugh. "You? What about me? What am I going to do without my sister watching out for me?"

"How do I watch out for you? I'm never out with you."

"You might not be with me, Rowan, but you always have my back. Whenever I need advice, reassurance—anything—you're there for me. Always. I've been thinking more and more about your bravery, and you've inspired me. You know, I think I'm finally going to ask Lark out."

I gasp, just a little, then bite my lip.

"What?" he asks, a little sharply. "You don't think I should? You think she'll say no?"

"I . . . I don't know anything about relationships," I say truthfully. "I think you should do whatever feels right." It felt right when Lark kissed me. But it was nothing like any kind of romance I ever imagined.

"Well, don't worry about that," he says, making an attempt to sound breezy. "You have enough to think about." I sniff. "Listen, I'm doing my best not to cry, too, so let's just look forward to the next time we can see each other. It will be soon, right?"

He looks so eagerly hopeful that I feel my throat tighten. But I manage to say, "I'm sure it will be." Then I fling my arms around his neck. I can feel his tears dampening my shoulder. Mine are falling, too. It's not fair. He should know.

But Mom, who has apparently been lurking just outside the door, bustles in and says it's time to go.

Ash takes my hand and we walk out into the main living quarters.

"It's only for a little while," Ash whispers, more to reassure himself than me, I think. "We'll be together again soon." I choke back a sob and hug him.

"Come on, we should go," Mom says.

"But you have to say good-bye to Dad," Ash says, with that same look of vague confusion I always see on his face whenever the issue of Dad's relationship with me comes up. Mom and I make sure it rarely does. She and I glance at each other now.

"Right," she says, nodding decisively. "He's in his room. Go on, but be quick."

I'd rather not, but with Ash watching, I should pretend there's at least some normal feeling between us. I knock softly at the bedroom door, but when I don't get an answer I just push it open slowly.

He's in striped pajamas, perched tensely at the edge of the bed. "You're still here," he says.

Oh, Dad, even now, even at the end, you can't just lie and pretend to just a little bit of feeling? Not a good luck, or an I'll miss you, or anything?

Nothing. So I steel myself and say coldly, though with a tremor in my voice, "For another minute, anyway."

He nods, looking down at his knees. I search for anything— sadness, anger—but his expression is unreadable. Mostly it seems like he's waiting. He's been waiting for sixteen years for me to conveniently disappear from his life, and now, if he can just hold out a little longer, he'll get his fondest wish.

"Okay then, Dad," I say, swallowing hard. "Good-bye."

I wait. Nothing except the crease of his frown deepening between his brows.

So I leave. Leaving him is the one thing I'm truly glad of in all this mess.

11

IT FEELS SO weird going out through the front door like a regular person. Mom glances at me like she's expecting me to be in shock at being outside for the first time in my life, so I do my best to look awestruck, to gawk at everything from what she imagines is a new perspective.

She leads me to the small arched outbuilding that holds our tiny car. I've read that back before the Ecofail, cars were huge monsters that ate fossil fuels with a gluttonous appetite. They actually burned gasoline, with engines that ran by caging explosions. They were violent juggernauts that thundered through the world by the billions like vast migrating herds of some destructive creature.

We still use the word "car," but the few that exist in Eden (almost all in the inner circles) are nothing like their namesake. Our water-fueled vehicle is an elegant deep-pink egg with a shell so thin we can see the world around us in a rose-colored haze. It reminds me of Lark's glasses.

We sit in comfort in the center, as Mom switches the controls to manual. Usually, you tell it where you want to go, close your eyes, and listen to music until you're there. Like the bots that zip through the city, Eden's cars are programmed to avoid collisions, and are usually completely autonomous.

Few people use the manual option. Of course, Mom doesn't want a record of where we're going.

I have to keep it together, I think as I stare out at the fleeting scenery, the landscape that, after a couple of nights out, now seems almost familiar. It is slowly sinking in how serious this is. Not just that it is the end of everything I know. Suddenly, the danger feels real. Before, when I snuck out it was scary, sure, but there was always an edge of excitement to it, like when I played laser hunt with Lark. Sneaking out was a challenge, and getting home again with adventure and experience under my belt was a victory.

Now, though, someone is apparently actively hunting me. This just got real.

I reach over and take my mom's hand, leaving her to drive with the other. She flashes me a quick, loving look, then fixes her eyes back on the road. It's about 3 a.m. and the streets are virtually deserted. Even the cleanbots are recharging. Still, she has to be careful. An accident would be disastrous.

"Out in the world at last," Mom says, squeezing my fingers as she maneuvers down one of the radial streets, away from the green glowing eye of the Center. "And you didn't even have to knock down the courtyard walls to do it," she jokes. "I always knew, right from the start, that it was going to be hard for you. But now my strong-willed little girl is growing into a strong-willed woman. Rowan, I am so proud of you."

She speaks the words very distinctly, as if she's trying to burn them into my memory.

"And now you're finally going to get the freedom you deserve."

"But the price!" I say.

She shakes her head. "I . . . we would have spent anything to help you have a normal life. Luckily we can afford it."

"That's not what I mean."

"I know," she says softly. "But there's always a price, to every decision. I've paid a heavy price since the moment you were born, a price of guilt at the life I've forced you to lead. And your father . . ." She breaks off, and I notice for the first time that she has my habit of clenching her jaw in moments of extreme emotion. I don't think I've ever seen her upset until the past few days. She always seemed so calm, so stable, so happy . . . though I wonder now whether she kept her equilibrium at home to make things easier for the rest of us.

"What about my father?" I ask sharply.

"It's . . . nothing."

Of course I can tell from her voice, from the play of muscles in her jaw, that it is the very opposite of nothing. "We only have a little while longer, Mom. You owe me honesty." I see her wince a little. "He hates me, and I don't know why. Is it just because I'm an inconvenience? An obstacle on his path to greatness?"

"Oh, sweetheart," she begins, and I can tell she wants to lie. But finally she says, "He doesn't hate you, Rowan. He hates himself."

In a halting voice she tells me what she herself only found out a few years ago, when my father was drunk and tired and weak and too crushed under the burden of his guilt to keep the secret any longer.

When my dad found out that Mom was pregnant with twins he took it upon himself—without asking her, without telling her—to try to abort one of us. During what was supposed to be a routine prenatal check he used a modified ultrasound device he created to try to destroy one of us.

Did he pick his victim at random? Did he let chance decide whether Ash or I would be a first child, an only child—or no child at all?

No. He wanted a son.

When there were billions of people still crawling on the planet, men and women weren't always treated equally. Ash and I used to laugh about that when we studied ancient history together. Imagine, anyone thinking women were lesser than men! Here in Eden, I believed that kind of prejudice didn't exist.

Dear old Dad, though—he wanted a child created in his own image. He wanted a boy to mold like him, to follow in his footsteps, to become a great doctor or politician.

"He aimed the ultrasound device . . ."

"Call it what it is, Mom," I say bitterly. "A weapon." I think of myself, huddled in the womb with Ash, safe and warm . . . with my own father aiming a gun at my head.

"He aimed it at you, but something happened. He was almost incoherent when he confessed, and I never spoke with him about it again, but he said that you moved at the last second. That you were close to Ash, that . . . that you hugged him. You pulled him to you, and the sound beam hit Ash instead of you. Your father shut it off instantly, but some damage was done. It hit Ash in the chest. It injured his lungs."

To my surprise, a tiny part of me almost feels sorry for the monster that is my father. For sixteen years he's lived with the guilt of the crime he committed. Every day he has to look at his ill son and think *That's my fault.*

But every day he has to look at his daughter and think *I tried to kill her, and failed.*

I feel sick inside.

There's one thing I can't understand. "You forgave him for that?"

She's quiet for a long moment, steering the car around a tricky curve as we skirt an algae spire.

"No," she whispers at last. "But it was best we stay together." She takes a deep breath. "Rowan, I know you want to talk more about that, but it isn't relevant now. The past can't be changed. But . . . it has to be understood. Listen carefully. I put something in your backpack. Something I found in the house long ago, around the time you were born. It . . . it changed the way I see things. It made me believe that . . . *Bikk*!"

I see her eyes widen at the vista ahead. "Oh, great Earth, no!"

Ahead of us are the flashing blue-and-green lights of a Greenshirt checkpoint. We've just turned onto one of the narrow radial roads that connect one ring to another. There are no side streets, and the road is barely wider than our car. We could turn around, but it would be blatantly obvious we were avoiding the checkpoint. They would be after us in a heartbeat.

I can see the choices flashing across my mother's face, foremost among them a panicked urge to make a run for it. I don't know. If I was on foot, and alone, I'd go for it. But cars aren't designed to go more than twenty-five miles per hour, and if we bailed, Mom couldn't run as fast as me. Plus they'd easily find out who owned the car.

Mom has an answer, though.

"Pretend you're asleep. Pull your hat over your face and curl up against the far door. I can probably talk my way through." She gives a weak chuckle. "After all, I work for the Center, and have friends in high places." Dropping my father's name would certainly help. How ironic, that he might actually save my life this time.

I have confidence it will work. I know that Greenshirts tend to respect anyone with a Center ID. Still, I can feel myself tremble as I tuck myself into a ball. We cruise slowly toward the checkpoint. It is such a long way away that it feels foolish now not to have turned around, but I have to trust Mom's judgment.

She talks to me in a low voice as we progress toward the barricades and flashing lights. "The surgery center is in a back office of a modification parlor called Serpentine." I understand. That's a place where the people who believe they should have been born into an animal body get their scales and claws and horns. "It's in the next-to-last circle, on the east side. An orange building, almost the color of your tunic. There's an electric fence around it, but third panel from the left on the southeast corner is turned off from three to four in the morning. You can climb over. Go to the back door and knock twice up high, and three times down low. Can you remember that?"

"Yes," I murmur into the sleeve that is curled over my face.

"And whatever happens, keep that backpack close. Keep it safe."

Wait . . . keep *it* safe? Not keep *me* safe?

"What . . . ?"

"Shh," she cautions. "There's something inside for you. Something that . . . Stay down! They're coming toward us. They have their weapons out." She gasps. "Are those *real* guns?"

It's too late for me to ask what she means by that, but I have a terrible idea I know. All Greenshirts carry weapons, the kind that slam you with an electrical charge carried in plasma. They're usually called guns. But before the Ecofail I know there used to be more lethal things, also called guns, which shot metal bullets that ripped through human bodies. They've been outlawed in Eden. Could Mom possibly mean . . . ?

I try not to move, but I know my rapid breathing will give me away if they look too closely. Try as I might, I can't calm my breath to sound like I'm sleeping. I listen as hard as I can.

"Step out of the car, ma'am," one barks right away in a deep, gruff voice.

I can hear the smile in her voice, and I silently applaud her cool. "I'm on Center business," she says, and I'm sure she is tilting her head at him so he can more easily scan her eyes. "My assistant and I were collecting some archival material from the outer circles, and I got turned around. Am I heading inbound now, or out?"

He doesn't answer her question, but only says, "Step out of the car."

Mom's voice hardens slightly. "I said I'm on Center business. There are very valuable documents that needed to be . . ."

"Step out," he says again, flatly. "Now."

I can tell she's starting to sound desperate, but to the Greenshirt she probably only sounds angry when she says, "My husband is Dr. . . ."

I hear the door open, and there's a tussle and scramble. "What do you think you're doing?" she shrieks. "Do you know who I am? You're impeding Center research."

"Quiet!" the Greenshirt commands. "I have orders to search every vehicle originating in the inner circles, no exceptions. Get your assistant out and scanned, and you can be on your way."

"She . . . she's asleep. I've made her work a double shift. Don't wake her, please." She's babbling now, and every nerve of my body yearns to spring to her aid. But I do what she told me, staying curled and helpless as a baby in the womb, even when I hear her say, "Let go of me!" followed by a cry of pain.

I stay immobile, following Mom's orders, trusting her to

protect me, even when I hear someone grasp the door handle on my side. A second later my body is shifting as the door I'm leaning against is pulled open. I turn my grunt of alarm into a sleepy sound and keep my eyes closed. There's a crunch of rapid footsteps. "Leave her alone! She's my assistant, traveling under my pass! You have no right!"

But I feel hands under my armpits, trying to haul me out. I want to kick, to punch, to run, to scream, but all I can do is curl up, eyes closed. I hate being helpless. But Mom said . . .

The hands let me go. Then comes a sound that makes my eyes fly open. A solid, meaty *thwack*. He hit Mom?

I search through the darkness, my eyes taking a while to adjust. There's a figure standing, and one crumpled to the ground. But when my vision resolves I find Mom standing, panting, with the Greenshirt's handheld eye scanner in her hand. The Greenshirt himself lies in a heap at her feet, groaning softly. There's blood on his temple . . . and on the scanner.

I've scraped my knees in falls, bloodied my fingers with a bad hold during a climb. But I've never seen blood resulting from violence. It chills me, even on a man I know to be my enemy.

Shouts come from the checkpoint. Three or four other Greenshirts are running at us, though I can hardly see them beyond Mom's body. Her shoulders are squared. She looks impossibly resolute.

"Go!" Mom hisses.

I just stare at the fallen Greenshirt.

She grabs me by the arms and shakes me. "Run, as fast and as far as you can. Get someplace safe, then tomorrow try to get to the surgery center. Promise you'll run and not look back. Promise you won't make this all for nothing."

She ducks into the car and, when she comes out, thrusts the backpack against my chest.

"I love you," she whispers. "Never forget that." Then she shoves me away from her so hard I stagger. "Run!"

And I do. She's my mother, so I just do what she says. Isn't that what good daughters are supposed to do?

Just like good mothers protect their children.

At any cost.

As I turn to run, I see her hurl herself, panther-like, at the first Greenshirt charging up. I freeze, uncertain. There's a flash of metal in the dim predawn light. He's trying to shoot me? But as Mom tackles him the shot goes wide. The sound is deafening, echoing in my ears. There's another shot, like an explosion from much too close, and I hear something whistle sharply past my head.

Real guns. Real, lethal guns.

As I stand there, tense and poised and terrified, there's one more shot. I see Mom pirouette with the impact, a scarlet flower blossoming on her chest. Her eyes as they sweep past me are already dimming, but I see confusion, fear for me, the question *Why are you still here?*

So I run. It's what I do best. I am speed without thought, without emotion, without pain. Only muscle and breath and the surge of my body as I sprint away from my dying mother.

12

I RUN LIKE a machine, unthinking, unfeeling, mercilessly fast and mercifully numb. All that matters is to move. I hardly even remember why. One leg in front of the other; repeat. Even when the sound of gunfire behind me ceases, even when the shouting, boot-steps, and other sounds of pursuit fade away behind me, I still run at top speed. Because there's nothing else I can do.

I used to run like this in my courtyard at home, the endless pounding of my feet driving away my frustrations, the exhaustion an anodyne. I never knew I was training to kill the ultimate hurt. I'm not running to escape the Greenshirts who are after me. I'm fleeing the look in my mother's eyes as she fell. The look that said she was happy to give her life so that I might live. It's too much. I don't want the burden of her sacrifice.

I should have stayed with her. I should have died with her.

But still I run, away, anywhere. I've lost all sense of direction. Wherever I am, the lights are dim, and it will be at least another two hours before the sun comes up. I can imagine I'm running in a world of nothing, a void. I can't even feel my own body anymore.

And I don't feel it at first when, miles later, my foot hits something in the dark and my entire body twists violently as I go down hard. I'm up in an instant, running again, but within three steps I'm hopping. I've sprained my left ankle.

I don't care! I have to keep going! I force myself to move, but every step is agony. I can feel the skin start to tighten as swelling sets in.

No! I can't let this stop me. Because if I can feel the pain of my injury, I'll be able to feel other kinds of pain, too. I clutch the nearest wall and hop through the darkness, putting my left foot gingerly down every few steps and wincing in agony. The pain shoots up my leg . . . seemingly all the way to my heart. I collapse in a dark doorway and the tears start to flow, huge heaving sobs.

Now that I've stopped running, everything hurts. Everything is swollen and bruised. Before, I couldn't stop moving. Now I'm sure I will crouch in this doorway until the end of time. I'll sink into this dead Earth and never rise again.

I cry until I can't breathe, until my sobs turn to ragged, hiccuping gasps. And when I have nothing left inside of me— no tears, no strength—a strange sense of calm washes over me. From my recessed doorway shelter I watch the sun come up.

As the sliver of sky I can see between buildings starts to glow pink, I wrap my arms around my knees and simply watch the world wake up around me. I know the grief will return, will never truly leave, but for a moment, in my mental and physical exhaustion I just experience the world. I wonder if this is what an animal feels like, in the moment, without regret or anticipation, simply *being*.

I don't remember whether I saw anyone when I was running—it was all a blur. Now, as the world lightens, I begin to see a few people moving furtively through the streets. They look as if they want to get to their destinations as fast as possible, unobserved. The light reveals a place of dirt and squalor. Debris is tumbled across the streets, and the sidewalk is as rough and broken as if it had been upturned by an earthquake. It's like nothing I've ever seen, or even imagined. I can't retrace my steps, but something tells me I've found my way to one of the outer circles. I think maybe even the outermost circle.

I clamp my jaw tight, press my lips together to keep them from trembling. This is the most dangerous place in Eden. Never mind about the Greenshirts chasing me. I've heard stories about the horrors of the outermost ring whispered when Mom thought Ash and I couldn't hear.

If the Greenshirts catch me, I might possibly get lucky and be imprisoned for life.

If even half of the stories are true, here in the outermost circle death is almost certain for all but the hardest, toughest residents.

I try to remember everything that Lark told me about the outer circles. Hers wasn't nearly as rough as this one must be, but there had to be some similarities. On those two long nights together when we talked about everything under the stars, she told me about the various gangs, about how to move through the streets without being noticed. She even explained a bit about the subtle signs that might be painted or scratched on a door to say whether that house might offer work, or food to the desperate. Other marks might warn people away from certain homes or entire buildings. She told me about the signs people flash to signal their affiliations, their intentions.

But all this came only in passing. It was entertainment, conversation just as an excuse to hear each other's voices. If only she'd told me more, in greater detail. If only I'd paid more attention to her words than to the curve of her mouth as she spoke . . .

Now I have to focus on survival. It's easy to say I'll just

sit here forever, but already I feel something stir inside of me, some urge to act, to save myself. My mother's face keeps looming before me, her loving, worried eyes, but I push it back. I'll cry again later—soon, I'm sure. But now I have to find a place to hide while I figure out how to survive the next hour.

Or minute. Someone is crossing the dilapidated street, heading right for me.

A man—or at last I think it is a man, based on his size—is shuffling in a zigzagging way, tacking unsteadily from left to right as he moves. He's a walking bundle of rags, a motley of faded, dirty cloth. His thick walking stick thumps at his side with each step.

Should I get up? Should I run? I remember reading a passage about predators in an Eco-history book. It said that predators couldn't resist chasing anything that ran. If you held your ground, a tiger might decide not to attack. If you turned and fled, it would pounce and snap your neck.

So I sit in my sheltered nook as he makes his ungraceful way to me. As he gets closer, I can see that his face is caked in grime. On the left side there is a curving smear of what might be dried blood, or else reddish clay. He wears cracked black-framed glasses with smudged lenses. I can't tell if he's young or old. Up close he smells terrible, like urine and moldy bread. Part of me recoils, but another part yearns to help him. But I have no money, no food, nothing but my too-flashy clothes and, I assume, a price on my head.

I'm so fascinated—in an appalled way—by his repulsive appearance and smell that I realize too late I'm staring at him with wide-open eyes.

Bikk! I'm done. I don't know what the Center would pay for information leading to my capture, but it has to be more than this poor bum has ever seen before. He'll tell the first authority figure he sees (though I haven't seen any sign of a Greenshirt or other official), and the hunt will be on again.

I know exactly what I should do. I should spring on him like *I'm* the predator, force him to the ground, beat him unconscious, or worse, to give myself a chance to escape. I'm sure that's what life is like out here on the edge.

I could do it, too. For all that I'm tired, I feel strong. The fear and sorrow combine to make my muscles bunch, my fists clench. I'll dive for his legs, take him down, do whatever I have to. I feel a sick ache in my gut . . .

But before I can act, the man backs away one shuffling step. "Blend in and wait," he mutters, at the same time using his stocky walking stick to scratch a number into the dust of the crumbling building that carpets the ground: 6572. He waits just a second and stomps it to oblivion, dust rising around his booted foot. He peels off his mended, dirty glasses and lets them fall casually by my feet. As he turns I see—or think I see—his eyes flash in multi-hued hazel, bright green, and gold.

Another second child! Well, not a child any longer. An old man, I think, though I can't tell how old beneath the filth. But he's survived this long. If he can do it, I certainly can.

I watch him shuffle unsteadily away. I want to run after him, to ask him questions, to beg him for answers.

And then I think: Is that my fate, my future? A scrabbling, unwashed existence on the fringe of society?

He's gone before I can decide what to do. So I put on the glasses to hide my eyes, and start to think. He's right: in this poverty-stricken circle I stick out like a sore thumb. There are a few people on the streets now, passing in their furtive way without seeing me. In stark contrast to the people in my home circle, they are dressed in dark, sober colors, faded black and muddy hues. Even though I'm dusty, sweaty, and disheveled, my clothes are obviously bright and expensive. I feel a twinge of shame. I never realized my life was easy until now.

I need to do something about my appearance right away. I might not have any money, but I envision myself being robbed for my clothes alone, stripped and abandoned on the street.

Or *not* abandoned, which would be far worse.

Can I get a change of clothes somehow? I wouldn't know where to begin. I'll just have to dirty up these clothes and hope the costly sheen doesn't show. If only I was in the pre-fail days, it would be easy—back then, there was real dirt. Here, though the street is filthy enough, it's all building dust, food waste, and mysterious oozy puddles. I scratch up dust from my doorway and rub it into my orange-gold sleeves. Then I add some to my sweat- and tear-soaked face. I pull my hair out of its braid and tug the strands over my face.

I know it isn't enough. Now instead of looking like an inner circle girl who's lost, I just look like an inner circle girl who's crazy. But it will have to do. The big question at the moment is: can I trust the bum? He gave me glasses to hide my eyes, but what about that number he scratched into the dust? It must be a building number. Or maybe a code? But to what? In any case, I can't stay here all day. I'm tucked away and unobtrusive, but with the sun coming up people will definitely notice me, and attention is the last thing I need.

To find shelter, I'll have to venture out into the open.

Look like you're not afraid. That's what Lark told me when I was nervous about walking among the poor, the street people, the gangs in her home circle (which seems so civilized now). *Walk like you belong here. Don't make eye contact, but don't look down either. Own the space you move in.*

So I gather my confidence and step out. In the growing light of day, the place looks like a war zone. How can anyone live like this? The idea that has been nagging me for days suddenly solidifies. How can this poverty exist in Eden? The principle of this survival city has always been sustainability. They're willing to kill me, and any second child, to keep the population in check so there will be enough food and water and other resources for everyone.

Why on Earth then do some people have so much, some so little? It makes no sense. The inner circle people don't need exotic nightclubs, decadent food, and luxury clothes. If they had a little less, the people out here would have a little more. Around me I see broken windows, skinny children with empty bowls outstretched, begging for a scrap. There's a crater in the road that looks like a bomb fell. There are no cleanbots, no securitybots . . .

Why doesn't EcoPan divide the resources equally?

I'm distracted from my thoughts by a group of people moving purposefully along the street. There are six or seven, all dressed in bone-white decorated with a dotted pattern. They look so clean against the grime that I'm immediately relieved . . . until they come closer and I see that what I took for abstract polka dots are really splashes of blood. It is bright and fresh.

"Lost, little girl?" one of them asks in a tone of slimy concern.

"Found, now," a woman says, and they all laugh at the weak witticism.

They start to crowd around me.

"What do you have in your pockets?"

"She doesn't have pockets."

"Must have something good hidden *somewhere*," one says with sly insinuation. "Let's have a look."

I feel a hand on me and something snaps. I punch the closest one in the nose, sending out new decorative sprays of blood and hurting my own hand far more than I anticipated. An elbow takes down another one, and that method feels much better to me. For a second they hardly react. They must not expect an inner circle girl to be capable of much. Some of them are even laughing at their comrades' injuries. They're that confident that I'm not a threat.

I'm not. But neither am I their plaything to rob or torment. I do what I do best. I run.

They must have had a long night. I smell alcohol and synthmesc. They make a token show of chasing me down, but even with my ankle screaming, my gait gimpy, I lose them within half a mile.

I feel the tears starting again, only this time they're tears of frustration. Is this my life now, being alternately accosted by Greenshirts and thugs until one of them finally wins? Isn't this supposed to be a nearly perfect society, a preserve for the last of the humans? Why are humans friendly and happy and easygoing and rich near the center, and trying to assault one another out here?

Someone is approaching. "Get the hell away from me!" I scream, only to see them cower and slink away. It's a middle-aged woman with a bundle under her arm. She wasn't a threat (was she?) and I treated her like a monster. What's happening to me?

I need to find the building the ragged second child told me about. If that's in fact what he meant. Most of the buildings aren't marked. A few have numbers with gaps where some have fallen off. Others have numbers spray-painted on them, half-obscured by graffiti championing one gang or another. That one says 5994 in dark green paint. I wander until I find another: 6003. I'm headed in the right direction, at least. It is a small victory, and my heart feels the tiniest bit lighter. But what awaits me there? An ambush from another gang, or

Center officials, or the strange old bum himself? Maybe he makes a habit of luring lost girls . . .

People look at me, either in curiosity or hostility or evaluation, and I glare back. Finally, though, I see the building he must have been talking about. It is gray and squat . . . and crowded. I smell food, and my stomach gives a growl. How is it that my body still thinks something like hunger is important?

It's a charity house, dispensing food to the poor. In other words, to every outermost circle resident who isn't strong enough to take, or keep what they need. Barefoot children emerge with flatbread smeared with a bland but nutritious basic algae paste. I think of the huge variety of flavors available in my home circle. The food there tastes (so they assure us) exactly like pre-fail food, even if it isn't actually made from fruits and vegetables. Here, it seems, taste doesn't matter. The children wolf their bread and algae down as if they're worried someone might snatch it away.

Then, on the periphery, someone does just that. A scrawny girl cries as a bigger boy yanks her dole out of her hands. She looks down miserably at the crumbs she managed to salvage in her fist. Suddenly the bum is there, moving swiftly through the throng, his motley rags flapping dramatically. No unsteady shuffling this time. He whacks the boy across the shoulders with his cane. The boy drops the bread and runs. It lands algae-side down. The little girl obviously wants to pick it up and eat it anyway, but the bum takes her hand and gently pulls her back toward the charity house. He's gotten a new pair of glasses since our meeting. With his free hand he raises them, flashes me a wink of his bright golden eye, and heads inside. I'll mingle with the crowd and wait for him to return. He has to be able to help me.

I watch mothers standing on the dole line with children

who scamper and cling and laugh and cry, all the things children do when they're bored and waiting. Though the mothers' clothes are worn and torn, though there is despair in the back of their eyes, when they look at their children they're exactly like my mother. They're so full of love and care and worry. They'll do anything for their little ones. My eyes get hot, my throat tightens, as two small children play tag around my legs. The mother examines me curiously, but doesn't seem to condemn me. She calls her kids over and gives me a little smile before turning away. Apparently I'm not a threat, but none of her concern. I relax just a bit . . .

. . . which, I'm learning, is generally a bad idea.

A murmuration goes through the crowd, and it starts to close in around me. I don't know what's happening, but they move like one entity, a multicelled animal with a mysterious but frightening purpose. I'm being closed in by a wall of people. No one is looking at me, but I can feel the heat of their bodies as some twenty people subtly move nearer to me.

Then I hear the voice, loud and commanding. "We're looking for an inner circle girl. Have you seen anyone who doesn't belong?"

They're trapping me! They're holding me for an easy capture, for the reward! I shove my way through, shouldering mothers and children out of the way, and break from the crowd.

"There!" a Greenshirt shouts, and I'm limping away again, a slow and painful half run. I look quickly over my shoulder. Behind me, the people move once more, like a school of fish, a flight of starlings, to get between me and the two pursuing Greenshirts. It is so smooth it looks accidental, circumstantial. The Greenshirts shout at them to move and force their way through after me. By now, though, I have a decent head start.

Then I hear a bullet hit the wall beside me. Without meaning to I skid a brief stop and look at the groove it gouged. That isn't an electrical charge. That's a real solid bullet that will tear apart my flesh!

There's nowhere for me to go but in a straight line. The Greenshirts will have a clean shot at me. Another bullet streaks by my side and I dodge, zigzagging in what I hope are unpredictable turns. I might as well be a difficult target. *Bikk!* Isn't there a place to turn? There are no alleys, no open doors.

"Hold your fire!" someone shouts. The voice is familiar. I hear feet pounding far behind us . . . but not far enough. They're closing in!

I'm too tired to run any faster. Before long, I won't be able to run any farther. My side cramps as if a claw was gripping my ribs, my swollen ankle throbs, and I can hardly catch my breath.

I have to get out of this open space. Finally I see a little side road between two buildings. I dodge sharply in and stagger against the wall as I run painfully on. But the walls get closer together! The road narrows into a dead end filled with piles of stinking garbage.

I whirl around, but it's too late. The two Greenshirts are blocking the entrance. One of them levels his weapon at me. I press against the wall, fall to my knees, curl up in a ball . . . and hope the end will be quick.

There's the sound of a tussle, a thump. I look up to see one Greenshirt standing, the other sprawled at his feet. The one who is standing holds a gun . . . but he's pointing it at the unconscious Greenshirt on the ground, not at me.

I recognize the burly young blond Greenshirt from my first venture into the city. Rook, was that it? He looks scared. Of me? That can't be. Could it be *for* me?

He beckons, but I stay cowering in the garbage.

"Come on!" he whispers urgently. "The others will be here soon."

Cautiously, I rise and approach. His face looks so young. It doesn't match his burly body and menacing uniform. "Do you have a safe place to hide?" he asks.

I shake my head. He looks down the road in the direction we came from. "Where *is* he?" he asks aloud to himself. "Look, I can't take care of you. It's going to be hard enough covering this up." He gestures with his gun to his unconscious comrade. "Just go and hole up somewhere. But come back to the breadline after dark. He'll find you."

"Who will find me?" I choke out, completely confused. "Why are you helping me?"

Apparently the answer to both questions is the same. "My younger brother."

His brother is another second child?

Before I can ask any more questions he curses, and hisses, "Run!" I see other Greenshirts approaching, marching swiftly in tactical formation. I stagger off, clutching my aching side, while Rook squares himself in the line between me and the other Greenshirts so they can't fire at me.

He fires, though. And he misses, deliberately, each time.

I turn toward the only place the Greenshirts might not follow me: the wasteland beyond Eden.

13

EVEN THOUGH ROOK is helping me, I know I'm far from safe. I have one ally, compared to the entire might of the Center, all of the Greenshirts, the security-bots that will cut me down, even the little cleanbots that will alert all the rest of my whereabouts.

But no, I think as I limp away at a half trot. There might be other people on my side. There's Rook's brother, whoever he is and wherever he is. Though I can't expect any help from him unless I can survive the day and sneak back to the bread-line tonight.

And then there's the hobo in rags, his second-child bright hazel eyes twinkling mysterious advice at me. And what had happened at the charity station? When all of those people—mostly mothers and children—crowded around me, I was sure they were part of a conspiracy to capture me. But then when I was spotted, and fleeing, they seemed to step between me and my pursuers. Did I just imagine that? It casts the first occurrence in another light. Though I'm a little incredulous, I think maybe when they closed around me they were trying to hide me, to protect me, to shield me.

But why? I'm a stranger from an inner circle. A second

child who threatens the very existence of Eden. Why would *anyone* help me?

The part of the outermost ring I've seen so far is dirty, crumbling, a place of desperation and squalor—but still, apparently, habitable. As I move outward, though, what was bad becomes so much worse.

Entire buildings seem to have been knocked from their foundations and lay sprawled across the streets like disheveled drunkards. There are huge holes in the road that look like bomb craters. I've read about the wars people fought back in the days before the Ecofail. They slaughtered one another for the flimsiest reasons: disputes over nuances of myths, or ownership of the toxic forms of fuel that gave the world energy back then. But these craters must have been caused by something else, right? Collapsed water pipes or faulty infrastructure. There's no way that the last remnants of the human species could engage in anything like a war.

Whatever the cause, this stretch at the extreme outer edge is like another world, an alien landscape of tumbled masonry and exposed pipes, of shadow even in the brightness of morning. Of loneliness. I don't see a living soul anywhere out here. The wind makes a mournful sound as it wanders through the wreckage of a city.

But alone is good. Alone is safe. Surely somewhere out here amid the devastation is a place where I can hide until nightfall.

Then I hear voices behind me.

"There she is! Get her!"

I dodge behind what was once the wall of a clothing store. A faded sign still clings by one bolt to the lopsided masonry, advertising the latest fashions at a reasonable price. Just as I disappear behind the cover, a spray of bullets embeds itself in the wall. I have the impression that this time the miss isn't deliberate.

"Take her alive!" I hear someone shout, but I can't tell if it's Rook. There are reasons other than compassion why the Greenshirts and the Center might prefer to have me taken alive rather than gunned down in the street. Torture. Interrogation. A public example to the citizens of Eden . . .

I break cover to dash as fast as I'm able to the next crumbled edifice. A quick backward glance shows them moving slowly in tactical formation, as if they're expecting to be attacked themselves. Maybe out here in this outlaw place they have more to worry about than me. I thank my lucky stars. I'm so slow now that if they pursued me at speed, I'd have no hope. But as long as they move in that cautious, stalking, defensive way, I can limp fast enough to stay ahead of them.

For a while, anyway. Until my ankle gives out, or I make a wrong turn and get cornered.

Panting, I lean against a wall riddled with what look like old bullet holes. What on Earth happened out here? My leg muscles are starting to twitch in protest, and my side is cramped, but my ankle has swollen enough that, for a little while anyway, the nerves are too pinched to hurt much. I know it won't last, and any minute the stabbing pain will start. I just hope the ankle can bear my weight.

I know I shouldn't rest, but my body has a mind of its own and I lean against that wall way too long. A bullet hits the masonry over my head, and with agonizing slowness I coax my legs into a run.

I round a corner . . . smack into a twenty-foot wall of twisted, tangled metal and wires, and concrete, all corners and sharp places. *Bikk!* The second they come around this corner, they'll have an open shot. The wall of debris is unbroken, and there's no way back except the way I've come. Back toward the Greenshirts. I try to climb—it's one of the things I do best—but every hold either slices my hands or collapses beneath them. The wall is impenetrable, unclimbable, and stretches as far as I can see in either direction.

I want to cry. Not from grief this time, but from pure self-pity. I'm so tired! I hurt so much! I'm thirsty and bloody and bruised and my ankle is screaming now and my hands are raw . . . I can't do this anymore. I can hear them coming.

I have no hope. I've reached the end.

I just want to lie down. What does it matter now? I let myself sink down, and the blessed relief of giving in to gravity—of giving in, period—is so welcome that I almost want to sprawl there, clasp my hands behind my head, and just gaze at the sky, waiting for the end to come.

But I don't. I can't. Not after Mom gave her life for me. I would be betraying her sacrifice if I just gave up.

Maybe I can't go *over*, but what if I can go *through*?

I scramble to my knees and begin to paw at the seemingly impenetrable wall of debris. It isn't long before I see it: a tunnel. Almost.

Go, my mother's ghost commands, and I drop to my belly and begin to slither through headfirst.

"Halt!" someone bellows as my head disappears. Bullets pierce the wall around me, sending concrete dust into my eyes.

"Stop!" comes another voice, Rook's voice, I'm pretty sure. But I can tell from his tone it's not an order. It's a plea. I'm shoulder-deep now, twisting and flexing to maneuver through the winding opening. "Come back!" Rook calls again as my hips almost don't fit through, then squeeze past with a small avalanche of dust. He's not putting on an act for the other Greenshirts. Something about his voice tells me he really believes that whatever I'm crawling toward is far worse than being captured by his compatriots.

My feet disappear, and the last thing I hear is one of the other Greenshirts saying, "Let her go. If she goes out there, she's dead anyway."

I don't stop. If I'm going to die, at least I'll die on my own terms.

I move through what feels like a maze of ruined civilization, wondering how this devastation came to be in our perfect society. Does everyone know about this, and I'm only surprised because I've lived a sheltered life? I'd think Ash would have told me about this if he knew. How many other truths have I missed out on for one reason or another?

I push and shove and wiggle and twist my way through, getting scraped by rough concrete and poked by shards of plastic. At the very least, why hasn't all this stuff been recycled? There are tons of reusable material making up this wall. It stretches as far as I can see on either side, and so far I've crawled through at least thirty feet of tangled mess with no end in sight.

In my weary, near-hallucinatory state I wonder if it will go on forever. I've had dreams like that, where I try to walk through a door that seems only across the room, and yet somehow I can never get through. What if this isn't just a wall but the world? What if Eden is surrounded by all the refuse and waste of humans' dead civilizations, pollution and garbage stacked up to our very borders and filling all the rest of the world?

I feel as if I've been crawling forever when the way finally opens up. I crawl over some archaic piece of machinery, through a tip-tilted pipe . . . and emerge in a monstrous fairyland.

Mom, who has access to all of the old pre-fail records, used to tell me the stories she discovered in dusty, crumbling books made from dead trees in the times before datablocks.

There was one story that was such a favorite I made her tell it over and over—"Jack and the Beanstalk." It's the tale of a boy who seems to make a foolish trade, giving up the security of a milk cow for the allure of magical beans. His mother is furious, but his gamble pays off when his beans grow a giant beanstalk that leads him to fortune and—more important in my childish eyes—adventure.

I think of that story as I look up . . . and up . . . and up. They stretch into the sky, leviathan plants, a green so dark it is almost black. No, not plants, I realize as I look closer. Synthetic stalks and technological tendrils and mechanical leaves that turn on whispering gears to follow the sunlight. These are like the artificial photosynthesis "plants" that decorate Eden, but on a massive scale. Each trunk is ten feet across; the leaves are as broad as houses. They are three times as tall as the algae spires, the tallest structures in Eden.

There are thousands of them.

They are so tall that they could probably be seen from the Center. And yet, when I sat on my wall, or on the abandoned spire with Lark, I never saw anything like this. Just the city, blurring into the distance, and a faint shimmer at my eyes' farthest reach that I assumed was heat rising from the blistering desert wasteland.

But even if I'm wrong, and you can't see them from the Center, surely I would have noticed them later, when out with Lark, or driving with Mom, or running from the Greenshirts. I definitely would have seen them loom over the wall of debris. They would have blocked out the sun! Had I been too blinded by excitement or anxiety to notice?

I look up at the gently undulating field of giant beanstalks. No, there's no way I could have missed these.

In the bean forest, I can only see the trees, so I decide to forge my way through. It feels unnaturally still. It shouldn't be like this, I think. In the faux-forests I've visited—the Rain Forest Club and the exciting laser tag arena—there were birds and bugs and the rustling of paws that step, and are still. There was life in those places, even if it was artificial.

Here, in this vast constructed forest, there is nothing but me.

I wander for hours, losing track of direction. The sun is mostly blocked by the canopy, and when it reaches the ground it is in confused angles, splitting shadows. Twice I find myself back at the debris pile, a wall that reaches to the artificial roots of the bean trees where they embed in the concrete. Finally, abruptly, the beanstalks stop in a uniform rigid wall and the desert stretches golden before me.

Heat hits my face like a slap, and I stagger back, turning my face away from the glare. I look into the cool shade of the bean trees to give my eyes time to adjust . . . and suddenly I think I know why I couldn't see the beanstalks from Eden. Why no one can see them.

They're camouflaged.

Not in a broken-pattern kind of way. When I look at the bean trees nearest to me, I can see them very clearly. But as I look down the row of them, they gradually vanish from my sight. Only the slightest imperfection lets me realize that the trees aren't just in this one patch. A bit out and the trees look a little fuzzy. Past that, there is a slight metallic shimmer. Then a little farther, and I can see a strange double vision—both the bean trees and the sky beyond them.

I have to stare and pace, move backward and forward across the burning sands to realize that each individual leaf, each stalk, is projecting an almost seamless image of the landscape behind it, as it would look if the trees weren't there. Like each tree is a datablock showing me an image.

When I was in the forest there was no illusion. Out here,

I can *just* tell it exists. If I was only a little bit farther away, I wouldn't have any idea the bean trees were here at all.

How can all of Eden not know that these beanstalks are out here? All my life, I thought I was the only secret Eden was hiding. Now I don't know what to think about my perfect city.

But now what? I can't go back, at least not for a while. Maybe after dark I can creep back and make my way to the breadline.

I turn to find a shady spot underneath the synthetic bean trees, away from the desert heat that is already threatening to blister my skin. It's a dramatic change, like stepping from an oven to a refrigerator. There must be a forty-degree difference between the forest and the desert, in just a couple of steps. In addition to collecting energy from the sun, does this artificial forest shield Eden from the heat of the wasteland the rest of Earth has become?

Suddenly, I think I hear footsteps. I can't be sure, though. Maybe the mechanical beanstalks are just moving. The sound is soft, stealthy, just the barest crunch. If the rest of the world wasn't so hushed I never would have heard it. I can't see anyone yet, but the huge trees are spaced widely enough that they don't offer much cover. In just a few seconds I'll be able to see whoever it is . . . and they'll see me.

I can't hide in the forest. It's too open. I'm too hurt and exhausted to outrun anyone, even a chubby new recruit.

So I make the impossible choice. The deadly choice. With a last gasp of cool shady air I limp into the desert and hope whoever is after me isn't foolish enough to follow me.

Funny that survival might hinge on being stupider than your enemy.

Within seconds my lungs are burning, scorched. The air is so dry the heat rises up in visible waves around me. It sucks the moisture from my body, and sweat beads and dries almost instantly. My eyes become so dry that my lids stick to my eyeballs on each blink with a gritty feel. Breathing through my nose helps my parched mouth, but it does nothing for the fact that my body temperature seems to be rising with each step.

But I press on, because survival somehow feels less important right now than not getting caught. I spent my life behind a wall. I won't be a prisoner again. Even if they kill me immediately after capture, even a moment of captivity would be too much. I'd rather die.

That's big talk, isn't it?

At first it is easy going. The sand is almost springy under my feet, and such a novel sensation after synthetic surfaces that I almost enjoy it. It cushions my aching feet as I hobble along.

After a while, though, the sand becomes loose and deep. My feet sink past the ankles with each step and I drag along like I'm wading through water. I fall, and the sand scalds my hands, but I drag myself up and forge on through this merciless sea of sand.

I start to sink deeper with every step, but in my dehydrated, almost delirious state I don't realize exactly what is happening. First my feet feel cool, and the sensation is so pleasant I just stop and enjoy it for a moment before moving on. But when I try to pull my foot out the ground seems to grab it and hold on tight. With a supreme effort I pull my leg up and take another step. When I pull my foot out, I can see that the sand is clinging peculiarly to my shoe. I try to brush it off, but it sticks to my hand, too. It almost feels wet, but when I rub a little between my fingertips there's no moisture.

Baffled, I try to take another step, but it is my bad ankle, and when I pull, it feels like I'm pulling my foot off. I have to bite back a scream. The sand feels like it's sucking me down!

Panicking, I turn, but my body moves while my feet stay still, and I topple in slow motion. I try to catch myself with my hands, but there's nothing solid. They slide right through the sand to the quicksand below and I pitch down face-first. The muck fills my mouth and nose as I thrash and gasp for breath; it blinds me.

Did I just say I'd rather die than be captured? In the space of an instant I learn better.

I thrash and kick and fail, and manage to get my head above the quicksand for one desperate, blessed breath before sinking down again. I can't swim; I've never been in water deeper than my bath. But I think even if I could, it wouldn't help in this strange, clinging sand. This is thick, clawing at me. It feels like a living thing trying to swallow me.

Like the Earth itself eating me up.

I can feel my body growing cool and soft. I stop struggling. For a second it almost feels good, to give up, to hang suspended here, to know that I don't have to run, or fight, or be lonely ever again.

Then something catches my arm, pulling me up. I'm being hauled out of the pit. Someone lays me on the scorching sand and I don't care if it's a Greenshirt with a gun to my head. I would kiss his boots if I had the strength, just because he gave me one last breath.

A hand wipes muck away from my mouth, my nose, almost tenderly. My eyes are still crusted with muck, and I can't open them. My head is swimming, my lungs convulsing so I feel like I still can't breathe.

Just before I pass out, I hear someone say, "You're a hard girl to save."

14

THE WORLD COMES back to me one piece at a time. In the beginning I can't move. I hardly even know I have a body. Am I dead? Sounds return before anything else, before I can even feel my own skin. First there's a rushing, a pulsing in my ears. I imagine the ocean sounds like that, surging to the shore in an endless cycle. My blood is like an ocean, the tides slowly rising in my veins. I lie in darkness, with no real sensation of my body.

A subtle smell comes next, warm and pleasant, an animal smell I would say, if I had ever encountered an animal. It makes me feel almost comfortable . . . until the rest of my body starts to wake. I feel heat in my muscles, coolness on my skin. And still I can't see, don't even remember how to open my eyes.

Then the pain comes, hitting me like a stone wall, and I groan, a deep, guttural sound. Everything hurts, with every kind of pain. Muscle aches and tendon tears, cuts and scrapes and sunburn and . . . a broken heart.

"Open your eyes." I can't tell if the voice is inside or outside my head. I feel fingers brushing the crust of dried quicksand away from my lids. Big hands. Gentle hands.

My lashes flutter. It is dark. Was I unconscious all day?

I blink, and the world snaps into place as I come fully conscious.

Golden kaleidoscope orbs look back at me, a mesmerizing mix of brown and hazel and copper. Second-child eyes. I know these eyes, I think. But they're in the wrong face.

I saw them before in the ragged hobo. But these incredible eyes are in a young man about my age, with longish chestnut hair pushed back from a broad brow and a long crescent scar curving on his left cheekbone. I've seen that scar before, I think, though I can't remember . . .

I frown in confusion, and the young man laughs at me.

It makes me angry to see his mocking face, so carefree beside all of my suffering. He's too close to me, too. It makes me uncomfortable to feel the heat of his body on my skin. Without thinking of the consequences I shove him away from me as hard as I can and try to scramble to my feet.

It doesn't go so well. My body seems to have locked up. I stumble over my backpack, then just sort of crawl and collapse.

I'm sure he'll fight me, but when I shoved him he just let himself roll backward like he was playing a game with a clumsy child. He's still laughing, damn him! Laughing at my pain and my inability to fight.

"Who are you?" I demand to know. I'm crouched awkwardly a few feet away, and feel a little more comfortable with some distance between us.

He rolls to an easy sitting position, still smiling. "I guess I need to explain a few things. You know what I am, right?" He stares intently, meaningfully, his golden eyes open wide.

I nod. "I know *what* you are. I want to know *who* you are."

"My name is . . . Lachlan." I notice the pause. Was he deciding whether or not to lie? Which did he choose?

I think about the familiar eyes and take a guess. "And you're the son of that old man in rags I met earlier?"

A hint of a smile twitches at the corner of his mouth, but he catches himself. "Not quite. I *am* the man in rags."

My mouth gapes.

"Pretty effective disguise, wouldn't you say?"

I can only barely believe it. In my mind I try to layer him in grime and stink, make his hair dirty and wild, clothe him in rags. If I squint, I can just see it.

"I use a few different disguises. Hobo, student, Bestial, woman. It makes it easier for someone like me to move around Eden without attracting notice." The smile twitches again. "Unlike you, I can't always outrun the Greenshirts. That was some impressive work."

"You saw me?"

Again, there's the slightest hesitation. I think if it wasn't for the fact that people are so new to me, so alternately fascinating and frightening, I wouldn't be paying as close attention. What is he hiding?

"I saw part of your escape. Just at the end. I'd been looking for you, you know."

I stare at him. "You knew about me?" He nods, and the pieces start to come together in my brain. "You're Rook's brother?"

Lachlan nods. "You should have heard the way he told the story. There you come out of nowhere, a second child, with his giant shoulders the only thing between you and that securitybot's cameras. *Stop*, he says, to keep you from getting in the bot's line of sight. And what do you do?"

I hang my head when I remember how I shoved Rook. He was helping me! I thought I was being so brave, and after all that was the thing that almost got me caught. Maybe it was what initially alerted the Center to my very existence.

"And he had to tackle the bot and hope that it couldn't get a good scan of you. His supervisor was so angry with him that he got transferred to the outer circles for a six-week punishment detail. Which, as it turned out, was fortunate."

"They would have killed me if Rook hadn't knocked out that other Greenshirt today."

"My brother is a good man. He joined the Greenshirts just to help . . . me." I want to tell him I notice the pauses, realize that there are things he's not saying, but I bite my tongue.

Instead I say, "I can't believe I'm actually looking at another second child. I always assumed there must be others, but I never thought I'd meet one. How many of us are there?"

He shrugs. "I don't know." Before I can ask whether he's met another second child, he asks, "How did you wind up so far from home?"

A spark of suspicion. "You know where I live?"

"One of the inner circles, I'd guess. That's where Rook ran into you. Or you ran into him."

I can't help smiling, and his answering smile makes my cheeks flush. I can't look away from his eyes. Another person like me! Meeting Lark was amazing, but this is something on an entirely different level. This is like finding family. My people. Well, my person, anyway.

"Where were you headed when the Greenshirts found you?" he presses. I open my mouth to tell him, but something urges me to be cautious. I'm almost overwhelmed by this incredible feeling of camaraderie, and I want to trust him, but I know that's just caused by the fact that he's also a second child. Or *seems* to be. Everything that's happened has made me suspicious. I met a man with eyes like a snake's. If he could do that, why couldn't Lachlan get contact lenses that make him look like a second child? What if this is a trap?

"I just went out to explore," I say cautiously. "I took an autoloop, and got lost, and . . . wound up out here."

He nods, but I can't tell if he really believes me. "It's tough out there for people like us."

"How have you managed this long?" I ask. "Do you live with your family?"

He bites his lip, and the gesture makes him look so much younger. "No," he says, a tiny word that speaks volumes.

"Tell me," I say softly.

He does, and by the end I have tears in eyes that I thought were all cried out.

He wasn't a twin, but an accident. Most women are sterilized after giving birth, but if there's any doubt about the first child's survival, they remain fertile until the danger is thought to have passed, several years at least, to be sure. They're supposed to be on infallible birth control, but apparently nothing is infallible. Rook was premature (though he certainly made up for it) and weak as an infant. Lachlan was conceived two years after Rook was born, and the parents—middle circle merchants, owners of a small chain of grocery stores—decided to keep him, to hide him.

"I lived like you must have lived—alone, always anxious, always a little angry, hearing about the world from the brother who was welcomed into it with open arms. My parents loved me, as far as I could tell, nurtured me. I was happy—mostly. But I know now how hard it was for them to live in constant fear of arrest. They were brave . . . but not brave enough. All along they were looking for a foster family for me."

"As they should have," I say, nodding approval. "It's the only way a second child can have a normal life."

"Until we change what normal is," he says, a fierce passion in his eyes.

So he left his loving home at age ten, and went to his new family. It was hard enough thinking about the prospect at sixteen. I can't imagine being torn from my family at the tender age of ten. His parents told him what a wonderful life he would have, hid their tears, and little Lachlan tried to put on a brave face. Maybe it wouldn't be too bad, he told himself.

It was worse. So much worse.

He didn't give me details. Part of me didn't want them anyway. But judging from the tension in his entire body, it was probably worse than anything I could imagine.

"They made me do things," he said flatly. "They said if I told, they'd turn me in. Me and my whole family. I couldn't say no. At least, not when I was ten."

They were supposed to get him the black market lenses so he could live a normal life. But they never did. He thinks they just pocketed the money his parents gave them. So even in his new home he was trapped, though he was often out at night, he said, doing the things they made him do.

When he was sixteen, though, his foster father died, and Lachlan left his foster home for good. He didn't say it, but I get the impression that he might have had something to do with the man's death. His big hands clench and unclench methodically when he speaks of it.

He went home again, maybe not expecting that everything would be like it was before, but believing that they would help him, hide him, that they'd had no idea what kind of life they sent him to. Rook welcomed him with tears and laughter. He'd been searching for Lachlan ever since he left. The parents, though . . .

The ten years of fear had been too much for them, and the last six had been a relief. They told Lachlan flatly that he was not welcome. They shut the door in his face.

"After that I lived on the street, getting what help Rook could manage. I've made a few friends, learned my way around. It's not so bad now."

I would express more sympathy for his story, but he tells it flatly, matter-of-factly, and I think somehow he wouldn't welcome too much emotion right now. For myself, thinking about someone else's suffering seems to dull my own. I want to tell him about my mother, unburden myself about everything. But I can't quite bring myself to trust him yet.

"Good thing you have a home, people you can depend on," he tells me. "You *do* have that, don't you?"

"I . . ." Secrecy kept me safe for sixteen years. Only when I abandoned it did my life shatter. I left my safe shelter. I trusted Lark. (No, she would never betray me. I know it. No, I *feel* it.) Instinct tells me to keep silent now.

"Why should I trust you?" I ask, glaring at him with hostility. Maybe I'm ungrateful. He saved me, after all. But I can't put my faith in anyone. Mom, Ash, that was all. Now it's just Ash, and he can't do anything to help me. Now he's nearly as alone as I am.

Lachlan doesn't seem at all surprised or upset at my suspicion. "You shouldn't. And I shouldn't trust you. Sure, we're both second children. We both face the same penalties if we're caught—and believe me, they're worse than you think."

"Worse than death?" I ask. "What could be worse than that?"

He swallows hard, and I can tell he's trying to control his emotions. "Pray to the Earth you never find out. But I'm sure a second child would betray another one in exchange for a promise of protection. People can be weak, or selfish, or just plain scared, and do terrible things as a consequence. I don't trust *you* . . . yet. But I think you can trust me a little bit, can't you? After all, I saved you, at considerable risk to myself.

The nanosand is designed to swallow up any living thing that crosses the wasteland."

"You mean, someone made that stuff? I thought it was natural."

"It's almost exactly like real quicksand, except it travels. It searches out signs of life, tracks them, hunts them . . . and eats them."

"*Eats?*"

"Bones and everything," he says. "After a while the nanosand secretes acids to digest whatever organic material it swallows."

I start frantically brushing the crumbling mud and sand from my limbs. "Easy, easy!" he says, lunging forward to catch my wrist. I freeze, and he seems to suddenly become acutely conscious of his fingers on my skin. I know I am. He lets go, but I feel the lingering warmth where his fingers pressed. "It takes a long time, and it becomes inactive in the presence of air. You're perfectly safe now."

And the funny thing is, when I look at him, I feel like I am.

He's the first stranger I've ever met, really. Lark wasn't a stranger, because I'd heard about her for so many years it was like finally being introduced to my best friend. I had casual contact with a few other people, like the other laser tag players. But this is in a way the first time I've sat down and looked for a long time into a complete stranger's eyes.

My brain tells me not to trust him—not to trust anyone at this point, no matter what the evidence says—but some other part of me, my heart, my skin, my blood, tells me that I can rely on Lachlan. Is it an accident of his face? That broad brow that inspires confidence, the straight strength of his nose, the earnest wide set of his eyes—he simply looks honest. Everything about him screams *Trust me*. That in itself makes me suspicious.

But I'm so tired, so sore, so sad. It would be easiest to lean on him. To trust him.

"And not only did I save you from nanosand," he continues, and I think I see a hint of a smirk returning. I start to hope for the rest of the smile. "I also carried you back through the desert and more than a mile through the beanstalks. And you're no featherweight." He winks. No one has ever actually winked at me before. "And that's *after* I chased you through most of the outermost circle. So I really went to great lengths to save you."

It's true. I immediately feel ashamed of my suspicions. He's Rook's brother, and Rook saved me twice. Lachlan's a second child himself. There's no reason to mistrust him. If it wasn't for him, I'd be slowly digested in a pit of nanosand right now.

And so, haltingly, I tell him about Mom's arrangement to send me to a foster family after getting the lens implants. I tell him how just a few hours ago I was shaken awake, taken to find the cybersurgeon who would perform the operation. How we were trapped at the roadbock. How Mom gave her life so I could get away.

I hug my backpack to my chest and start to weep silently, my body shaking.

I feel his arm around me. I stiffen, then relax, then lean into him, wetting his shoulder with my tears.

"I'm so sorry about your mother," he says.

"And now I'm all alone," I say miserably. "I can never go back home. My father wouldn't want me, and even if he did . . . the Greenshirts will find out who my mother is, and find my dad and brother through her. What will happen to them?"

"I don't know," he says gently. "Right now, we have to focus on keeping you safe. After that, maybe we can help them."

I have no idea how that can be possible. The two of us against all the might of the Center? Still, there's something about him that gives me hope. He sounds too confident, too competent to be wrong.

Or is he just telling me what I need to hear right now, so I can get through the moment?

Either way, I'm grateful.

"Thank you for saving me," I say shyly from under the crook of his arm. He loosens his comforting hold, and I sit up . . . and scoot a little away. "I'm . . . I'm glad I have you with me. Another second child. Do you think we're the only ones?"

He's silent for a long moment, staring at me so intently that I want to look away. But I hold his gaze until at last he whispers, "I have an entire family of second children, Rowan."

15

FOR A MOMENT I can't breathe. More second children? A *family* of them?

"Are you strong enough to move?"

I nod vigorously. If it means meeting more second children, I'm strong enough to do anything! Sleep has relieved many of my aches, given my cuts time to scab, and even my ankle is a little less swollen. I won't be winning any races, but I can walk.

"Where are they?" I ask, and my eagerness must be apparent on my face because he laughs and says, "Easy now. You've waited sixteen years to meet more second children. You can wait another hour or two."

"Are they out here in the beanstalks? Are they in the outermost circle?" I'm rewarded with another one of his sly, mysterious smiles.

"Second children are everywhere," he says. "All over Eden, right under your feet, and you'd never know." He springs to his own feet and offers me his hand. Even though I feel a lot better than I did twelve hours ago, I'm grateful for his help getting up.

"We have to travel fast, and be inconspicuous," he says. "What do you have in that pack? Can you leave it behind?"

I scoop it up and sling it onto my shoulders. I haven't even looked inside it, but it is the only thing I have from home, from Mom, and no force on Earth will make me part with it.

"That answers that question," he says, and starts walking. I scurry to catch up, feeling somehow that he's disappointed in me.

"When we get back into the city, you need to do exactly what I tell you. Understand? They're actively looking for you, and the next hours will be extremely dangerous. Luckily, I know someone who can reduce the risk considerably." He slows to wait for me. "Good thing you're tall. You'll look the part."

He knows an easier route through the tangle of rubble than the one I took, and I make it through with hardly a scratch. We emerge at the back of a building and he leads me inside, through a door barely hanging on its hinges.

"Are *these* the second children?" I ask. In the dim light I see bodies sprawled in corners, lying on makeshift mattresses or on the cold bare floor. It's hard to make out details, but their faces look gaunt. As we walk swiftly through, I see a young woman with a band tied tightly around her upper arm. Below it, blue-black veins bulge. There's a needle in the crook of her arm . . .

Lachlan takes my elbow and hustles me away. "No. We'd never let a second child come to this. We take care of our own. We protect each other, from the Center, and from ourselves—to the death."

I feel a deep shiver run down my spine.

"Don't these people need protection, too? Even though they aren't second children?"

I think I touched a nerve. "They have every opportunity that legitimacy can provide," he snaps. "If they choose to destroy themselves, it's not our problem."

I don't know. There's something in his eyes as he looks at the addicts that makes me think his inner thoughts don't quite match his words.

We're through the building in a moment, exiting onto a narrow alley that takes us within a few steps to another building. We slither through a street-level window into an empty basement apartment, and wend our way through corridors until we emerge somewhere else. Over and over we do this, traveling mostly through basements of decrepit buildings, through abandoned warehouses and empty businesses, emerging only for a few seconds at a time, using the structures like a warren of tunnels to travel out of sight.

It isn't long before I've lost all sense of direction. I don't know if we've traveled miles toward the Center or in a circle. Finally we slip from one basement into an adjoining building, climb five flights of stairs, and stop at a door locked with a thumbprint scanner. Lachlan presses his thumb to the pad. He seems to shift it restlessly as he presses down.

I frown. "Is it a good idea to have your prints on record?" I ask.

"Good thinking," Lachlan replies. "Luckily the scanner is just a decoy. The door unlocks from the rhythm I just tapped in with my thumb pressure. It only scans the fingerprint if someone doesn't tap the code. Then we can track whoever is trying to get in without authorization."

Clever. There's apparently a whole world of trickery in Eden that I never imagined.

Inside we find a businesslike middle-aged woman in the sort of suit typical of a Center official. Instinctively, I flinch behind Lachlan, but he greets her by name. "Hey Rose, do you have the day's roster?" I peek around his shoulder and look at her eyes. They have the flat, dull sheen of the implants. Not a second child, then.

"Of course, whippersnapper. When do I *not* have the roster?"

He gives her a quick hug, a peck on the cheek.

"Who's this then?" she asks.

"No one—yet. I'm taking her to the others."

Rose raises her eyebrows and looks me over. "Has she been tested yet? She really shouldn't be here if she hasn't been tested."

Lachlan glances at me. "In the last day she's been tested as much as many other second children."

"But not as much as some," she replies, looking at him hard. "Still, if you say she can be trusted . . ."

"I do."

"Then follow me." She leads us to a back room, and then to a closet full of Greenshirt uniforms. "The usual lieutenant for you, Lachlan?"

"Rank without too much responsibility, that's me."

"And I'm guessing recruit for this one." She pulls two uniforms off of the racks and thrusts one at me. "Change. There." I step behind a screen and strip off my dirty, torn clothes, feeling so strange being naked in the same room as strangers, my height making my shoulders and half my chest stick up over the screen. When I've struggled into the uniform I step out and Rose yanks the fabric into order. "Straighten your gig line, recruit!" she says, pulling my belt into alignment with my zipper.

I look at myself in the mirror, wearing the uniform of the enemy. My eyes look frightened . . . until Rose hands me a pair of darkly tinted glasses. Then I look as menacing as any Greenshirt. I'm a little scared of my own reflection.

Dressed as authority figures, we move through Eden unmolested. In the outer circles, people sidle out of our way. Closer to the Center, they mostly ignore us, though some nod in greeting, believing their elite position in society means they have nothing to fear. Some of the time we travel by autoloop, but at the end we're on foot again. For my backpack, which would otherwise look out of place, Rose has given me a large tag that reads "Evidence." I'm just a recruit finishing up a case.

There is a brief moment when I recognize streets I walked along with Lark, and the memory brings a pang. I look at each face, thinking I might see her. But she'd be in school, and wouldn't recognize me in this uniform, and I couldn't dare approach her even if I saw her.

Then Lachlan's pace quickens, and he leads me through streets at such a pace that I get disoriented again.

Suddenly he says, "Do you trust me?"

"Yes," I say at once, not even thinking about whether it is true. People keep asking me that.

"Then follow me."

He pulls me abruptly down a side street, kicks a loose grate aside, and points to what looks to me like a bottomless black pit. It is only just wider than my shoulders. I take an inadvertent step back.

"Don't think. Don't question. Just jump." He looks a little excited, like he's wondering what I'll do, whether I'll disappoint him.

I've never been afraid of climbing. Though I'll never have an opportunity to climb a mountain, I know for a fact that no matter how high I ascend, it will never bother me. Falling, though, the very antithesis of climbing, scares me to death.

What if this is all a trick, a trap? What if he's working for the Center and this is a pit to my doom? What easier way to get rid of a second child than to convince her to voluntarily leap to her own death. This might be an abattoir filled with the bodies of . . .

He pushes me.

My hands claw for the edge but I'm falling down . . . down . . . the passage narrows. The sides are perfectly smooth, nothing to grab onto to slow my descent. The walls are closing in. I'm going to be wedged in here forever, left to die . . .

As my body brushes the sides, though, the tunnel begins to slant and instead of falling I'm sliding smoothly. The slide levels out, and before I know it I'm skidding to a gentle stop. Now that it's over and the adrenaline leeches from my body, I decide it was rather fun. I'd like to do it again—without all the fear of death part.

I find myself in a stone chamber. Stone! Rock! Real natural minerals just like the walls of my own house! This must be an underground cave system. Phosphorescent strips along the floor offer a gentle glow, and I wonderingly examine the whorls and crevices of the cave, the formations that hang like jagged teeth from the ceiling. I'm so lost in the marvelous sight that Lachlan bumps me from behind when he slides down.

"I told you to do exactly what I say," he tells me brusquely. "There's no time for indecision in a second child's life. Any mistake can be your last."

Then it is a race through twists and turns that leave me baffled. I try to pay attention to our direction—and I try to admire the amazing natural cave system I never knew was under Eden—but Lachlan pulls me along at breakneck speed. Once, I'm sure, he leads me past the same rock formation three times.

It is such an utterly baffling labyrinth down here! I realize that these confusing tunnels are the best layer of security imaginable, probably more effective than armed guards. Even if they found the entrance, which didn't seem likely, the impossible maze down here would thwart any invader.

Finally he slows, in a passage that looks like every other— arching stone walls, dim lights barely illuminating our feet.

"We're here," Lachlan says, and turns to smile at me. "Are you ready? You're about to meet your brothers and sisters. An entire family of second children." He takes my hand and squeezes it quickly before releasing it.

I feel my breath coming fast, and smile back. People like me! Second children who have made a life for themselves! I have no idea what kind of life that is, but I am giddy at the thought of finding out.

Lachlan presses a hidden panel in the end of the cavernous chamber and the rock seems to split. A crevice opens up that turns into a door, cleverly hidden in the stone. It creaks slowly open to a black void.

"Go on," he urges, his smile so joyful and welcoming. I don't repeat the mistake I made at the pit. Without question, without fear, I step through into the impenetrable darkness.

There's movement, hands on my body, something heavy and wet forced over my head so I'm trapped, suffocating.

"No! Let her go!" I hear Lachlan bellow. "Rowan! No!" I hear the sound of fighting, but I'm being dragged away. I feel a prick in my arm, and the world goes blurry for a while . . .

When I come to my senses, the heavy bag is still over my head, cinched tight at my neck. I can feel the cords of the drawstring draped over my shoulders.

"She's awake." I hear a slosh, and someone dumps freezing water over my head. It soaks through the bag, making it cling tightly to my nose, my mouth. I can't breathe! When I shake my head, I manage to make a small gap between the canvas and my mouth, just enough to suck in a little air. But it's not enough, I feel light-headed, drowning on dry land.

"Tell us your name."

I turn toward the unfamiliar voice. A hand grabs the back of the bag, along with some of my hair, and yanks my head back, exposing my throat. I am exposed, vulnerable. "Where did you get those uniforms? Who is that boy with you?" He shakes me until my teeth rattle. But I say nothing.

For some seemingly endless time they question me, about my own identity, Lachlan's, where I'm from and where I was headed. I don't say a word, not even a lie. Not when they slap me hard across the face. Not when they tip me backward under a faucet that sends a steady drip, drip, drip of water onto my nose and mouth. I suck in pitiful amounts of air through the sodden bag, getting more water in my lungs than oxygen.

I pass out twice, and each time they haul me upright, pull the bag away from my face to give me a little more breathing room until I'm fully conscious . . . then tip me backward again. I don't know how long it lasts. It feels like hours.

The voice comes close to my ear, growling through the bag. "This is only going to get worse. If you talk now, you can be a Center witness against the others. You'll get off easy." He sounds almost reasonable now. "That boy doesn't care about you. You're just a pawn in his traitorous schemes. He's *using* you."

"No," I start to babble. "He saved me. He was taking me someplace safe."

"Where?" the voice demands.

"I don't know. Please, let me go."

"What is your name?"

I bite my tongue.

"What is his name?"

I shake my head, and he cuffs me on the temple.

The questions begin all over again, in an endless nightmare. I feel like if I could see my captors, look them in the eye, I could bear it better. But these hard hands and harsh voices coming at me in the choking darkness are almost more than I can take. I don't want to tell them anything. But I have a terrible feeling I will if this lasts much longer.

I start to cry, and every time I breathe I can taste the salt of my own tears. I talk, begging, pleading, swearing I know nothing . . . and as the questions continue, I think I hear triumph in my interrogator's voice. I might not be giving him useful information yet, but I'm talking, terrified, desperate, and he knows it is only a matter of time now.

Then he makes a mistake. In one of his good-cop moments when he's leaning close to my ear, making tempting offers of clemency in exchange for information, swearing I'll be safe if only I tell him what he needs to know, he says the wrong thing.

"Your mother didn't die so that you could protect scum like that boy we caught you with."

A white-hot rage rises up within me, burning out my fear. How dare he talk about my mother! Was he the one who killed her? Him, or someone like him.

I all but snarl beneath my soaking hood. My mother died for *me*. She died so that I could have a chance at a decent, safe life.

No matter what this man promises, I'll never have that with the Center or the Greenshirts. Maybe I'm caught. Maybe I'll be imprisoned, or killed. But if what Lachlan said is true, there is a community of second children, living the safe, happy life Mom wanted so desperately for me. For their sakes, and for Mom's memory, I won't tell them a thing.

My interrogator's head is still close to mine as he murmurs his persuasive words. His fingers clutch my shoulders.

"Get your hands off of me, you *bikking* Greenshirt!" I snap, and head-butt him in the nose.

I hear a deeply satisfying crunch, a curse . . . and Lachlan's voice saying, "That's enough, Flint. I think she's proven she won't break."

16

THE WET BAG is stripped from my face, and I find myself in a stone room without right angles, a rounded, cave-like chamber. Lachlan is standing a few feet from me, his face hard. There's another man in the room, too, an imposing man in his forties with silvered black hair. His eyes are blue-gray, almost as flat as implant eyes, but the dark blue rings around the irises mark them as natural, and him as a second child. Blood drips from his slightly off-center nose.

"Everyone breaks, given time," Flint says, his face impassive.

I look from one man to the other. "This was a test?" I ask, incredulous. "This wasn't real?"

"It was completely real," Flint says. "They'll do that to you, and worse, if they catch you. We had to know you wouldn't talk. At least, not right away. I'm responsible for every second child here, and I can't risk their safety by letting in someone who is weak or untrustworthy."

Part of me is relieved. I was sure the nightmare would continue until it was unbearable, ending only in my death. But another part—the part that head-butted Flint in the face—is furious that they fooled me, frightened me, tortured me.

Of the two, Lachlan is in arm's reach. The knuckles I split

punching that outer circle gang open up again on his cheekbone. I don't care, because his face splits, too, right across that long crescent scar beneath his eye. He takes it without flinching, without the smallest movement of retaliation.

Flint wraps his arms around me and effortlessly picks me up, turning me around and setting me down out of reach of Lachlan. I'm shaking, and I clench my hands together so they won't see . . . and so I won't punch anyone else. Violence doesn't seem to have much effect on them anyway.

"How the hell could you do that to me?" I ask, my voice furious and hurt. "Lachlan, I thought this was supposed to be a brotherhood, a family of second children. I trusted you with everything about myself. Why couldn't you trust me?"

I expect an apology, but he looks at me levelly and says, "The Underground is bigger than any one person, more important than one night of suffering. We've only known about you for a matter of days, so we know less about you than we typically do about second children. Most we find when they're very young, even babies, or before birth. Our hunting methods are sophisticated—more so than the Center's, anyway. But we missed you entirely, and only found you by luck. Most second children come here so early they *are* part of the family. They're loyal. But you . . ."

"We don't know where your loyalties lie," Flint supplies.

"I've been a prisoner all of my life because of Center policies!" I rage. "I've been in constant danger of prison or death. The government killed my mother! Do you really have any doubt about my loyalties at this point?"

"People can be surprising—even to themselves," Flint says. "You don't know what you'd do in the worst situations, until they happen to you. But for now, I'm willing to let you into the Underground. You're one of us . . . sister."

He offers me his hand. I stare at it, considering. I understand why he did what he did. I really do. In theory. But the fact that he did it to *me* makes it different. There's a world of difference between what is rationally necessary and what a good person should actually do. Logic shouldn't always win.

But my hand rises and clasps his firmly. Something seems to surge through me. Flint is a natural leader, I can tell. Just looking at him makes me feel like he has everything firmly under control. He's inspiring, and I feel like I can rely on him. *Sister . . .* I'm no longer alone.

But when Lachlan holds out his hand, too, I glare coldly at him and then deliberately look away. We confided in each other. We talked about our lives. He shouldn't have let that happen to me. I understand why Flint did it, and forgive him, but somehow I can't forgive Lachlan. It might not make perfect sense, but there it is.

"Come," Flint says, touching me lightly on the shoulder. "Let me introduce you to the Underground." We exit the torture cave—just a room now—and step out into something I could never have imagined.

I'm inside a jewel. A faceted, glowing, many-hued jewel.

"Are . . . are we still under Eden?" I stammer, not believing my eyes.

I look out over a huge crystal cavern, maybe half a mile across. The entire roof and most of the walls of the gigantic cave are covered with clear bright jutting stones that look like colored ice. In subtle shining shades of palest pink and amethyst, of smoky silver and water-blue and pure clear diamond they surround me, catching the dim artificial light, so beautiful that for just a second I don't notice the even more remarkable thing below them. In the center of the twinkling crystal cavern, rising almost to the ceiling and spreading its canopy more than a hundred feet across, is a tree.

A tree. *A living tree.*

The trunk is massive, twenty, thirty feet across, lumpy and gnarled. Roots spread aboveground for around the trunk before plunging into Earth. Earth? Dirt? It can't be. The ground of the cavern looks like a forest floor, Earth covered in brown fallen leaves.

My eyes rise to the tree again, and for the first time in my life I make the gesture they make in temple. My fist rises from my belly to my face, my fingers branch out, like a seed growing, sprouting. I feel reverent awe, like I should fall to my knees, hide my face in the presence of something so radiantly beautiful, so perfect as a tree.

Then dawn breaks over the green, living canopy, making the crystals above seem to dance, and tears fall silently from my eyes.

"It can't be real," I whisper. But I can smell a sharp-sweet scent, and beneath that something rich and moist. Leaves, and Earth. I've never smelled anything like that—no one has, for generations—but some part deep within me recognizes the scents right away. Somewhere in my blood is a memory of nature, and it rejoices.

The sky goes from gray to pearl touched with pink as the sun breaks an unseen horizon and bathes the world with gentle morning light. That part has to be illusion, technology. We're deep underground, with rock all around us. Somehow they've made an almost perfect simulacrum of breaking dawn. But it's not just color, or light. I feel a flush of warmth hit my skin from where the sun is rising. The crystals in the roof and walls shine brightly beautiful.

"The tree is real," Lachlan says from beside me. I'm so awestruck I don't even think to move away from him. "And the Earth."

"But . . . there aren't any more trees." That's what we've been taught. The world is dead, the dirt is toxic, all living things extinct except for a few hardy lichens, single-celled organisms . . . and a handful of humans.

"There's one," Lachlan says.

"But how?"

"Aaron Al-Baz, of course," Flint says, his voice low and reverent. "The man who saved us. The man who will save the world. He made a perfect Eden, and humans corrupted it. We mean to bring Eden back to the paradise he intended it to be."

"What is this place?"

"The backup Eden," Flint answers. "This is where humans would have had to live if Eden wasn't ready in time, or if the world was more toxic than predicted. Underground. He kept it as a secret fail-safe in case humans managed to ruin things once again on the surface. It is self-contained and self-perpetuating, set up on computer controls and automation entirely separate from EcoPan."

That's amazing, I think. We've been taught that EcoPan took over control of every computer and electronic system on the planet.

"But he knew man can't live completely apart from nature," Flint went on, "so he managed to preserve this tree. The dirt is real organic soil from the surface, clean, good, uncontaminated pre-fail dirt. It goes down fifty feet, so the roots can bury deep. Hidden panels among the crystals simulate sunlight. As far as the tree knows, it's still on the surface. It gets sunlight, water, nutrients, seasons . . . and it gives us almost all the oxygen we need to survive down here with the place entirely sealed."

"He must have loved us, Rowan, to give us all this," Lachlan says. I won't look at him. "He must have loved humans so much, to save us from ourselves."

"I have work to do," Flint said abruptly. "Lachlan, show her around."

I try to protest, but Flint turns on his heel and is gone.

Lachlan reaches for my hand, but I shake him off before he can so much as touch me. Every time I look at him, I feel like the wet bag is over my head again, and I'm choking. He steps back and nods, gesturing for me to precede him, giving me space. I want to stay up here gazing at the tree, but then he says, "I know you want to touch it."

I can't resist that offer. I storm ahead of him, but it's all I can do not to smile.

The walls are high, ringed with galleries at multiple levels. I can see many cave-like rooms all around. The interrogation chamber I just left is four stories up along the curving walls of the cavernous hall. I fly down stairs cut into the stone, getting curious glances from a few people. I'll look at them later. Just a few days ago, other humans were exciting. But a tree! For the moment, nothing else exists.

I sprint across the smooth stone floor until suddenly my feet hit dirt. I skid to a stop and look down at my boots. Lachlan is behind me. "Take them off," he urges, and I do, laughing as my bare toes grip the real, natural packed Earth. I touch it with my hands; I kneel. Ecstatically, I kiss it. I must look like an idiot, dirt on my lips, but I don't care. I never thought I'd experience this in my lifetime. Everyone in Eden must endure artificiality for generations so that one day our descendants might know the glory of nature.

I meet Lachlan's eyes, still smiling . . . and remember my night of torture. My smile dies, and I stand, turning away from him.

The tree looms before me, a true behemoth, dwarfing me as I creep closer. I pick up a dead leaf from the litter at my feet and rub it gently between my fingers, releasing a burst of that sharp, stimulating smell that permeates the air and makes me feel so alert and alive.

And then I'm touching the tree, tentatively at first, like a newfound love, then pressing my cheek against the rough, fragrant bark, embracing it. My tears wet the bark, soak into it, and are gone.

With my arms wrapped around the huge tree, my chin on the trunk, I look up into the canopy with all its myriad shades of light and dark green. As I look, a leaf detaches from its twig and drifts slowly down, tacking left and right in elegant swoops. I catch it in my hand. Can I keep it? One leaf is more precious than a jewel. I don't care if I hang for it—I slip the leaf beneath my shirt, nestling it close to my heart. It is a gift from the tree to me.

"Stop! Look out!" a voice calls from behind me, and I whip around on high alert, ready for Greenshirts, for anything.

Anything, except being under attack from a horde of tiny people in patchwork clothes.

I haven't seen children since I was one, and then only Ash. It feels strange to see this pack of screaming, laughing, tiny humans, and I brace myself as they surge toward me, having no idea what they will do, no real comprehension of childish behavior.

But they're not running for me. As one they tackle Lachlan, clinging to his legs, squealing with glee and pretend aggression. And that big, hard man, the one who allowed me to be tortured, is suddenly on the ground beneath a pile of children, laughing, tickling them, letting them put him in headlocks, giving them rides on his back . . .

Which is the real Lachlan? The one who said that torturing me was perfectly fine? Or the one who is currently letting a four-year-old girl in pigtails pull his hair?

He flashes me a quick, almost apologetic smile before a little boy does a belly flop on his head and brings him down. "Lach!" they squeal. "You're back! We missed you, Lach!

What did you bring us? Did you fight anyone? Lach, tell us a story of the Above!"

"That's quite enough of that, kidlets," says a plump but solid maternal-looking woman as she bustles up behind the children. "Let Lachlan breathe."

The tiny girl in pigtails looks up at the woman with huge, sincere eyes and says emphatically, "But Lach is our *favorite*."

The woman nods. "I've heard that before, perhaps a bit too often." She looks archly at Lachlan as he rises and brushes the dirt from his clothes.

And I realize, as the children gaze lovingly at Lachlan, that this is what he did it for. These little second children are the reason he thought it was justifiable to torture a girl who had just lost her mother, who had been hunted through the streets. They need to be protected, at any cost. Now that I understand, I wonder if I would do the same thing myself. I don't know . . . but I understand why Lachlan did it, and I find that I can't be mad at him anymore.

The woman holds out her hand to me. "I'm Iris, house-mother of the Underground. Welcome." I introduce myself, and she tells me to come to her if I need any clothes or personal items. "A ruffian like our Lachlan here wouldn't think of creature comforts like lotion and nail files and such. We might be a bit primitive down here, but I like to think we manage to hold on to the best parts of civilization."

She gives my shoulder a friendly squeeze and herds the children away. The children all say hello as they pass, making me feel welcome. All except the little girl in pigtails. She shakes my hand very formally, and then says, "You can like Lach a little, but not too much. He says *I'm* his favorite girl. Don't you forget!" She shakes a warning finger at me and scampers off. I manage to keep a straight face until she's gone.

"I'll take you to your room," Lachlan says. "I know you

need to shower and change. Do you have clothes in there?" He nods to my backpack.

I don't even know. I haven't had a moment to open it.

"I'll see what I can scrounge up in your size."

"Thanks . . . Lach," I say, and he grins sidelong at me as he leads me to my room.

17

ONCE I'M ALONE, the bed looks so inviting I want to flop down on it, curl beneath the crisp new-leaf green sheets, and sleep for years. But I'm so filthy I can't bear to dirty the sheets, so I go into the little shower alcove and let the cold water wash over me until I'm approximately, if not completely, clean.

Being in this room—in the Underground itself—is like being in the heart of the Earth. The rooms are carved directly into the stone, and every surface is smooth, connected, without the edges and corners and seams of the rest of Eden. I know the rooms are man-made, not natural caves, but because the material is all-natural it feels almost like the Earth made this place for them.

For *us*. I'm a part of all this now.

Finally I lie in bed, still damp and cool from my shower, and stare at the ceiling, somewhere between happy and sad and drained. My backpack is on the floor beside me. I know I need to go through it soon, take stock . . . but I also know that once I delve into the last thing Mom did for me, the sorrow I've kept at bay will return. I will grieve forever, but I know I can't let myself weep forever.

So I think about this wonderful, strange place I find myself in. Lachlan said there are about two hundred people living here, from infants to elders, all second children. The community has been thriving below ground for around fifty years, ever since a second child rediscovered the hidden world. Even though many of its members venture out into Eden for supplies, it is separate enough that it has developed its own culture.

I haven't found out exactly what life is like down here, but I can see the difference even in the clothes. In Eden, styles are brash and sharp, deliberately loud and provocative. Here, colors are a little more muted, more natural. The cut is easy, flowing, and often the material is a beautiful patchwork, made up of complementary fabrics interspersed with occasional jarring—but oddly fitting—elements that make the whole outfit extraordinary. The effect of the pieced-together motley somehow isn't one of patching and make-do, but of a deliberate choice, taking the best of everything and fitting it together into something even better.

Almost everyone I see is wearing a piece of crystal. Most have a simple chunk on a piece of cord around their necks. One pretty young girl has a purple piece at the center of a circlet in her flowing hair. I see one older man with no visible crystal jewelry reach into his pocket and pull out a piece of clear, polished crystal which he rubs meditatively as he talks to me.

I don't see one on Lachlan, but I notice a thin cord around his neck, braided red and orange in a snake-like pattern. Maybe he has a crystal, too.

I haven't met anyone beyond Iris and the children, but attitudes here seem so relaxed, so low-key. No one is hurrying to work or entertainment like they do in the inner circles, or hustling in search of money, or away from danger, as they do in the outer circles. People down here seem to operate on a different internal clock. No one seems hunted, harried, like they do up in Eden. Everyone up there, now that I think about it, seems caffeinated, driven, a little too sharp.

Maybe it's the tree that calms them down, the soothing proximity of nature. Maybe it is a relief to finally be in a place they truly belong.

I start to feel it myself, breathing in the leafy scent, feeling the cool cavern air touch my skin. Eventually, I feel centered enough to go through my backpack.

The first thing I pull out almost makes me lose it: my ragged stuffed chimpanzee. Mom must have rescued him from the garbage and stuck him in the pack when I wasn't looking. I hug him tight to my chest . . . but then set him gently aside.

There's one change of clothes, and a pair of soft shoes. A pretty filigree hair ornament Mom often wore. A new sketchbook and a set of pencils.

And, in a tightly sealed bag, a notebook.

Its pages are made from a substance I don't quite recognize, a plastic of some sort, I think. We use a kind of plastic that is completely recyclable, but I learned in Eco-history that people used to use plastics that couldn't be easily broken down, that persisted in the environment forever. Plastics choked entire oceans, and the animals that lived in them. I shudder when I touch it . . . though I have to admit that such an enduring substance makes a perfect medium for a book. Waterproof, virtually time-proof, whatever is in here will last through the centuries.

Written in cramped, awkward hand is a manifesto, or maybe a confession. Sometimes the words are perfectly lucid, textbook-clear. In some passages, though, the language rambles incoherently, the handwriting becomes almost illegible, as if the only way the author could squeeze the words out was to scribble them as fast, as unthinkingly, as possible.

I have a sneaking suspicion who the author might be even before I turn to the last written page. The page is at the end . . . and at the middle. That is, the last half of the notebook has been cut out, carved raggedly, hacked, even. The scrunched signature has been added in a different ink on the last remaining page that grips the binding weakly, flapping loosely in the space where the missing pages used to be. I stare at the signature.

Aaron Al-Baz. Prophet of environmental doom. Founder of Eden. Savior of Earth.

And, if these, his own words, are true, a deluded, psychotic monster.

I read through the notebook, and then read it again to be sure I understand. It takes me hours to parse the tale, and when I have, I still can't believe it. Aaron Al-Baz is a hero, half-god, the whole reason any humans still survive and the only reason the Earth will one day flourish again after the global devastation we caused. Every textbook says so. Every temple hails him as near-divine.

I need to tell someone about what I've read, I think at once. But at that very moment there's a knock on my door and Lachlan walks in without waiting for an answer. I shove the notebook under the bedclothes and force a friendly smile. It must look pained, but he doesn't say anything. He knows I have plenty to be distraught about.

I need more time to digest what I just read. Society is held together by a common belief. What will happen if that belief is shattered? I have to think. The secret has been kept for more than two hundred years already. It can keep another hour or two.

But I'm numb when Lachlan takes me to meet some of the more prominent members of the Underground. There are cooks, clothiers, musicians, storytellers, healers, and even clergy for the Underground temple. I've always wanted to go to a temple meeting. Now everything about the ritual would ring false.

No, not everything. Not the message of hope, the desperate need for us to revive and reconnect with the environment, to love and cherish and respect it.

But as for the focal point of that worship, the man behind it all . . . My lip curls involuntarily. I can hardly pay attention to what I'm doing. I forget to smile, forget names, stand dumb like a post.

Before I've met everybody, Lachlan makes my apologies. "She needs rest," he says, "and peace. We'll give her time."

Understanding, the beautiful, happy, mellow people go about their lives. They seem ready to accept me no matter how churlishly I behave.

Lachlan leads me back to the roots of the tree. Some of them snake above the ground before plunging into the Earth. As soon as I get near the tree I feel calmer.

"Do you know what kind of tree it is?" Lachlan asks. His voice is soft here, gentle.

There were once thousands of kinds of trees in the world. In my Eco-history books I've read about a few of them. Grand oaks, delicate silver birches, maple trees milked for their sweet syrup, fir trees treated with such profligacy that they were chopped down and brought indoors for winter festivals, decorated with lights.

But I don't know what this tree is. "It is called a camphor tree," Lachlan explains. "They grow into giants—as you see— and the oldest one at the time of the Ecofail was more than two thousand years old."

"And that's why . . ." I can't say his name. "Why the creators of the Underground chose this species?"

"Partly, and for the smell." He inhales deeply. "Think of all of our bodies crammed down here, sealed off from the outside. I don't like to imagine what this place might smell like without the scent of camphor leaves filling the air."

I want to tell him so much, if only to share the burden of knowledge. But I bite my tongue, and he goes on.

"The tree has medicinal qualities, too. We don't harvest much, of course, but the oil of camphor can treat lung problems, even some heart problems, in small doses. At larger doses it is poisonous."

That's interesting, but I still just want to marvel at the fact a tree exists at all. I want to touch it again, to feel its leaves between my fingertips.

"But this tree, this one tree out of all the others, is particularly special. It is a symbol of nature's ability to survive no matter what terrible things humans do. Do you remember in your History class reading about a great conflict called World War II?"

I do, vaguely, but in my memory it merges with all of the other senseless conflicts in our history.

Then he refreshes my memory about one part of the war in particular—the time when one group of humans dropped an atomic bomb on another group of humans. Not on a battlefield, even, but on a city full of schoolchildren and mothers and shopkeepers and gardens and playgrounds.

The city, the people, the trees, were incinerated in a heartbeat. They said nothing could have survived, nothing would ever grow again.

But when spring came, a small number of charred stumps sprang forth with new, green life. Nature had withstood the worst that humans could do at the time.

"This tree was grown from a cutting of one of those survivor trees," Lachlan says, touching the bark reverently. "A miraculous symbol of nature's regenerative ability. Aaron Al-Baz hoped—we all hope—that the Earth will be as forgiving again. Unfortunately," he adds, "humans aren't so forgiving." His voice hardens. "We make bad choices, we neglect our fellow man." He looks earnestly at me. "We are all we have left! And yet we make part of our population illegal. I know that supplies will run out if there's uncontrolled reproduction, but can any civilized society actually kill its own children, for any reason? There has to be another way!"

He pounds his fist on the bark. I'm a little shocked, but the tree can take it.

"There's so much wrong with Eden, so much that can be fixed. We've gotten so far from Aaron Al-Baz's ideas of kindness and compassion."

I make a choking sound, and he looks at me strangely. I have to tell him!

"Rowan, we second children are not just hiding down here. Not just surviving and enduring. We are the children of Eden." He pauses a moment while this sinks in. "We're making a plan to take back Eden and make it a place where everyone is safe, everyone is equal, everyone is free. We have allies above."

"Like your brother?"

He nods. "And many others besides. The plight of the second children is small, in comparison to the plight of the poor. There are a few hundred of us. There are thousands of the underclasses, the poor, the desperate. You've seen the outer circles. How can there be poverty and crime in the perfect Eden that Aaron Al-Baz designed? His utopia has been corrupted by power-mad leaders. Al-Baz would never forgive us for what we've let Eden become."

His voice is low, but deep and reverberating. He seems to stand taller. "Rowan, the revolution is at hand, and we need your help."

I'm so taken aback I momentarily forget what I just

learned from the Al-Baz manifesto. "*My* help? What on Earth can I possibly do?"

"You can give me your lenses."

I blink, as if the implants are already in my eyes. "I don't have them yet."

"But you know where you were going to get them, right? You know the identity of the cybersurgeon?" He is tense and eager, leaning forward as if on the verge of springing for something. For me?

"Mom told me where we were headed. I think I could find the place again."

"Tell me."

And then, I don't know, something makes me hold back. I feel like if I give up this important information there might not be any more use for me. It feels like a power, almost, or at the very least a bargaining chip. My description is vague, misleading, confused. He shakes his head and says he can't think of any place matching that description. "Which circle is it in?"

"One of the outer ones. I could find it," I offer. "I think once I saw the area, Mom's description would come back to me. I could get you there."

He looks at me for a long moment, and I'm pretty sure he's aware I'm saying far less than I know. But as long as I'm willing to take him there, he seems content.

"Let's go right now!" he says. "Are you rested enough?"

I look at him skeptically. "Do you really think it is safe for me to be on the surface again right away? And . . . it *is* daytime, isn't it?" The light panels on the cavern ceiling say so, but my body isn't sure.

He sighs. "You're right, of course. I've just been waiting for this chance for so long! Do you know how long we've been searching for a cybersurgeon skilled enough to make lenses that pass? We've had a lead—just a whisper—about this person you're going to, but we haven't been able to track him down. There's a rumor of someone so skilled they can hack the EcoPan itself, but we have no idea if they really exist. Your parents must have used all their government connections—and plenty of money—to find him and hire him."

I tell him I had no idea it was such a big deal. The way Mom presented it, other second children had gotten black market lenses before.

"Some have," he says. "But they're not very good. They give the visual appearance of first child eyes, and some can pass a basic identity scan, but no one has ever managed to make lenses that bind fully to the neural networks, that are good enough to fool any Center official or securitybot or the EcoPan itself. If the rumor is true, this man can. I need to find him, and get the lenses he has ready for you."

I feel a momentary qualm. My mom gave her life so that I could live like a first child. My only chance of being normal is to have those lenses. Then, somewhere above my head, a family is waiting to take me in. Is that even still possible? Do the authorities know too much for the original plan to ever work?

I bow my head. Of course it could never happen. And I have the Underground now. It's not what I had planned . . . but then, what is? Of course I can give up my lenses.

And then I realize what this means, and to my shock I find myself upset. "You mean, you are going to have the lenses for yourself?" I ask. "You're going to pass as a first child and live aboveground in Eden?" Unspoken are the words *while I stay down here, trapped again.* I wouldn't admit it aloud, but already a small part of the appeal of living here in the Underground is that Lachlan is a citizen. I don't want him to go.

"We have a plan to infiltrate the Center at the highest

levels. It has been in the works for years, and everything is in place except for the last component—the lenses. Once I have those, there is a place arranged for me with an inner circle family that is deeply sympathetic to our cause. There's a place for me at Oaks Academy."

I give a quick intake of breath. That is the most exclusive school in Eden, just for the children of Center officials. Ash goes to a really good school . . . but Oaks Academy is for the truly elite of Eden.

"Believe me, it took every bit of blackmail, bribery, and threats we in the Underground possess to set this up. Flint is going crazy because he's used to taking point on all of our operations. But this is a long-term plan that needs someone to get close to Eden's top families, and there's no way he can do that. And obviously he's far too old to go to Oaks. But when I get into Oaks Academy with my cover story, I'll be in a perfect position to get at the Center—through their sons and daughters."

It makes sense. An adult like Flint can't just appear from nowhere, but a young man, a supposed orphan moving in with relatives, could insinuate himself more easily into that social milieu. Lachlan is charismatic enough to do it, I think.

But part of me has been building vague fantasies of friendship here in the Underground, and I don't want to lose him this fast. It makes no sense, but I suppose now that I don't have anyone of my own I'm more prone to cling to the few connections I make, even if our acquaintance is only a few hours old. I like him, to be truthful. He alternately annoys and enchants me. I want to know him better.

"Tomorrow night, after sunset," he says. "For now you can learn more about us, and then get plenty of rest before we set off."

I'm nervous about venturing up into Eden again, and

anxious about what I learned about Aaron Al-Baz, but before long I find that the people of the Underground have a soothing effect. I feel instantly at ease with all of them. At home, even. The talk ranges from simple, even trivial topics—my favorite foods, curiosity about the latest fashions above-ground—to impassioned discussions of politics, equality, and freedom. I'm shy and closemouthed for a while, but eventually the air of calmness surrounding me allows me to open up.

Lachlan comes and goes, checking on me periodically to make sure I'm doing okay. Every time I see him I want to pull him aside and tell him what I've found out about Eden's founder. But every time, he leaves before I can overcome my uncertainty. It's so huge—blasphemy! But he, and Flint, and all of Eden should know the truth.

I'm just talking with an elderly man about deeper caves beneath the camphor tree cavern that might have challenging rock faces to climb, when an alarm pierces my ears. I look around frantically as the deafening noise assaults me, but I can't see any danger.

All around me, though, the aura of calm instantly evaporates. Those happy soft people are all at once hard and focused. Weapons appear from nowhere. People are running here and there, taking up positions, crouching, aiming . . .

"What's happening?" I ask, grabbing Lachlan's arm as he races past.

"Get down!" is all he has time to say before he races off to a nook in the cavern wall, slings a long rifle over his shoulder, and begins to scale the camphor tree.

I still don't see any danger, but the wailing, pulsing sound of the incessant alarm is drilling into my head. I'm not going to stay cowering on the ground. I don't know where to run, so I make a quick decision and follow Lachlan up the tree. Instinct says to climb.

He looks surprised to see me following him, but not angry. I wish I had time to enjoy the climb. It is so different from the rock face that it takes me a while to find my rhythm. Near the base I climb using crevices and knots in the trunk. Higher up I have to wrap my arms around thick boughs and shimmy, and then higher still I wrap my legs around limbs and climb with my entire body. It is exhilarating, exhausting.

High in the canopy, not far from the crystal roof he stops, wedging himself in a crook. He gestures with his eyes to a similar spot a little higher up, and I climb there as he settles himself low against the branch, clinging with his thighs as he props the rifle at an angle, aiming toward the main entrance. I can see the doors easily through the leaves, but anyone on the ground would have a hard time singling me or Lachlan out. He has the perfect sniper position.

The Underground is primed for battle . . . but nothing happens except that the dreadful alarm finally shuts off. Lachlan holds his position for another five minutes, and I bite my lip, waiting.

Then there's a second alarm, a softer repetitive buzz. I see Lachlan's tense shoulders relax.

"All clear," he says. "Soon you'll be given your orders for defense drills, but you did well. You kept out of danger, out of the way, and you can act as a spotter from up here. Good job."

He slings the rifle back over his shoulder and starts his descent. I follow—and going down is much harder than going up.

"You mean there's no real threat? This was just practice?"

He pauses in his descent to look up at me. "Make no mistake, the threat is real. The Underground is in constant danger." He throws a wry smile up at me. "After all, we're at war."

18

AFTER AN EARLY communal supper of simple but delicious food served by the children (trying, and failing, to look very serious), I go immediately to bed. With the mission to find the cybersurgeon waiting for me the next night, I think I'll have trouble falling asleep so early. On the surface it would be nearly dark, and down here the ceiling panels are mimicking a gentle orange sunset that shines through the camphor tree boughs as I wearily make my way to my chamber.

I shut the door—it has no lock, which is worrying, but I suppose there's no danger down here, except from the outside, the Above, as they call it. I fall into bed, expecting to stare sleeplessly at the ceiling. But I must fall asleep almost immediately, because the next thing I know I'm in another place.

Part of me knows it is a dream, but somehow that doesn't make it any less disturbing. I'm walking through a meadow of flowers and tall grass. I can see it. I can smell the green scent that rises as I crush the herbs beneath my feet. It feels completely real. Up ahead I see shapes, low to the ground, and I approach, smiling, thinking they might be animals.

The stench hits my nose just before I can make out what they are. Corpses, human corpses, scattered across the beautiful meadow, their limbs twisted and contorted, their faces twisted in final agony and frozen in place until their flesh rots. Which it is definitely starting to. The scent of the flowers turns sickly, too sweet, and then dissolves into a smell of blood and decay.

At first I can see the grasses beneath the bodies. But as I walk—and because it is a dream, I can't stop walking, can't weep, or run away—the bodies grow thicker on the ground until it seems as if the Earth itself is sprouting them from the dirt. A crop of human corpses.

I forge my way through, almost wading, until the bodies are piled on top of one another and I have to step high, then climb, and finally crawl up a mountain of bodies. Their rotting flesh sloughs off beneath my fingers as I scramble upward. I can't stop, because there's someone standing atop this mountain of the dead. A tall, slender man with dark hair, a neatly trimmed goatee. I know I have to reach him.

He looks down at me, and his eyes are so gentle. How can that be, when he's standing on ten thousand corpses? Corpses he made. Because of course, the man is Aaron Al-Baz.

He reaches out a hand as if to help me to the summit, but I hold back. He tilts his head, looking at me curiously, and says, "Extinction is natural."

This wasn't a natural extinction, I want to say, but in my dream I'm mute.

"Humans evolved to the point where they could wipe themselves off the face of the Earth," he says in that soft, reasonable voice. "They would have, eventually. It was just a question of how many other species they took with them. My way was best."

Dream Me manages to shake her head.

"It was a hard thing to do," he says, a shade of sorrow crossing his face. "But the right thing. You will see, in time."

Unable to resist, I reach for his hand. But instead of pulling me up to the summit he shoves me violently backward and I'm tumbling, cartwheeling over the pile of bodies, landing in a tangle, trapped in a net of corpses that pull me under like quicksand . . .

I wake up screaming!

I'm out of bed and down the hall before I really know if I'm awake or still asleep. No one wakes, no one peers out of their bedrooms. The solid rock must have shielded the sound of my screaming.

I could go to Flint. He's the leader, he's responsible for all of these people, and for me now. I should tell him what I know. I could go to Iris, let her take me in her plump maternal arms and comfort me as if I were one of her brood of second children.

But instead I go to Lachlan. I'm drawn to him, irresistibly, in my moment of need.

He showed me where his room is, in passing, as he was giving me a tour of the Underground, but he didn't invite me in. His room is one of the few occupied dwellings on the upper story of galleries. As I race up the stairs I realize that if the Eden authorities ever found this place and launched an attack, Lachlan would be first in the line of fire. Of course, he would also be the first one with a clear shot at the invaders. Knowing him (and strangely, I almost feel as if I do), he probably thought of both when picking his room. He would be either a shield, or a sacrifice for the vulnerable second children he was defending down below. Whatever was required, he would do.

I pound on his door. I don't have the composure for a polite knock. Almost instantly the door opens a crack and I see not his face, but the muzzle of his weapon, the glint of his eye barely visible behind it.

The first words out of his mouth are "What's wrong?" He opens the door another inch and looks beyond me for danger.

"I . . . I had a nightmare," I confess.

He visibly relaxes, and I wonder if he looks a little disappointed in me. Like he expected me to be able to get through something as trivial as a nightmare on my own. He doesn't realize it is so much more—a nightmare about a terrible truth.

He pushes the door open with a sigh. "I'm not sleeping anyway. You might as well come in."

Somehow I expect his room to be stark and ascetic: bare walls and weapons. But it's like nothing I imagined. Standing racks of clothes are almost decorations in themselves. I realize they're costumes, the disguises he uses to move freely around the city. The bright colors of inner circle fashions dominate, muted here and there by various uniforms—of reclamation workers, deliverymen, and other Eden workers who could pass virtually unnoticed. I even see the collection of pieced-together rags that made up his hobo disguise, complete with false hair and beard.

But it is the walls that are the most surprising. Every square inch is covered in artwork. Mesmerized, I move closer to look. Most of the pictures are obviously drawn by children, bold and colorful depictions mostly of small grinning little stick people holding the hand of a tall stick man obviously meant to represent Lachlan. Without exception, the balloon-headed Lachlans the kids draw wear huge smiles.

Though the kids' drawings dominate, there are other more skilled and subtle works, too. One is a simple pencil sketch of an elderly woman sitting in a kitchen, a lump of dough on the table before her. The lines are sparse but evocative. I can almost smell bread baking. In one corner is the title, *Nana*. In the other is the artist's name: Iris. I can see Iris's life all in an instant—raised by a beloved grandmother, bereft and alone when her grandmother died. And now she's here, grand-mother herself to a huge family. Why did she give this draw-ing to Lachlan? To remind him that everyone here is family?

And then there are a couple of paintings that can only be described as masterful. They're done on rough material, inexpertly mounted, and attached to the rock walls with ad-hesive . . . but the skill is astounding.

Each picture shows an animal in the center, in a pose that suggests it has no idea anyone is watching. A leopard lolling in indolent magnificence; a squirrel hanging by its hind feet, nibbling a nut held in its forepaws; a dolphin breaching the surface of the foamy sea just enough to snatch a breath, its eye murky beneath the water.

Near the beasts, their environment is depicted in vivid, minute detail. The leopard's jungle is lush and green; the dol-phin's sea is speckled with sargassum and silver fingerlings. But as the color stretches to the outer edge of the canvas, the details begin to fade. The richness is diminished, the colors become muted. Their world is vanishing. Suddenly I can see prescience in the animals' eyes. They know their existence is ending.

In the right-hand corner, in scratchy black letters, is the artist's name. Lachlan.

"These are incredible," I say, and I feel like that pat praise sounds insincere. I want to gush about them, about what his paintings make me feel, the autumnal nostalgia for something I never experienced, the loss that happened before my time. But I feel shy, and can't find the words.

Lachlan shrugs. "Just something I do in my spare time," he says, dismissing his own skill. "Not that I have much of that."

I try to explain my reaction to the paintings. "They cap-ture that feeling of things slipping away, the inevitability of it . . . There was a time, I'm sure, when people knew the end was coming, that there was no stopping the Ecofail. When they still had their cars and air-conditioners and pesticide-laden crops and could pretend everything would go on like that forever, but they knew the edges of their world were dissolving, and there was nothing they could do about it any-more." I'm frowning, struggling to express myself.

"One man could have done something about it," Lachlan says staunchly. "Aaron Al-Baz tried to stop the man-made catastrophe, and no one would listen. He couldn't stop them from destroying the world, but he could save them. Save us. We have to live up to his memory so we're worthy when we can finally go out into the world, when it heals."

"He's your hero, isn't he?" I ask softly.

"He's everybody's hero."

"What if he wasn't?" I force myself to ask.

Lachlan is fiddling with his weapon, doing something the purpose of which I can't fathom, but it is taking his concen-tration. He seems to think I'm suggesting something hypo-thetical, an intellectual exercise in debate.

"If he wasn't a hero, why were our ancestors all saved in the final human refuge: Eden?" he asks absently as he makes a minute adjustment to the sight of his weapon.

I make myself speak more firmly. "Lachlan, I mean it. What would happen to the people of Eden, of the Underground—to you—if you found out that Aaron Al-Baz wasn't the good man everyone thinks he is?"

I have his attention now. His head comes up, his entire body is tense like he just spotted danger.

"The fact that we're here, when every other animal on the planet is gone, seems to me like proof of his goodness." His voice is challenging, almost antagonistic, and a part of me wants to let the whole thing go. "If the people of Eden found out otherwise . . ." He looks confused for a second. He can't conceive of quite what I'm getting at, or what the consequences might be. "It would disrupt everything. Everything that everyone believes in."

"I found something," I say in a small voice. "My mother gave it to me, before she . . ." I swallow hard. "She found it in our house, hidden behind a stone wall. The house belonged to Aaron Al-Baz just after the Ecofail."

And so I sit down on his bed and tell him what I learned.

Aaron Al-Baz was a visionary, who saw the imminent destruction of the global ecosystem long before anyone else. He was a genius, who put technology to work, first to stop the devastation and then, when that proved impossible, to fix it. He made the machines, the computers, the programs, work for him to begin the generations-long process of saving the planet. But before that, he decided to get rid of the thing that had poisoned and burned the planet in the first place.

It wasn't the Ecofail that killed off the human species. It was Aaron Al-Baz. He did it to save the rest of the planet.

It made sense, in a sick, inhumanely logical kind of way. The planet was dying because of people. He could either try to fix the harm humans had done . . . or go straight to its source. At some point the brilliant, mad genius developed a virus that would kill nearly 100 percent of the population. His talent knew no bounds; he simply created a program that would devise an unstoppable pathogen, and let his mechanical minions create it. Then when the scientists unleashed their particles into the atmosphere in an attempt to reverse global warming, Al-Baz released his disease.

Of course, he made sure that he himself was immune to it. His family, too. As for the rest of humanity, he left that up to chance.

Natural selection, he calls it in his manifesto.

He reduced the human population to a fraction of its original billions. Then he gathered up some of the survivors and installed them in Eden, to await the day humans could repopulate the world.

And the rest of the humans who survived the plague? The ones he didn't take into Eden? They were left to fend for themselves, to die slowly in the dying world along with all of the other animals.

"No," Lachlan says flatly when I finish telling him what I've learned. It is the first word he's spoken throughout the tale. The whole time he sat still and silent on his bed next to me, almost expressionless except for a slight downward turn of his brow.

"But I have proof," I insist, thinking he doesn't believe me. "Aaron Al-Baz's own admission. I can show you." I start to get up, but he pulls me back down onto the bed.

"No," he says again, softly but so firmly.

"But . . ."

He holds my hand in his, so I don't even try to rise again. I look down at his knuckles, at the seams of white scars where the skin has been split countless times. So many punches, so much fighting. That has been his life. But he's calm now. Almost unnaturally calm. The only sign of his agitation is the nervous way he strokes my skin with his thumb, over and over again in the same place.

"Have you told anyone else?" he asks. I shake my head. "Don't. Please," he adds, and I can see a deep worry in his eyes.

"Don't people deserve to know the truth?"

He looks down at my hands for a moment, and I wonder what he reads about me there. Short fingernails, ragged now, though clean after my shower. Callused fingertips from climbing my courtyard wall day in, day out. Split knuckles of my own, fresh and crusted over with a scarlet line. My first battle scar. First of many? I feel like I'm on the cusp of something big, and dangerous, and sublime.

"Aaron Al-Baz isn't just *my* hero," Lachlan says. "He's the patron saint of Eden. What we plan to do—the revolution that will make all citizens of Eden free and equal—will be launched in Aaron Al-Baz's name. He is our touchstone, our inspiration."

"But he was a monster!"

"No one knows that," he tells me. "No one can know. It will lead to chaos. That's the last thing we need. The Center is doing terrible things, but at least Eden is whole and sound. Water flows, people eat, and the deadly environment outside is kept at bay. We mean to make a smooth transition."

"You said you're at war," I remind him.

He nods. "A subtle war. A battle from within, as bloodless as possible. Do you remember the craters you saw in the outermost rings?"

I do.

"They're from the last time the outer circles staged an uprising. They're from bombs."

I'm shocked—almost moreso than when I read the truth about Aaron Al-Baz. "What do you mean? There has never been an uprising! No one ever dropped bombs inside Eden. It's not in the history books."

"What *is* in the history books?" he asks sharply. "Ancient history of pre-fail Earth. The life of Al-Baz. Environmental history. But what do the books say about the generations that have lived in Eden?"

I think about it. There are civics books, explaining the tenants of Eden. There are books about the governmental system. Lists of previous chancellors and cabinet ministers. But history? Of the years humans have spent in Eden? No. I assumed that was because nothing much happened. We simply lived our lives, waiting for the time when we could reenter the world. It never occurred to me that history could be happening in Eden.

"It's not in the books, and the first children . . ." He breaks off, rubbing his forehead. "It's like they have no memory of it. I've tried to talk with some of our allies about it, and they get confused, or laugh, or flatly deny it. Craters? They say those must be from collapsed underground water reservoir tanks. But the second children remember. At least, the oldest do, and they passed it on to us."

It was seventy years ago. The poor of the outer circles tried to seize more power for themselves, armed with stones and staffs and a few guns. Pitifully few. The Center retaliated. Brutally.

"Why don't the first children remember?"

"I don't know," Lachlan admits. "Some kind of brainwashing? Mutual agreement to ignore the unpleasant parts of life? I have no clue. But the important part is that we can't square off against the Center with weapons and fighters. We'll fail, people will die, and the poor will be worse off than ever. Someone has to infiltrate the Center at its core. From there, influence, blackmail, yes even violence, will be put to work to effect change. In the end, all of Eden has to be behind us, rich and poor, first and second children alike. That's why it is so vitally important that Aaron Al-Baz's name remain untarnished. They won't all get behind me, or Flint. But Al-Baz is someone everyone can believe in. We need to have the people on our side, but then the major shift has to come from within. The ones in power have to concede to it, and give up their power to the people."

"It sounds impossible. Why would they do that?"

"We won't give them any choice," he says, and the steel in his voice makes me tense up. He feels it in my hand. "Don't worry, I'll make sure you're kept out of it. After tomorrow, that is. Once you take me to the cybersurgeon you can relax and enjoy being a real member of a welcoming society for the first time."

He flops back on the bed, still holding my hand, smiling up at me.

But I don't think that's fair. "What if I want to help?" I ask. "There must be something I can do."

He looks proud of me for making the suggestion, and I feel a little glow inside. But he says, "You've been through enough."

"Not more than you," I press.

"But no one should have to go through that much. If we win, no one ever will again. Peace, safety, prosperity, for everyone in Eden."

I look down at him, lying on the bed weary and impassioned, and I'm overcome with a mad impulse. I remember Lark's kiss in that quiet moment together, the way it haunts me, confuses me, elates me. And I wonder, would kissing Lachlan be the same?

He sits up suddenly, as if he just realized his vulnerability. "I have something for you." He fumbles in a pocket and pulls out something. He holds it out in his closed hand. All I can see is a bit of cord woven in and out of his fingers.

I put out my hand, and he covers it with his own, letting his knuckles rest there a moment before uncurling his fingers. I feel something drop into my palm. When I look, I find a stunning piece of pale pink crystal, two inches long, its six sides beautifully smooth.

It is so clear! I hold it up and look at Lachlan through it. His face is softened to rose tones.

"Every second child has a piece of crystal from the cavern. It is a symbol of our unity. You're one of us now."

"It's lovely," I say, stroking the cool stone. "It's perfect."

Overwhelmed by the gift—and more by what it implies— I lean toward him, intending to kiss his cheek. At the last moment he turns his head, just a bit, and my lips touch his. Just the lightest touch. I don't retreat. Our eyes lock, second child eyes, and I hover, his breath on my mouth, waiting to see what he'll do. What I'll do. The memory of Lark's kiss fills me, then fades a little as I look at Lachlan. I have no idea what I want. But Lachlan does.

Suddenly his hand is in my hair, pulling me to him in a kiss that is fierce, delightful, frightening in its intensity. I feel wildly alive . . . but as I reach to take his face in my own hands his fingers twine in my hair and pull me back. I gasp.

"You should get some sleep before we leave," he says firmly, though I notice his breath is coming fast, too, and his pupils are huge and luminous.

I know what he means, of course, but I pretend I don't. I don't want to be alone.

"Good idea," I say, and stretch myself on the bed beside him, my head nestled in the crook of his arm. I can hear his heart racing.

He doesn't tell me to leave.

Though my body is comfortable, I'm also too tense with the strangeness of it to fall asleep right away. My mind is whirring, bouncing from the terrible truth I discovered about Eden's hero, to the kiss, to Lark, and back again.

As I listen to the soothing sound of his steady breathing my mind clears, my body relaxes, and I fall asleep . . .

19

I AWAKE WITH a jolt, thinking someone's trying to break the door down. I'm confused, first to not be in my own bed at home, then even moreso when I realize Lachlan is lying beside me. I'd thrown an arm over him in my sleep, and he peels it off to roll over my belly and spring to his feet. His gun is in his hand.

"What's wrong?" he asks as he pulls the door open, the same words he spoke to me when I knocked. He must always be on edge, waiting for the worst.

I shrink back, suddenly aware that I'm in Lachlan's bed in the middle of the night. Fully dressed, to be sure, but whoever is at the door is going to think . . .

"We can't find Rowan." It's Flint's voice, and he sounds angry. "She's not in her room, not in any of the common rooms. You said she could be trusted. If she slipped out and betrays us . . ."

With an inscrutable smile on his face, Lachlan slowly pushes the door all the way open, revealing me sitting awkwardly on his bed.

"Oh," Flint says, and looks at Lachlan with raised eyebrows.

"It's not—" Lachlan and I both begin at the same time, but Flint interrupts.

"Get up, Rowan. I need you. Now." He starts toward me.

"What's this about?" Lachlan asks, and I notice that he subtly imposes himself between Flint and me. I'm indescribably touched by the instinctive protective gesture.

"We've captured an intruder snooping around the tunnels."

"What do you need Rowan for?" Lachlan asks, glancing back at me.

"You'll see."

Baffled, I smooth my disheveled hair and follow him. Lachlan stays close at my side. Once, I think I see his hand start to reach for mine, but he seems to check himself. Still, it's good to have him so close.

Flint leads us swiftly around the gallery and down two flights of stone steps. I stop dead when I recognize our destination: the interrogation chamber. I can feel the wet bag suffocating me, and I have to bend over, breathless, hugging myself as I try to breathe.

Lachlan has an arm around me, bends low beside me. "In through your nose, out through your mouth. Slow. Easy. You're going to be okay." It takes a minute, but my breathing returns to something like normal. I stand up straight and try to maintain my dignity, but it is hard when I remember the torture I received in that room.

Flint enters first, then Lachlan. He blocks my view with his shoulders, but I can see two people inside. One, a woman I met briefly beneath the camphor tree, holds something in her hand that looks like a small sock filled with sand.

The other person is tied to the chair and has a bag over their head, and my lungs convulse again, though I keep myself visibly under control. I see bare arms covered with bruises, and as I watch, the Underground woman—Flora, that was her name—cocks her arm back and hits the prisoner in the shoulder.

The prisoner groans. "Please . . ." The gasp is muffled

under the soaking bag, but I know that voice, know the down of golden hair on those poor bruised arms.

"Lark!" I shout, and surge toward her. Flint grabs me roughly by the shoulders and forces me back.

Her head inside the bag turns toward me. Suddenly I see her entire body go rigid, straining tightly against her bonds. I push against Flint but he won't let me go. Then Lark's body starts tembling spasmodically. Her head thrashes back and forth, then after a long moment her body goes completely stiff again, then slack.

"She has seizures," I cry out, kicking uselessly at Flint's shins. "Let me help her!"

"Did you lead her here?" Flint growls, ignoring my struggles, and I remember that this is the man who tortured me. He's been so pleasant ever since, his tone cordial and inspiring. Now I recall the voice of my interrogator, and I try to shrink away from him. But he holds me in an iron grip and shakes me. "Did you send her a message? Who is she? Who is she working for?"

"Let her go," Lachlan says, and if his voice is soft, his intentions clearly are not. His fists are clenched, his jaw set, and I think he's ready to attack the leader of the Underground. Flora looks over her shoulder, surprised, and Flint lets me go abruptly. The two men stare at each other for a long, tense moment. Then Flint takes a step back.

"You know this girl?" Flint asks, keeping a more respectful distance from me . . . and Lachlan.

"She's my friend," I say. Lark's head is turned toward me now, and I want to rip the bag off her head, comfort her, but I don't quite dare.

"I thought you said she was kept strictly in her house all her life," Flint says to Lachlan.

"She was, until just a few days ago. I don't know who this girl is, though."

"She's my brother's best friend," I explain. "I met her when I snuck out. She knows I'm a second child, but she'd never tell—ever! She's an outer circle girl, and she . . . she helps people." I really don't know what Lark does, but I know she's somehow involved in resisting the Center.

"What was she doing snooping outside?" Flint wants to know.

"Why don't you ask her, instead of beating her?" I say, looking levelly at Flint. Then I slip between the two men. No one tries to stop me when I start to fumble with the cords that tie the wet canvas bag around Lark's neck. The water has made the knots swell, though, and I can't undo them.

"Here, let me," Lachlan says, and whips out a folding knife with a curved blade. He slices cleanly through the ropes, and I trust him so much I never even worry how close the deadly edge is to my friend's neck.

I pull the bag off, and strangely, it is Lachlan she sees first. The two people I've kissed, meeting face-to-face under these strange circumstances.

Then she looks at me, and her face floods with relief. "You're alive!" she gasps.

I use the hem of my shirt to blot her face dry.

"What are you doing here, Lark?" I ask, very close to her ear, so close it is almost a kiss.

"I've been looking for you. I had all my contacts from the Edge searching."

"You're with the Edge?" Lachlan interrupts.

"Bunch of amateurs," Flint mutters. "Deluded do-gooders."

Lachlan shoots him a disdainful look. "At least they're trying. What's wrong with trying to do good? Anything is better than nothing."

"Until they get in our way, or expose us, or bring the Center sniffing around where it doesn't belong."

"What is the Edge?" I ask.

Lark answers. "The Edge is the opposite of the Center. We try to bring people together, people of all circles, all incomes, all educations."

"A social club," Flint scoffs.

Lark looks at him furiously, so impassioned even though she's still tied down that my heart thrills for her courage, her strength. "We're doing what we can. We let inner circle people know about the problems the outer circle people face. We raise money, we try to help the poor. We hide rebels. We help second children."

Flint looks incredulous. "What second children have you ever helped?"

"Rowan, of course. She's the first I ever met. Ever since then members of the Edge have been keeping an eye on her house, following her when she sneaks out to make sure she's safe."

I feel my heart sink in my chest, as Lachlan and I exchange looks.

"You *told* someone about me?"

"Only a very few trusted members of the Edge. I've known them for years. They're absolutely reliable."

"You idiot!" Lachlan thunders. He steps toward Lark, looking furious, and for a second I'm afraid for her. But then I see that once again he's getting between Flint and his intended target. Lachlan is angry, but when I see Flint's face I start to shake. He looks murderous. I think if Lachlan wasn't between them, his hands would already be around Lark's throat.

"Lark," I ask softly, "how could you do that to me?"

Her face falls. "I . . . I thought I was helping you. I trust them."

"Then you trust a traitor," Flint snarls at her. "Which makes you a traitor, too." He jabs a forefinger in my direction. "This girl lived in perfect safety until you told one of your 'trusted friends' about her. Now her mother is dead, because of you. The Center is hunting her, because of you."

"I didn't mean to!"

"And did your Edge friends follow you here? Are they alerting the Center now?" She shakes her head, looking desperately at me.

I'm confused, and turn away from Lark even as her flowing tears beg me to comfort her. I never truly believed that she would betray me. And this . . . She didn't mean to, I know, but it is still her fault that Mom was gunned down in the street. I trusted her.

"Rowan, I'm sorry!" she wails, pulling at the cords that still tie her, as if she would fly into my arms if she were free. I start to walk away . . . but I can't.

"She made a mistake," I say firmly to Flint and Lachlan. "She thought she was helping me. But she didn't turn me in. She didn't betray me." I look at her sweet, sorrowful face. "I trust her," I say, and I'm absolutely certain that what I'm saying is true.

"Trust," Flint spits, scowling. Then he seems to relax, and shrugs slightly. "What motivated the girl doesn't matter. She's here now, and done is done. Flora, get patrols up to monitor the streets outside the entrance, and put everyone on alert. I want sidearms carried at all times by everyone over twelve years old until further notice."

She nods brusquely and leaves to make it so.

"And now I think you should go, too, Rowan," Flint says, and a sudden deliberate gentleness in his voice gives me pause.

"I'm not going anywhere," I say staunchly.

"You don't need to see this. You've been through enough."

Perplexed, I look to Lachlan.

"Do you really need to do this?" Lachlan asks his leader.

"She's been in the Underground, and she's not a second child. What other choice is there?" He turns to me again. "Rowan, go." Then he opens a drawer in a rolling cart and takes out a syringe.

Lark understands before I do. "No! Please!" she shrieks. "I'll never tell anyone, I swear! I'll tell them I was lying about Rowan, that she's not a second child! I'll leave the Edge forever. No! You can't!" She twists in her bonds, trying to get as far away from Flint as possible. "Rowan, please! You can't let him kill me!"

I stare at Flint in disbelief.

"I know it's hard for you to understand," Flint says, "but we can't let anyone know about us. Not yet, and not for a long time. We've managed to keep this place secret. I won't put all of us—all the children and families, the tree—in jeopardy because of one stupid girl. Maybe she just made a dumb mistake. But dumb is deadly, and we can't take any chances. The girl has to die."

I hurl myself on top of her, protecting her with my body. "Lachlan . . . ," I beg in a whisper.

He looks torn. "Flint, I appreciate everything you do to keep us safe, but . . . she's just a young girl, not a Greenshirt or a Center official. There has to be another way. You don't even know how she found the Underground yet."

"No," Flint admits. "Flora reported that she hadn't yet elicited that information from the girl." He looks at Lark with a touch of grudging respect. "She withstood interrogation well."

"Then let's find that out first. How she came here—and *why* she came here. *Without* beating her. Then, when we're all cooler, we can decide what to do with her."

"You're just delaying the inevitable, prolonging the suffering for Rowan, and the girl," Flint says. "There's only one option."

"There are always more options," Lachlan insists.

Flint agrees, obviously reluctantly, and I hold Lark's hand while he and Lachlan ask her questions.

———

THE EDGE MEMBER assigned to keep a discreet watch on my house followed us when Mom and I went out to get my lens implants. They saw everything—the roadblock, Mom's murder—but couldn't help me without giving themselves away. They gave Lark my last known location, and she came searching for me, along with other members of the Edge who were in on the secret of my existence. But no one could find a trace of me.

In despair, Lark went to her star tower, the glorious rooftop where I got my very first, very confusing kiss. And there, by a strange coincidence, she looked down over the edge to the city below and saw me.

She was sure she was imagining it. Of all the vast number of people in Eden, how could it be that she happened to spy the one person she was searching for. She almost stayed on the rooftop, knowing it was only wishful thinking . . . but in the end she dashed down the stairs. She lost us for a long time, but finally spotted Lachlan and me just as we were slithering through the grate that led to the Underground.

How could she know me from so high up? I wondered. I had been up there at night, of course, but even in daylight I doubt I could have picked out any one person from so high up. Could her story be true? I want to believe it.

"No one else knows," she swears. "Just me, and it was just luck."

"Why did you want to find Rowan so badly?" Lachlan asks.

"I didn't just want to find her. I *needed* to find her!"

"You care about her that much?" Lachlan asks, half-respectful and, I think, half-suspicious.

"I do," Lark says amid her tears. "And I had to tell her something."

"What?" I ask, coming closer.

"It's your brother, Rowan. They've got him."

My heart seems to sink in my chest with a sick thud. "Who?" I ask, knowing only too well.

"The Greenshirts came for him when you were missing. They dragged him out of his classroom."

I can't believe it. Not Ash. Not poor, weak, innocent, loving Ash.

"His trial was already held, quickly and in secret. He's going to be executed in three days."

My hand covers my mouth. He's done nothing wrong! Holding back sobs, I force myself to ask, "And my father? Has he been arrested, too?"

"Oh, Rowan," Lark says with such sorrow you'd think *I* was the one bound in a torture chamber, my death looming. "Your father is the one who condemned him."

20

"UNTIE HER," I say, and when no one makes a move, I scream, "Let her go now!" I feel like I'm losing it. Not Ash. Not sweet, gentle Ash . . .

"Rowan, I think you should . . . ," Flint begins.

"No," I shout, and I'm surprised at my own strength, standing up to these two men. Where Ash is concerned I can do anything. "She's going free, and she's going to help me rescue Ash." I stare evenly at Lachlan. "And you're going to help us."

"Out of the question," Flint answers for him. "Even if we let her live—and that's still very doubtful—she can never leave the Underground. We can't take the risk. And I'm very sorry about your brother, but we simply can't help him. Neither can you."

"You can't stop me from trying to save my brother!" My voice comes out in a snarl, fury rising in my throat.

"We most certainly can. It won't be pleasant, but we can lock you up, drug you . . . whatever it takes to protect the Underground from exposure."

"You mean I'm a prisoner? I thought this was supposed to be a free society, where second children could lead normal lives."

"There's no such thing as normal on this Earth anymore," Lachlan interjects.

I ignore him. "You're all about protecting second children, right? Well, my mother and brother have been protecting one for sixteen years. My mom gave her life protecting one! My brother has been arrested because he kept me safe for so long. You have to help him."

"Rowan," Lachlan says very gently, "your brother must be in the Center prison. I'm so sorry for him, and for you. To lose everyone important to you all at once . . . ." He breaks off, and I see his eyes glisten with tears that don't fall. He blinks them quickly away. "But there's nothing we can do. There's no way any of us can get inside the Center prison."

"I can get you in," Lark says.

———

WE LISTEN TO her idea. It sounds feasible, but . . .

"No, it wouldn't work," Lachlan says. "That would get us in, but once inside we'd have to maneuver within the building. We'd need IDs, clearance. None of our contacts have that kind of power. We'd have to have someone very high up on the inside to give us security codes, access passes."

I think for a moment. "Someone like the next vice chancellor?" I ask.

They look at me in surprise as I let them know my father has been handpicked by the chancellor to be his second in command.

"But he would never help you," Lachlan protests. "Not if what Lark says is true." He asks Lark, "Did he really turn in his own son?"

She nods. "My father overheard some Center officials talking about it, though I don't think anyone outside the government knows yet. I don't know how he managed to protect himself, but your father's job—and his life—are secure. And he's the one who signed his own son's death warrant."

I hear Lachlan suck in his breath, feel his hand on my arm. I shake him off.

"I don't need your pity—I need your help. I know my father is a wicked man who would do anything to save himself." No, that's not quite true. I never, ever imagined he would do this to Ash, his beloved son. I always knew he would have turned on me, turned me in, if it wasn't that Mom and Ash would have suffered, too. But Ash? I wouldn't have thought it possible, even from him.

"We can't help you," Lachlan says again, so gently. "It's an impossible mission. Suicide. We can't put what we have here, and our future plans, at risk." I can see the strain in him, the tension of believing that two opposing things are absolutely right. He wants to save Ash, for my sake, and because Ash helped a second child, and, I think, because Lachlan simply believes that it is his duty to help people in need. But he also has an unshakable commitment to the Underground, to keep it safe no matter what the price. He would give his own life for the Underground. He will give Ash's life, too.

Would he give my life? I wonder.

"Not *can't*," I correct him. "Won't." I stare at him without flinching so he will understand how deadly serious I am. "If you won't help me, I won't help you."

For a moment Lachlan's mouth works without uttering a sound as he tries to process, to come up with an argument. But I think I see something in his eyes that tells me he approves. He can't go along with it, but if I give him no other choice . . .

Flint spins me around by the shoulder, and this time Lachlan doesn't intervene. I think I understand why. "What do you mean?"

I regard him coldly. "I mean simply this: if you don't help me rescue my brother, I won't help you get the implants you need from the cybersurgeon."

Flint starts to fume and sputter, a far cry from the collected leader I've come to know. "This is preposterous! We take you in when you have no one, nowhere else to go. You depend on us. If it wasn't for us, you and every other second child would be dead. And you think you can defy us?"

My only reaction is to blink once.

"You heard me," I say evenly.

"You stupid girl, do you think we won't *make* you tell us what you know?"

I raise my eyebrows slightly, though I can already feel my lungs tighten. "You tried that before," I tell him, trying to throw as much disdain into my voice as I can. "Didn't get very far, did you? As I recall you didn't get any useful information out of me even when I thought you were a Center official. What do you think you'll get now that I know you're just a cringing second child skulking in an underground lair . . . with my brother's very life at stake." I'm talking so much more bravely than I feel.

"You'd break," Flint says, but he doesn't sound so sure.

"She would," Lachlan says to my surprise. "But how long would it take? We need to get the lenses soon. Particularly if there's any risk that the traitor in the Edge might know about us. We need to set our plan in motion, and it can only work if I have the lenses. Of course you can break her, eventually. But what if it takes days? What if she dies in the process?"

I know exactly what he's doing, but I give no sign. Flint looks uncertain, and the uncertainty makes him angry. I don't know much about government, but I don't think easy anger is a good thing in a leader.

"You want to save what you love," I point out. "So do I."

"Outside," Flint snaps to Lachlan and turns on his heel. Lachlan follows, and as he passes me he winks.

Alone, I wrap my arms around Lark and hold her tight. I can feel her body trembling, and I embrace her until the tremors start to subside.

"What is this place?" she asks.

Maybe I shouldn't tell her anything. What she already knows—or must have figured out by now—could get her killed. But she's my friend, and she should know. She made a mistake revealing secrets before. She'll know to be more careful now.

"It's called the Underground. It was designed as a backup for Eden, if anything went wrong. Now it's a secret sanctuary for second children."

Her face lights up, as if she's forgotten all about her torture, her uncertain fate. "You have a home! A place just for you! I'm so happy for you. But . . ." Her face falls, and I can see her lively mind calculating. "But won't I be able to see you? Won't you be able to leave, or can't I visit?"

"Lark, there's so much I don't know yet. I don't know what the Edge does, but the Underground is serious. A lot of lives depend on this place, and keeping it secret."

She looks a little sulky, then shakes her head, her lilac hair lashing her cheeks. "You'll sneak out," she says with confidence, a mischievous smile on her face. "You'll come to me. I know you will."

And even in the middle of danger and doubt I feel the irresistible pull of her, and know that no matter what happens, no matter what the risk, I'll try to see her again.

Lachlan comes in, stopping short when he sees us embracing, our faces so near, Lark's eyes sparkling. A quick frown darkens his brow, clearing almost before I know it's there.

I pull away from Lark awkwardly, one finger catching in

a snarl of her disheveled hair. I don't know which one of them to look at. I owe so much to both of them. But what I feel—for both of them—doesn't stem strictly from obligation. Feelings, new and strange, swirl in me, and right now there's only one thing I can do. Ignore them. It's like being awed by the grandeur of a mountain peak, and fearing the coming struggle to climb it . . . while you're still fording the raging river at its base. The mountain of Lachlan and Lark, of their kisses, looms, inescapable before me. But it's not immediate, and I have to turn my mind away from it.

"So?" I ask, making myself defiant with my hands on my hips.

"Flint has agreed," he begins, and by a quirk of his mouth I can tell the more accurate words would be *has been persuaded*, "to let me help you rescue Ash."

With a quick gasp of relief I reach for him . . . and stop myself.

"With certain conditions," he adds. "First, Lark will be drugged before we leave. She'll be unconscious, and when she wakes she probably won't be able to remember much of the last twenty-four hours. Is that acceptable?"

I look to Lark, and she nods.

"Not that we don't trust you, but," he narrows his eyes at her, "people make mistakes." She bows her head, cringing. "I'll come for you later, you'll get me inside the Center, and you will never make any attempt to find the Underground, or contact Rowan, again."

"But . . . ," both Lark and I say at the same time.

"Never. If you're seen anywhere near any of our entrances, or in Rowan's company, you'll be killed. No second chances."

"But she's my friend," I protest.

Lark doesn't object, just takes my hand and gives me a look that says *Agree, for now*.

I've snuck out, I've risked myself to be with her before. Later, anything can happen. For now, Ash is my priority. That, and making sure Lark leaves the Underground safely. Raging river first. The mountain will always be there.

And then I think, did that condition that Lark and I never meet again come from Flint . . . or from Lachlan?

A pleasant-looking young man with bottle-green second child eyes comes in with a syringe, and Lark holds out her arm obligingly. "See you on the other side," she says, and it is only as the clear liquid plunges into her vein that the thought occurs to me.

I whirl to Lachlan in a panic. "It's just to make her unconscious, right? Not the lethal syringe?"

"Rowan, what do you take me for?" He looks genuinely hurt.

"Swear it!" I cry, grabbing him by the shirtfront.

He takes hold of my hands. "Rowan, I swear it. Trust me."

Why does everyone keep saying that to me?

It isn't long before Lark starts to drift off. As her eyes grow heavy, I give her a kiss on the cheek. On the periphery of my vision I see Lachlan avert his eyes. A little while later a large man comes in and scoops Lark up like a limp doll. I feel an emptiness when he takes her away.

"He'll bring her to her house. She should be reviving at that point. She can let herself in, and with luck, forget about her little adventure in the Underground."

"But remember enough to help us."

He looks at me for a long moment. "I think that girl would do anything for you."

I bite my lip, and don't know what to say.

"How did you convince Flint?" I ask instead, changing the subject in what I hope isn't a too-obvious way.

Lachlan laughs, and it is such a relief to see. I like the

smiling, joking Lachlan. He makes me so comfortable, so . . . happy. I just don't know how to react to the other Lachlans: the fighter, the leader . . . the man.

Lachlan drops his voice to a low confidential murmur. "I think what got him was the very real possibility that I might die in this raid on the Center. We've always butted heads, and you know he thinks he should be the one to get the implants, and alter our plan. So he's letting me help you. Me, alone. His reasoning is this: When I don't come back, when I've failed in the rescue, our part of the bargain will be done. We tried, and now you'll have to take him to the cybersurgeon."

What a merciless man Flint is. The fight to save second children shouldn't be a power struggle between its two most charismatic leaders. "I wouldn't give him the lenses if you . . . didn't make it."

He touches my shoulder, then seems to realize what he's doing and jerks his hand away. "You held out admirably before, but make no mistake—he would have made you talk. His ways are . . . not my ways. I don't believe that causing pain can ever bring about a better society. Death, perhaps, under certain circumstances. But there's enough cruelty and suffering in the world. I won't add more if I can help it."

I feel such a warmth for him, filling my chest, spreading along my limbs, making my fingertips tingle. Why is my body reacting in such a visceral way? Why is it reacting to two different people? Is it only that I've never met anyone before? Maybe I'm enamored of the idea of people . . .

"Isn't there something you can do to get the better of Flint?" I ask.

"A girl after my own heart," he says with a wink. I feel my cheeks flush. "There's no convincing Flint to help you—or help me, for that matter. But there is certainly a way to force the issue, with your help." He leans close and whispers in my ear. So—if you're agreeable—we're going to turn the tables on Flint. Tonight, we go to the cybersurgeon and get my lenses."

I have a flash of suspicion. If I help him, and then afterward he refuses to help me save Ash . . .

But no. I trust him.

"And then not only will it be too late for Flint to get the lenses for himself, but I'll be so valuable to the Underground that they won't dare risk letting me break into the Center alone. He'll have to commit a few more people to help me. I'll have a much better chance of success with a little backup."

It was brilliant, and I beamed at him. But one thing was wrong.

"Not just help *you*," I say. "*Us.* I'm going, too."

And though he tries for a long time, nothing he says can dissuade me. I won't let him go alone into danger.

21

SO MANY THINGS, so fast. I stultified for sixteen years, and now a lifetime of danger and grief and wonder and emotion are all compressed within a few days.

We set out shortly afterward by a different passageway than the one I'd entered through. We enter a labyrinth of winding, confusing tunnels that double back on themselves. Once we come to what looks like a dead end, but Lachlan shifts a rock and a low stone door slides open on silent pneumatic hinges. We crawl for a while, then come to a place we can stand again. I'm utterly lost, but Lachlan knows the way unerringly.

I'm supposed to be snug in my bed while Lachlan takes the risk for me. I can't quite believe that Flint hoped (or nearly hoped) Lachlan would fail. Lachlan, though, seems perfectly confident as he sneaks me out of the Underground by a series of twisting, gradually rising passages. Excited, bouncy even.

"You just don't know what this means to us," he must say a dozen times as we make our way to the surface. "Having real lenses will change everything."

I want to know how, exactly, but whenever I ask, he's vague, or changes the subject. I know he wants to infiltrate the highest levels as an elite student, but what else? What next? I feel a swell of resentment. I've trusted him so many times—with Lark's life, with the secret of my lenses. I understand the danger of confiding in someone—look what happened when Lark told people she trusted about me—but when I'm the one shut out of secrets, it hurts.

"The next to last circle," I tell him definitively as we step out into the blackness. Eden doesn't respond to him any more than it does to me, and the ground at our feet stays dark.

He looks at me, apparently amused. "So you remember now?"

I don't know whether to pretend anymore or not, so I only look at him sidelong. "It's all coming back to me. Slowly."

He laughs, a low chuckle that warms me. "As long as you're on my side, I don't mind if you take your time telling the truth. Believe me, I get it."

It's strange how walking around Eden feels almost natural now. True, we sneak and skulk in the shadows, avoiding the few souls abroad tonight. But to be out, to move, to be part of the city now feels normal. The danger exists . . . but that feels normal, too, somehow. My body feels alive, eager, tingling with excitement. I feel ready.

We emerged only one circle away from our destination, and it isn't long before we cross the radius and head right, toward the east side.

"There's a modification parlor somewhere around here. Serpentine, it's called." Mom's words are burned clearly on my memory.

"I know that place," Lachlan says. "It's very popular with the Bestial crowd. But I had no idea there were shady dealings going on there. It's not in a great neighborhood, but the place has an air of respectability. Now, if you'd just told me it was the Serpentine in the first place you could be back in your nice safe bed dreaming of a better world."

"Dreaming gets you nowhere," I tell him as we walk. "I want to *make* a better world. Even if there's not much for me to do."

"You're giving up your lenses." He stops in the middle of the dark street and turns to me. The look on his face is one of respect, and maybe, I think, a little bit of awe. "You're giving up your chance to be part of a world you must have longed to join all of your life. You could walk away from the Underground, from me, from all of us, and take your chances up here in Eden, with your new eyes and maybe even the family your mom set you up with."

I look at him skeptically. "I got the impression Flint wouldn't have given me a choice."

A hard look flashes across his face, but then he cracks a smile. He makes light of things whenever he can. "I think you've gathered by now that Flint and I have slightly different approaches. Your lenses may very well save the Underground, and change Eden forever. But I believe in free will, and self-determination. Those things are at the core of what we're fighting for. If you had decided that you didn't want to give up your lenses, I wouldn't have forced you." That hard look casts another quick shadow across his face. "And if Flint had tried, I would have stopped him."

I wonder when this conflict between Lachlan and the leader of the Underground will break into all-out war, and what it might mean for the secret world of second children.

But I can't worry about that now, or about the dozens of other things plaguing my mind right now. We've come to Serpentine.

It is, as Mom described it, a glaringly orange building. Unlike most other structures in this overall squalid next-to-outermost ring, Serpentine is gently illuminated, a golden glow holding back the dark.

In there I would have become normal. In there, I would have found a real life . . . but one away from my family, my first friend. A life, sure, but it would really just be a different kind of a lie. Another kind of hiding.

No, I decide, firmly and absolutely. I don't want the lenses. I don't want to be part of a society that doesn't want me. Since there's no scenario in my future that doesn't have me hunted, a pariah, I'd rather just commit wholeheartedly to being what I am: a second child, among other second children.

A sense of relief washes over me. I'd been perfectly willing to give up my lenses to Lachlan and his cause, but that had been a rational decision. Now it was an emotional, gut choice, too. I realize I'm so much happier at the prospect of just being me, with my vivid second-child eyes, not something altered and corrupted by the Center, changing just to fit in someplace I only now realize I don't really want to be.

The electrified fence around the modification center gives off a low, menacing hum. Lachlan cocks his head up at it. "I wish you'd told me about the electricity ahead of time. It's going to take me a while to disable it, and I don't want to be outside here any longer than necessary."

"I can get us in," I tell him, and repeat Mom's instructions. "They turn off the electricity to the third panel from the left on the southeast side." I have a moment of doubt. "South*west*?"

He gives me a wry look. "You *do* know the voltage level is very likely fatal, don't you?"

"Southeast. I'm sure of it." Fairly sure. "It's off between three and four in the morning."

He checks his watch and nods. "I guess this place has dealings with a few people on the wrong side of the law. Nice of them to give their friends a back door inside." He leads me around the back of the building, and we count three chain-link superconductive panels from the left.

I lean close to try to listen for the telltale buzz of a charge, but the whole thing is humming and I can't tell if this panel is deactivated. I look around for some debris to test it with. Maybe if we throw something at the fence we'd see a spark? I'm not really sure how this works.

"Can we . . . ?" I begin uncertainly, but in what I'm beginning to realize is a characteristically Lachlan approach he hurls himself at the fence . . . and doesn't sizzle to death. He grins over his shoulder at me. "Coming?"

I can't help laughing. And then . . . I can't help racing him to the top. Despite his head start, my hand clasps the top before his. I feel strong, capable.

We drop down on the far side and make our way to the back door. As Mom told me, I knock twice up on the high corner of the door, pause for a breath, and knock three times near the bottom. There's a long, tense wait, and finally we hear footsteps approaching from within.

I don't know what I was expecting—a middle-aged scientist, a businesslike doctor in a white coat? We're greeted by a young woman with red hair pulled severely back from her face, her eyes heavily lined in black, in an otherwise bone-pale face. Her paleness is further set off by her all-white clothes. She's not wearing the traditional doctor's coat I'm used to seeing my dad in, but rather an edgy ensemble of strange angles, accented with sleek steel fastenings. Against all that stark whiteness her slicked-back hair is like a lava flow, her eyes like burning coals.

She stares—no, glares—at me for a moment, then her eyes widen slightly. "*Bikk!* Where the hell have you been?" she hisses. "And who the hell are you?" She turns those smoldering eyes on Lachlan.

"I'm . . ." he begins, but she obviously has no patience for an answer. She grabs us each by an arm and jerks us inside.

"I don't want to know who you are. And Rowan I know

quite well. At least from your mother, and from physical schematics of you. I'm Flame." The name suits her perfectly. "Why didn't you show up yesterday?" she demands.

In as steady a voice as I can manage I tell her about the roadblock, Mom's murder.

"She said someone was onto you," the cybersurgeon muses. "*Bikk!*" she swears again, stalking away from us. We drift in her wake. "I should have destroyed the lenses the second there was even a hint of trouble."

"You didn't though, did you?" Lachlan asks, and Flame looks at him sharply.

"What does it matter to you? Never mind." She turns to me. "Are you ready? The procedure will take about an hour, but we'll have to monitor you for a while afterward. Then follow-up visits for twelve weeks. It will be six months at least before the lenses fully bond to your neurons, and you'll need a final check after that. Until then if they're removed or damaged you'll have to start from scratch. After that, they'll be a permanent part of your body. But don't do anything to screw this up, because this is the only pair I've successfully made, and frankly after I implant them I'm out of this business. I don't need the trouble. The money, yes, but not the risk of death."

I try to get a word in edgewise through the whole monologue, but I don't have a hope until she runs out of steam. Then I finally blurt out, "I'm not taking the lenses. I want Lach—my friend to have them." I realized just in time that I probably shouldn't give his name.

She doesn't even stop walking. "Nope. Not gonna happen."

I trot to catch up. "But I don't want them. And he needs them."

She dramatically pantomimes blocking her ears. "I don't want to hear it. I got paid enough to move Serpentine three rings in, and that's the only social issue that matters to me. You go fight the Center or turn yourself into a turtle or feed the hungry or uplift the poor—it's all the same to me. Just don't *tell* me."

"You don't need to know why," I try again. "Just give them to him, not me."

"Kid, don't you understand? These are *your* lenses. Yours, no one else's."

"I know my mom paid, but . . ."

"This isn't about money." She gives a mirthless chuckle. "First and last time those words will ever pass my lips. Do you realize that no one outside the Center has even successfully made lenses that will bond to the individual? That will feed into the EcoPan like these do? This is my masterpiece! Me, with all my training and degrees, who spends her life implanting horns and scales onto Bestials, finally came up with something brilliant. These are not just any lenses. Your mom gave me scans of your eyes, your brain, a personality assessment, basal temperature readings, metabolic data . . . These are custom-made for you. They won't work in anyone else."

I'm stunned. I don't know what to think. At one point I was desperate for a normal life, but when that became impossible I decided I absolutely didn't want the lenses. I want to stay me. My eyes, my identity, even if I have to hide it all my life. Even if I have to die for it.

I'm about to say *Forget it, destroy them, we're leaving* . . . when Lachlan grips my shoulder. I don't think he means to, but he's clutching me so hard it hurts.

"You have to get the lenses," he says between clenched teeth. "You have to take my place."

I start to shake my head. "No . . ." I begin. But he pulls me out of the room, muttering "*Excuse us*" while the cyber-surgeon shrugs and makes a gesture of aggravated dismissal.

"This is our only chance," he hisses at me the second

we're alone. He's pulled me so close. I suddenly feel uncomfortably warm. "There's a very narrow window. And the way I've set it up, a very narrow age range. Someone our age has to infiltrate the school, the inner circle families, or this entire operation is shot to hell."

"I . . . I'm not like you. I hardly even know what's going on!"

"You're more like me than you realize. I know you have a sense of justice. I know you want fair treatment for second children, and all children of Eden."

"But I can't! You're . . ."

"I'm what? What can I do that you can't do, or learn? I'm nothing special. A kid who was kicked around, kept down, until he decided to fight. You're a fighter, Rowan." He rubs his cheek where I punched him. But that was different.

I shake my head. "I'm just . . . me."

"Never think that 'just you' isn't enough. Rowan, listen to me! Everything is riding on this. I've prepared for this, trained for this, thought about nothing else for the past year."

"But I haven't! I don't even know what to do. I don't want—"

I was going to say *I don't want to*, but he cuts me off, and probably thinks I'm going to say something noble, like *I don't want to let you down*. But that's not it. I was just getting used to the idea of peace, underground. Of companions, safety. A new family.

"I'll help you. I'll be with you all the way—or as close as I can get. I'll be your handler." As if to illustrate, he links his fingers through mine. I feel a strange mix of elation and trepidation. My handler? As if I'm a puppet, with him pulling the strings.

"It will be easy. All you have to do at first is go to school, make friends, act normal."

A laugh bursts out of me, uncontrollable. "*That's* easy? Until a few days ago, I knew three people, of which only two liked me. Make friends? Act normal? If you put me in, your mission will fail in the first five minutes!"

He smiles gently and squeezes my fingers in his. "You're more charming than you imagine," he says softly. "I believe in you, Rowan. Believe in yourself and you can do it. I wouldn't ask you if I didn't think you could. The mission is too important to trust to someone incompetent." He strokes one of my knuckles with his thumb. "And your life is too important to risk if I didn't think you'd succeed."

"Why?" I ask. I'm not fishing for compliments, not asking out of vanity. I really want to know why he values my life so much.

He flushes, actually turns pink. His eyes drop to my fingers, our fingers.

"I'll just pick one reason," he says, lifting his gaze to mine again, but not releasing my hands. The small room feels warmer than ever. "The way you fight for people you care about. For Lark when she was in danger. For your brother. You forget yourself, and think only of the person you love. That makes you extraordinary." He sighs, and there's a tremor in that sigh so deeply sad. "I only wish once in my life someone had fought for me like that."

I only have one question for him. "If I say no, will you still help me rescue Ash?"

"Yes," he answers without hesitation.

And because he says yes, I say yes.

Within minutes I'm in a brightly lit room, being prepped for surgery. A few breaths later, I slip into blackness . . .

22

... AND AWAKE to gunfire. Only, I'm not really awake. I can't be, because even though my eyes are open I'm still seeing dreamlike images. My eyeballs tingle. Not just sensation, but movement, a rapid vibration that is maddening. I see ... I don't know. People, in a chrome room sickly with a green glow that seems to emanate from above. Small animals, hairless and pink, helpless in cages. Wires protruding from tubs of bubbling gel. The images dance incoherently, but I can't tell if I'm seeing them with my eyes or my imagination. There's shouting, too, and another bang. Another gunshot? Real or imagined?

No, it's the sound of my own body crashing to the floor, jarring every bone. Except my skull. A hand holds my head, saving it from the hard ground. I sense a warm pressure on me, and feel unaccountably safe.

Finally my vision comes into focus, and I see Lachlan. He's pressed against me, holding me down on the floor. I smile. I don't know which parts are real, but this feels right.

"We have to get you out of here," Lachlan says. "Did you hurt yourself when you fell? The hand that's not cupping my head begins to feel along my body. I giggle when he brushes my ribs. The strange look he gives me when I do suddenly cues me in to what's real, what's not.

Gunfire. I had my lens implant surgery. We're under attack.

I look around wildly from my prone position. I'm practically under the operating table. Strange, sharp instruments are scattered on the floor around me. I try to get up, but Lachlan holds me down.

"They're at the front. Two, maybe three Greenshirts. Luckily your talented cybersurgeon is also a skilled hacker, and seems to have modified a couple of securitybots to do her bidding, and they're keeping the Greenshirts at bay. Can you stand?"

"I was trying to," I say testily, afterimages of some strange room haunting me, stamped on the back of my eyelids.

"There's no sign of Flame." There's a gun in his hand. I don't even know where he wore it. I didn't seen a trace of it on his body.

"We have to get out of here." He's looking at me strangely, and my hand creeps to my eyes. I want to see them, but it isn't exactly an opportune time to find a mirror. They're puffy and tender, but the world looks the same as ever through them now. Those other images must have been a hangover from my anesthesia.

"The shots are coming from the front," I mumble, trying to piece together the layout of Serpentine from the small amount I've seen. "Can we get out the back?"

"Maybe. But the fence is electrified again."

We're kept prisoner by the thing that is supposed to keep people out.

"Can you turn it off?"

"There should be a control box somewhere, but . . ."

I follow the direction of his gaze.

"It's probably in the front," I conclude dismally. "What are we going to do?"

"*You* are going to stay here. *I'm* going to give those ally securitybots a little help."

"But . . ."

He flashes me a wry look. "You're really arguing with me at a time like this?" I draw breath to protest again, but he places his fingers on my lips. "Hush. Stay."

And because I'm afraid I'll just get in his way (and maybe afraid in general, too), I stay, while he crouches, his gun held low and ready, and opens the door a crack. The shooting has stopped for now, and I can't hear any movement. Have the Greenshirts been defeated, or the securitybots disabled? If the Greenshirts are down, I want to be glad. But then I picture Rook in his uniform, sprawled and bleeding. I don't want anyone else to die, not even someone who wants to kill me.

Lachlan is looking through the crack, listening intently. His body is still and tense, so much power held in check. He can only see a sliver of the next room, but I can tell he's using every sense to search for danger. After a long moment, though, I can see the tightness in his shoulders relax a bit.

He turns to me with a reassuring smile. "Looks clear. But stay down."

I see his mistake in slow motion, though it takes place in a fraction of a second. He starts to push the door open just an instant before he turns his smiling face away from me, having lingered for a fatal moment. Is it my fault? Did I hold him with my gaze, releasing him too late?

His guard is down, just for a moment. But it is the wrong moment. There's a shot, close and deafeningly loud, and he staggers back. I see a fine spray of blood fly through the air, but I can't see the wound itself. He stumbles over a low stool and goes down, but he has the presence of mind to kick at the door as he falls.

For a second I hope . . . then a black boot jams itself against the frame and the door bounces open again. The Greenshirt shoulders it open and points his much, much larger gun—a rifle—at Lachlan. I don't know if size matters in these things, but suddenly Lachlan's weapon looks like a toy.

The Greenshirt doesn't see me, on the ground concealed by the operating table. Not yet.

"Get up," he barks at Lachlan.

Lachlan moans and rolls to his injured side. The Greenshirt kicks him, and it is all I can do not to cry out as Lachlan flinches and curls into a ball. I can't tell how much blood there is, how badly he's hurt. Is it worse than I thought? I think he was hit in the arm—bad enough—but had it gone through his chest and exited his arm? Why isn't he fighting? He's just lying there now, not moving at all. I have to clamp my hand over my mouth to keep quiet.

The Greenshirt screams at Lachlan to get up, then, with sneering mouth and a growl of disgust, slings his rifle over his shoulder, takes a pair of handcuffs from his belt, and kneels beside the apparently unconscious Lachlan.

Do something, Lachlan, I silently beg. But he doesn't move. The Greenshirt clamps one handcuff on with a click that echoes in the room.

Instantly Lachlan comes alive, using his handcuffed arm—his uninjured one—to pull the Greenshirt on top of him. The Greenshirt, surprised, doesn't let go of the cuffs in time and sprawls. Lachlan lets out a groan as his wounded arm grinds into the ground . . . but he never stops fighting for an instant. He jerks the handcuffs out of the Greenshirt's grasp, flips the dangling end up so that it covers his knuckles, and punches the Greenshirt in the side of the head once, twice . . .

But the Greenshirt shifts his weight and pins Lachlan's arm. Oh, great Earth, there is so much blood! They're slipping in it as they struggle, their boots trying to get a grip on the slick floor as they grapple for position. Lachlan rolls the Greenshirt, and for a moment he's on top. Then the Greenshirt reaches up and tears at Lachlan's bullet wound with clawed fingers. Lachlan's face drains white, and I think he's going to pass out as the Greenshirt flips him, punches him in the face, and finally remembers his rifle.

He's straddling Lachlan, a knee on either side keeping him pinned down. The Greenshirt takes his time now. He's that confident he's won. Easily, as if there's nothing at all urgent about the situation, he unslings his rifle and points it at Lachlan's face.

"Second child, huh?" The Greenshirt uses the rifle muzzle to turn Lachlan's face so he can examine his eyes. The length of the weapon makes for an awkward angle, and the Greenshirt has to lean back to give himself room to maneuver the weapon. "Do you know what they're going to do to you at the Center?" He laughs, an ugly sound. "I'd be doing you a favor to shoot you now." He presses the barrel to Lachlan's forehead, and I squeeze my eyes shut. Lachlan, please do something!

Then my eyes fly open. Why am I waiting for Lachlan to act?

The Greenshirt doesn't know I'm here. And right beside me, scattered when Lachlan hauled me to the ground as bullets started flying, is a scalpel. The blade is small, but deadly sharp.

The Greenshirt is talking, loudly, gloating about the horrors that await Lachlan. What he's saying turns my stomach . . . but strengthens my resolution. Silently, I slide my feet under me, picking up the scalpel. It feels so slender in my grasp, too delicate for violence.

But sharp enough for the threat of violence.

The Greenshirt, so intent on his taunts, doesn't hear me as I creep up behind him and lay the edge of the scalpel against the side of his throat. I have my threat all ready: *Drop your weapon, stand up slowly, or I'll open your veins*. We'll tie him up. We'll escape.

But the second my blade touches his throat, Lachlan bucks upward, and the scalpel slides in without resistance, as if the Greenshirt's skin is the finest silk.

I pull away—*throw* myself backward—but it is too late. A gush of blood sprays from his throat, pulsing in time to his heartbeat. As Lachlan grips the rifle and wrestles it away, the Greenshirt tuns to me with a look of surprise that breaks my heart. His eyes are big, he looks like he's about to say something . . . then he slumps, almost gracefully. The blood pulses more slowly now from his slashed throat, pooling in a crimson lake around his body. Once more. And then both the Greenshirt and his flowing blood are still.

Lachlan twists out from under him and stands unsteadily. I can't take my eyes off the dead Greenshirt. I did that. I ended a life . . .

There isn't even blood on my hands.

Lachlan is tugging on my arm. "Come on, we have to go."

I can't move.

"We need to get out of here, get you someplace safe." He drapes one of my arms over his shoulder and hauls me bodily toward the door. It should be the other way around. I should be supporting him. My legs don't seem to be working right. My feet drag.

"I can't . . ." I begin. But I know I have to.

The world begins to blur, the edges dissolving. Images like the ones I saw when I first regained consciousness threaten to barge into my sight, or my mind. Figures in white coats. A monitor tracking someone's pulse and other vital signs. And, wonderfully, in a vision I don't want to fight, a forest so real I can smell the damp Earth.

But I push it all back, and I see Flame in the doorway, beckoning. Lachlan trains the rifle, liberated from the Greenshirt, on her, but she ignores it. "Thanks a whole *bikking* lot!" she snaps. "There I was, all set to upgrade Serpentine and relocate to a posh ring, and now—this!" She squints at me, at my eyes. "You shouldn't be standing."

"Not much choice," Lachlan says between clenched teeth. "Where were you?"

"Had to do an emergency override of my securitybots' safety protocols. Thought a little judicious lethality might be called for here. My bots took care of the other one. *Bikk bikk bikk!*" She rubs her forehead and paces. "Can I come up with *any* kind of story to cover this up? I can melt the bodies, of course. We get rid of lots of unwanted bio bits here." She keeps up a monologue as she strides, kinetic and intense, and I have the strangest feeling that despite all her cursing, this disaster is no more than a setback. She looks up, and there's the strangest little smile on her lips.

"Do you kids have a place to go?"

Lachlan nods. "And you?"

"Think I've spent my life on the black market fringe without having a bolt-hole or two? But you go on. I've got this covered." She frowns down at the dead Greenshirt. "I think." Then she shrugs, and shakes her finger at Lachlan, other troubles apparently forgotten. I'm realizing she may be slightly insane. "You get her someplace she can rest, for at least a day. She needs to be lying down so the pressure doesn't build up behind her eyes. Don't want to go *pop*, do we? And her neural network will be confused for a while. After all, you're linked—more or less—into the EcoPan now."

I blink, my eyes burning. So many implications.

"I linked you with the identity your friend provided, instead of the one your mother had arranged. This boy has some connections!" She sounds impressed. "The identity your mother set up for you was compromised, I'm sure, since they were on to you. But this guy has the specs of another identity all set up." She gives him a significant look. "Almost as if he's planned all this for a long, long time. Had to fiddle with the details. Gender, for example. But now EcoPan will officially recognize you as Yarrow. It will take a while to gel, so there will be glitches for a few months. Some bots might not be able to get a read on you. But just to be safe, don't go anywhere you don't want the EcoPan knowing about."

I gasp. I can't go back to the Underground? Where else can I go? I can't go home. I feel panic rising. I'm alone, homeless, adrift.

Then, like the strange visions, but even clearer, I seem to see a flash of soft lilac before my eyes.

"Lark," I say decisively. "Lark will take me in."

23

SHE TOOK ME by her home on one of our nights out. I remember gazing at the small, comfortable residence. Most houses in Eden are connected, apartments built around a courtyard, or rows of upper-story apartments in commercial districts, but hers was like ours, detached from its neighbors. It was much smaller than ours, but as we stood outside, our shoulders touching, her lilac hair brushing my dark locks, I thought that it looked so warm and homey. Even at that late hour there was a golden light in one of the windows, where, she said, her father was working far into the night.

This is where Lachlan and I go when we flee Serpentine.

"Are you sure you'll be able to stay?" he asks. "She'll let you, and keep you safe, and secret?"

"I'm positive," I say. "Will you make sure Flint's order that we never see each other is rescinded?"

"Of course. I'm not completely happy about this . . ."

"What choice do we have? It's not like I have a lot of first child friends."

"Take this, just in case." He tugs up his shirt and pulls his gun out of his waistband.

I back away a step. "I can't," I stammer. "My mother . . ."

"I know," he says, so gently, and he brushes a strand of hair from my cheek. "But if the worst should happen, maybe this will keep you from sharing her fate."

I squeeze my eyes closed . . . but reach for the gun. "I don't know how to use it," I say as I heft its unfamiliar weight. It is small, but dense.

He shows me how to slide the gun from its form-fitting holster (I'm so ignorant I think it's part of the gun) and where the trigger is. "Finger off the trigger until you're ready to fire, like this." He demonstrates, cupping my hand, laying his forefinger over mine.

"I don't think I'll be able to use it," I protest, but he shakes his head.

"You don't know what you're capable of. None of us do, until we're put to the test. But you've been tested a lot lately, and you've shone. Back in Serpentine when that Greenshirt was going to kill me and you—"

"Don't!" I say sharply. I can still smell the blood. I think I will forever. I don't want to think about what I did. I try to tell myself that it wasn't really my fault, that I would have only threatened the Greenshirt, that he only died because Lachlan shoved him upward. An accident. Forgivable.

But I know in my heart that if he hadn't dropped the weapon, if I really thought he was going to ignore my threat and kill Lachlan, I would have plunged the knife into his throat deliberately, an act of will.

The knowledge frightens me. So does the way I don't make Lachlan take the gun back, but instead slip it under my own shirt, where it presses, cold and hard, against my belly.

I have things inside of me I don't understand. Things I don't like.

But they're things that are useful, that will keep me, and the people I care about, alive.

When he's about to leave, I experience a moment of panic. "Stay with me."

He shakes his head. "You can pass with Lark's parents. You've got the eyes for it." He winks his own second-child eye at me.

"I haven't even seen them yet," I say. There wasn't exactly time to look for a mirror when we were under fire. "How are they?"

I expect him to say they look just fine, maybe even to call them beautiful. Call *me* beautiful. Instead he cocks his head and ponders far too long for comfort. "They're . . . not you."

I feel myself crumble. I don't want the stupid lenses. I just want to be *me*, safe and happy. I hang my head so he can't see my eyes.

Lachlan takes me by the chin and makes me lift my head, makes me look at him. "Rowan is inside. You're not all this." He makes a sweeping gesture that encompasses my body from head to toe to head again. "You're this." His palm comes to rest on my heart. I can feel it beating wildly against him.

He pulls me closer . . . but only kisses me on the forehead.

"It's almost dawn. Get inside. I'll come back for you after dark."

Without another word he strides purposefully away, and in a moment he's lost in the night's last darkness.

I turn to knock, and as I do so I see a light in one of the rooms, softened by a curtain. It's not the same window I saw illuminated before, Lark's father's room. The curtain moves, and I see a glimpse of a face. Is that Lark? Did she see Lachlan touch me, kiss me?

I knock, and wait. And wait.

When the door finally opens, it's not Lark, but a woman in her forties, face a little puffy from sleep, her long fair hair tied in a hasty knot on the top of her head.

"Yes?" she asks, more in curiosity than concern.

"I . . . I'm a friend of Lark's," I manage to choke out. Even though I know I cleaned myself thoroughly in a public convenience on the way here, I feel an overwhelming desire to check for telltale smears of dark red dried blood. I force myself to look at her, to look pleasant, normal.

"An odd hour for a social call." Her voice has that bit of a twang common in the outer circles. I never noticed it in Lark, but of course she's been going to school here. "Are you early or late?"

"What?" I ask, confused.

"Up early to study for tomorrow's test, or out late from last night's party?"

"I . . ." I gulp. "Early?"

"Right," she drawls. "Don't worry, none of the parents talk to me, and I'm sure yours are no different. I won't be blabbing to them. Was it a good party?" I can't think of an answer, and she laughs, standing aside to motion me in. "Get your story straight before you try it on your parents."

When I'm inside, I feel a heavy pressure pushing against my eyes. I'm going to cry. I can't cry ever again. If I do, I'll never stop.

It's just . . . I know I don't have a lot of experience. Maybe every house feels like this. But Lark's place is somehow so obviously a *home*. There's a warmth, a smell of last night's cooking. There's a *feel* to it that I can't define. An aura of love, of safety, of family.

"It's not much," Lark's mom begins, almost apologetically.

"It's . . . it's perfect," I say, so ardently that she laughs.

"Let me see if Lark is awake. She probably is, just like her namesake. I feel like she never slept for the first three years of her life. Up with the larks. Lark!" she shouts. "Your friend is here!"

I flinch at the sudden volume of her voice. "Won't you wake her dad?"

"No, he's night manager at Water Reclamation. Water flows by sun and moon, he always says." She rolls her eyes, but she's grinning, thinking about her husband. I bet they love each other, and get silly together. I bet they're completely and totally happy. I'd like to see them together.

Lark comes out, looking fresh-faced and awake. The only sign of her ordeal is the fact that she's wearing long sleeves. I know they hide the bruises she received during her capture and interrogation.

"I forgot we were going to . . ."

"Study," I fill in, and then before she can accidentally introduce me by my old name, I hold out my hand to her mom and say, "I'm Yarrow."

"River," she replies.

"I can call you by your first name?" I ask, surprised. I've been tutored in politeness, for the day I would finally be out in the world, and I wasn't expecting to be so informal.

She gives a little shrug. "Outer circle folk like us don't tend to be sticklers for the rules." There's a note of defiance in her voice. She wants to remind me that she and Lark aren't privileged inner circle people.

It makes me wonder again why there are poor and rich, why there are inner and outer circles, why some have everything they could want and more, and some are literally starving. Eden isn't just supposed to be a shelter against the dead world, a place of survival and hibernation. It should be a utopia. There's no reason for inequality.

But Lark drags me away to her room and that conundrum slips away.

The second the door closes behind us, she has her arms around me, her head resting between my neck and shoulder.

"I remember," she says. "They said I wouldn't, and it was all a bit blurry for a while, but when it wore off I remembered everything." She turns her head, pressing her lips to my throat. "You were so brave. So strong. You saved my life."

She pulls back, looks into my eyes, and gasps.

"Your eyes! They . . ."

She doesn't say any more, but I can see disappointment in her face. Was I just something exotic to her, a strange-eyed second child? Even though she lived in the inner circles she mingled with the poor, the Bestial, the odd . . . Was I just another oddity on her list? A way for her to feel special?

Now that I can pass as a first child, am I just like everyone else?

Lark seems to sense my mood. "I have just the thing to cheer you up. So you lost a little color in your eyes. We'll just have to give you more color somewhere else!"

She sits me down on her bed and takes a contraption out of a small chest.

"I used to change my hair color all the time. Now I'm pretty set on this shade." She twirls a lock of her lilac hair. "But sometimes I put a streak in for something different." She sits me down on the floor, and perches on her bed, a knee on each side of my shoulders, my hair in easy reach. "Now, do you want to pick for yourself, or do you trust me?"

I stiffen. Stop asking me that, I think. But once her hands start to caress my hair I lean back into her and relax. She takes this as assent. "Ultramarine, I think, with a bit of turquoise and jade. Nothing overwhelming, and mostly underneath. I want your natural dark hair to dominate." She strokes the machine along strands of my hair, combing it out with her fingers. I wish this could last forever, me with my head on her lap, safe under her care. But nothing lasts.

"There!" she says finally, and jumps up to bring me a

hand mirror. At first I hardly notice any difference. "Shake your head," she instructs me. I do, and the colors suddenly emerge, vivid streaks in my dark hair.

"I love it," I say honestly. But my gaze keps being drawn back to my dull, flat, lifeless eyes. The hair can't make up for that. But I don't want to say that to Lark after she's been so kind.

She must be looking at my eyes, too, though, because as she looks at my reflection from over my shoulder she asks, "How did you get them?"

"I . . . It's probably better if I don't get into it. The more you know, the more they'll think you're a dangerous liability."

"Are they going to kill me for having contact with you?"

"No. Lachlan will take care of that."

"Lachlan." She repeats the name as if tasting something bitter. "Where did he come from, anyway? How well do you know him?"

"He saved my life."

"You don't know him as well as you know me, though, do you?" She sounds younger, smaller, weaker, not her usually vibrant and confident self.

"Do you trust him?"

I resent her questioning. "He's not the one who let the Center know about my mother," I snap before I can stop myself. "He's done everything possible to keep me safe. Can you say the same?"

"How dare you!" she seethes, stepping back from me. "I'm taking you into my home. I'm putting my father—my whole family, myself included—at terrible risk to help you! I made a mistake trusting other people, I know, and there are no words to tell you how sorry I am. But I meant well, and I'll never trust anyone again. No one except you."

Her voice has grown steadily softer, her anger dissipating.

She glides closer to me, but this time I'm the one who takes a step back. Trusting anyone is dangerous.

"You can trust Lachlan, too," I say.

"Oh, really? What did you have to do to get those lenses, then?"

"Nothing! What do you mean?"

"I saw you from my window. He looked like he owned you. *You* looked like you didn't mind being owned. That's not the Rowan I know."

"Is that what this is about? Me and Lachlan?"

I don't want to fight. I'm tired, so incredibly tired, and I hardly even know why she's mad. If anyone should be mad, it's me. But I'm here, because I need her to help Lachlan and me save Ash. "I'm not the Rowan you know. I'm not Rowan anymore. I'm Yarrow. And I'm going to bed."

Before she can say another word, I throw back the deep plum-colored covers of her bed and slide in. I pull them resolutely up almost all the way over my face as I turn toward the wall. "We'll meet Lachlan after dark," I mutter, and close my eyes. "Be ready to put your plan into action."

"Rowan, there's something I've been meaning to tell you. It just never seems to be the right time."

What could she tell me? How sorry she is, again? Exactly what she feels for me? I really don't want to hear it now.

I pretend to fall asleep quickly. All the while, I don't hear Lark move. Finally I do fall asleep. I know, because at some point I'm awakened by another body sliding under the sheets beside me. She doesn't embrace me, doesn't touch me. But she is there, the warmth of her body filling the bed.

But against my stomach the gun is still cold as death.

24

I SLEEP ALL day, and at night I take Lark to the location I told Lachlan we would meet him—an innocuous little take-out place with enough traffic to make us completely inconspicuous. But when we arrive, there's no sign of Lachlan.

As we wait, I look longingly at the takeout, kebabs redolent with salt and synthetic fat, because I haven't eaten in forever. I feel like at any moment we'll be too obvious even here, standing for a long time without buying anything. It is apparent that Lark and I are waiting, impatient.

"I thought you said you trusted him," Lark snaps.

"I do," I assure her. "Maybe . . ." But the list of maybes is too long, and for the most part too terrible to articulate. Maybe he was captured. Maybe Flint turned against him.

Maybe, now that he knows that Flame can make convincing lenses, he's decided not to risk his life helping me save Ash. Maybe he'll convince her to help the second children. Maybe he'll even turn her over to Flint for his particularly unpleasant brand of "convincing."

"We can't wait any longer," I say at last. So with great reluctance I leave the rendezvous site and make my way to my house.

I know the heart is just about pumping blood, an engine

and nothing more. It's not the seat of emotions, the repository of love and hope and happiness. All the same, when I stand at the base of my courtyard wall at the sheltered side where no one else can see, and look up at the walls that held me in all my life, the walls that held everything I knew and loved, I swear it is my heart that hurts. A pain, that must be physical, seems to stab me in the chest.

Home.

Without Mom and Ash inside it is really nothing more than an empty shell. Still, it was *my* shell.

"Give me about ten minutes," I tell Lark. "Maybe fifteen. With luck he's not home. He used to work late all the time, but now, I don't know. I'll let you in the front door."

"What if he is home?" Lark asks.

"I don't know."

"I do," Lark says, and I'm surprised at the fury in her voice. "If he's there, he needs to be punished for what he did to Ash . . . and to you."

My father, who hated me, who betrayed his own son to the Center, deserves to be punished. If Lachlan were here, so strong and capable, with so much violence lurking just beneath his usual joking exterior, he would willingly be the one to mete it out. But could Lark? Could I?

I find myself hoping he'll be out. Not because I wouldn't relish the sight of Lark beating his face to a bloody pulp . . . but because I *would*. That frightens me. What am I turning into?

"Whether he's home or not, I can get in silently. I've spent a lifetime doing it. Then after I let you in we can get his credentials. With them, we'll be able to move anywhere inside the Center."

When my fingers curl around the first handhold, I feel that stab again, but I take a deep breath—which turns into a sigh—and start to climb. I can feel her eyes on me, but I don't dare look down. I'm barely holding on. Literally.

The outside of the wall isn't as intimately ingrained on my memory, my fingertips, as the inside. But still it is connected to some of the happiest moments of my life, the bittersweet ending to each clandestine night with Lark. All the more bittersweet because of what came of our friendship. Each touch of a new rock beneath my hands seems to spark a new memory. Lark showing me the stars from the rooftop. Lark's kiss.

After tonight, I may never see her again. I'll be embedded in my mission, under my new identity. It's probably for the best. I can't look at her without thinking how her careless trust of the wrong person cost my mother her life, and ultimately condemned Ash to his death sentence. I know she didn't mean to, that it tears at her almost as much as it does me. Still, it might be best that we're going our separate ways.

At least I'll still have Lachlan, helping me with my mission.

Don't cry, I tell myself firmly as I climb down on the inside. All your tears are already shed. Now is the time for strength.

My feet hit the moss inside the courtyard, and in an instant I feel caged again. What if I'd never ventured outside of my familial prison? What would have been different? Would I have found a way to grasp at happiness? I manage to walk across the springy moss Mom tended to so lovingly without a single salty drop falling. Sure, my eyes are already heavy and wet, but that's just from the surgery.

I let myself into the house. Everything is just the same, as if I'd never left. I half expected new locks, a regiment of Greenshirts stationed inside. At the very least, some sign of chaos. Broken knickknacks, an overturned chair. An unwashed dish left on the countertop in a moment of grief, or even distraction. Dust.

But everything is perfect. Just as if Mom is still there, ruling so sweetly over the family.

I move through the quiet house, touching things, smelling Mom's side of the sofa, the place where her ponytail would rest when she flopped down after a long day at work. And I listen for the sound of my father. The house is silent.

Cautiously, I creep toward my parents' bedroom. There, finally, is a small sign of disruption. The bedclothes are disheveled. Did he forget to make the bed, plagued by guilt? Did he simply not know how to perform a task Mom usually did? Or has he been unable to sleep in their bed since her death? I don't know, but at least something is different.

If it wasn't made mostly of stone, I'd like to burn this whole house to the ground.

The bedroom is empty, and so is the rest of the house. My father is out. Maybe at work, maybe scheming to destroy someone else. Maybe, if he has an ounce of goodness in him, getting drunk and nerving himself up to jump off the tallest building in Eden. Bitterness consumes me, a hate that hurts, but I can't fight.

I let Lark in. "We're alone," I say, and lead her to my father's office. We're looking for his security pass. I can only hope that he's not staying late at work, but out somewhere else. If he's at work, he'll have his ID on him. I have no idea what we'll do then. We might also need other security codes to pass Center security. Lachlan would know exactly what we need. I'm not so sure myself. Where is Lachlan?

I start to go through various documents in my father's office.

"Can't you find it?" Lark asks, glancing anxiously in the direction of the front door, listening for sounds of approach. I'm beginning to panic that I won't be able to find it. What if he still has it on him? Do we wait for him to come home, and take it from him by force?

Finally I find it, shoved haphazardly in a drawer as if he just wanted to get rid of it in a hurry. "I've got it!" I cry excitedly, holding it up. "I think this is all we need. My father doesn't seem to be very security-conscious."

"Then let's go," she says urgently. "He could be back any minute."

"I want to see if there's anything else useful here. I don't know what else we might need once we're inside the Center." I also wonder if there might be anything incriminating in here, leverage to use against my father. Or maybe something that would be useful to the Underground. I scan each page as quickly as I can.

"Come on!" Lark says anxiously, bouncing on the balls of her feet.

But it's too late. I hear the doorknob turn, my father's heavy tread, stumbling.

I reach under my shirt and touch the gun pressed against my navel.

"No," I say, very softly, reminding myself that I'm a good person. Better than my father, at any rate.

If he doesn't come in here, if he goes straight to bed, we can slip out the front door.

He's talking. Did he bring someone home with him? I step closer to the closed over (but not completely closed) door and listen.

"It's not my fault." His voice is wheedling, pathetic. I've never heard him sound like that before. "It wasn't supposed to happen like that."

I wait, but there's no answer. He's alone, talking to himself.

"In here, quick," I say to Lark as I pull the trick bookcase out on its silent and smooth pneumatic hinges. She steps into the secret alcove behind and I close the door over. Not all the way, though. Once closed, it can only be opened from the outside. If anything should go wrong, I don't want Lark trapped in there. I creep out. I'm being foolish, I know, but I feel like I need to see my father. I haven't decided yet if he needs to see me.

"I was supposed to be the good example, the man who puts Eden before family. The incorruptible leader who isn't tainted by his family's transgressions." I hear a meaty thud, and another. When I poke my head carefully around the corner and look into the kitchen I see him striking the sides of his head with his hands.

"Oh, Ash, what have I done? They promised me!"

He slams his head down on the counter, and when he stands, swaying unsteadily, there's a bloody gash in his forehead.

Good, I think. I'm getting used to blood now.

Another part hurts for him. Whatever else he is, he loved Mom. And Ash, I thought.

I step into the room. "What did they promise you?"

He whirls, and the stench of alcohol hits me hard. For a second he looks overjoyed to see me. He starts toward me, arms starting to open. At the same time I stiffen, and he seems to remember how he has felt about me all my life. He comes to an abrupt halt.

"You're alive."

"So are you," I counter, my voice low and steady. Remarkably steady, given my inner turmoil. "But you shouldn't be. You gave up Ash to save yourself."

"N-no," he stammers, swaying where he stands. "It wasn't like that. The Center needs stability, or the circles will not hold. That's what they told me. They said they need an example. I thought they meant me. A *good* example."

He babbles on, slurring and incoherent at times, telling

me how the chancellor told him removing him from the vice chancellorship would be disastrous at this point. Everyone knew that he'd been tapped to fill the position, and if they changed their minds now, if he was brought down by a terrible scandal, it would make the Center look weak. So they decided to make my father look like the hero of Eden, the self-sacrificing kind of leader who would turn in his own beloved family for the sake of right and law and the preservation of our precious sanctuary.

"They've painted your mom as some kind of activist." He spits the word. "No one knows you're our daughter. They think your mother was just part of an underground network of people helping second children. Your mom, and Ash. They're telling everyone I turned her in. They . . ." He falls to his knees, overcome. Maybe begging for my forgiveness? "They're calling me a hero," he chokes out between sobs. "A real hero of Eden. A second Aaron Al-Baz."

How ironic, how fitting, that Dad should be compared to that monster.

"And Ash?" I ask coldly.

"They said they needed an example. Oh, great Earth, I didn't ask questions! I just signed whatever they put in front of me. I was so afraid. I could be executed for keeping you safe."

"Instead, your own son is going to be killed, while you assume the second-highest position in Eden. Always protect yourself, right?" Almost as if it has a will of its own, my hand creeps toward my stomach, my fingers twitching at the hem of my shirt. I can feel the irregular bulk of the gun beneath my clothes. Dad can't see it, though. Not yet.

"It wasn't supposed to be that way!" he moans, rocking back and forth on his knees. "He was supposed to be kept in prison until everything died down, set free somewhere far from the Center."

"Oh, so you just wanted to ruin his life, shuffle him away to the outer circles where he could starve?" A step above execution, barely. I shake my head slowly. "You've been a rotten father. Even to the child you actually love. You burned a hole in him while he was still in the womb, and now you're finishing the job of killing him."

He looks up at me, aghast. "You knew?"

"Recently. Mom told me, before the Greenshirts gunned her down." I sound so hard and cold. My voice doesn't seem like my own anymore. My father winces, cringes, seems to shrink inside himself.

"What can I do?" he asks, holding up his hands helplessly. But his hands are empty, powerless. There's nothing he can do to make this right, except . . .

I pull the gun out from under my shirt and point it at his head.

I expect him to shout, to weep harder, to beg, to lunge at me. But he just kneels at my feet, looking sadly up at me, accepting.

If he had begged, I would have shot him. But this broken man waiting quietly for the end . . .

I'm so focused on my father that Lark, swooping in behind him, is a blur of movement. She has a heavy lamp in her hand, one my Mom never liked but which we kept because it had been her own mother's. With a grunt of effort Lark hits my dad hard in the side of the head. He crumples to the tile floor, unconscious.

"Why didn't you let me shoot him?" I ask Lark. She doesn't know that I had already controlled myself.

"You need to have a clear head tonight," she says with a lighthearted wink that reminds me of Lachlan. "Do you think you'd be calm and collected if you'd just executed your own father?"

She's right, of course. She understands me.

"Let's go," I say, and lead her from my house.

Lachlan is outside, lurking in a cluster of faux palm trees planted near our doorway.

"Where were you?" I demand at the same time he says, "Why didn't you wait for me?"

Then we both notice I still have the gun in my hand. I realize I don't even know if it is lethal, or will only stun. With my jaw clenched tightly I tuck it back into my waistband.

"Do I even want to know what happened in there?" Lachlan asks.

I shake my head.

"Do I even want to know why you didn't show?" I ask him.

He flashes me a crooked grin. "Probably not. Just a few simple acts of thievery."

"Me too," I say guardedly.

He looks down where the gun is now concealed against my belly. "Any other crimes?"

"No," I say, then after a pause I add, "If I'd even consider shooting him a crime."

"Don't get hard, Rowan," he whispers to me, touching my arm lightly with his fingertips. "If the world calls for someone hard . . . call on me. I'm already broken."

25

"NO," I SAY when I look at the route Lark has arranged for us to break into the Center. I feel a gut-wrenching shock of revulsion. "Not a chance. Not even for Ash will I go into that."

"I know you don't mean that," Lark says.

"My head and heart don't, but my nose and gut do." But I press my lips together (I wish I could do something not-too-obvious to stop up my nose) and stand stoically looking over the huge underground reservoir that seems to contain the human waste of all of Eden.

We're underground, having traveled by conduits where Eden's water flows. Up until now it was what Lark called gray water—liquid that had been used for showering, washing dishes, brushing teeth. It wasn't exactly clean, but it wasn't disgusting. This, however, is everything that was shunted from the inner circle toilets.

"This is part of being human," Lark says philosophically. "Especially when lots of humans live together. Rich or poor, bodily waste all smells the same."

Lachlan looks just as calm at the prospect as I try to pretend to be, but he's quick to voice an objection in his usual sardonic tone. "If all goes well, we hope to not meet anyone the entire time we're inside," he tells Lark. "But in my experience, things rarely go as well as they should. Failing that, we hope, with her father's ID, to be able to pass as employees or messengers to a cursory glance." He sniffs deeply. "Do you really think anyone will buy our cover story for a second if we lurk around the most important, most secure place in Eden stinking like a sewer and covered in feces?"

Lark flashes him a disdainful look. "You really don't have a high opinion of my covert skills, do you? Oh, that's right, we Edgers are just dabbling dilettante do-gooders." She presses at a section of the wall and a door pops open. Inside are several sterile full-body contamination suits, along with disposable full-face masks.

I look at them dubiously. They don't seem watertight.

"Don't worry, they shrink to fit and then make a biofuse once you put them on. There's a built-in rebreather with enough for at least an hour. Nothing is breaching that. At least, nothing floating in there. When you get to the other side you can strip them off and shove them somewhere."

"And if we have to leave this way, too, instead of the main entrance?" Lachlan asks.

"There will be more on the other side. They're everywhere. Every time something goes wrong or gets clogged someone has to dive underneath the sludge. It's actually a very efficient system, overall. Just not one that takes human dignity into consideration. My father used to have this job, before he got promoted. Now he just decides when someone else has to do this job."

"And we'll come up right underneath the Center?"

"Right inside," she says. "There will be an access hatch. My dad has taken me all over Eden underground. I can travel anywhere, unseen—if I don't mind getting a little dirty. Most of the tunnels aren't bad, though."

"I wish we knew about this," Lachlan says. "We have our own system, passageways left over from when the Underground was first built, but we know nothing about the water and sewage system. When this is all over, would you be willing to share maps with us?"

"Of course. Assuming we live."

I try to ignore that comment.

"You're not coming," I tell her.

"But . . ."

"No," both Lachlan and I say. "You've done your part," I go on. "You've risked yourself enough for us."

"No, not enough. Never enough." She's looking intensely at me. "Ash is my friend." She turns to Lachlan. "And Rowan is . . . more than that."

Lachlan raises his eyebrows at that comment, but luckily doesn't look at me. Despite everything else that's going on, I know I'm blushing at that statement. "Rowan has the right to go. Ash is her brother. But you're just one more person to give us away, to make a mistake, to get hurt . . . to have to leave behind." He pauses to let that sink in. To him, she's the expendable one. If he has the chance to rescue anyone, it will be me, not her. She'll be on her own.

She sighs, but knows she's beat. Instead she busies herself helping us put on the underwater hazmat suits.

I look at the lake of foul sludge in distaste. "Are you sure we can actually swim in that?"

She chuckles. "It's just on the surface, about four feet of it floating in a layer on top of the water. Once you clear that, you just have to swim."

I suddenly see another obstacle I somehow never thought of. I've never been in water deeper or bigger than a bathtub. "I can't swim."

"Luckily, you don't have to," Lachlan says. "At least, not

really. It only counts as swimming if you have to get to the surface to breathe. All you have to do here is not panic. You can do that, right?"

I remember the nanosand crushing me, filling my nose, my mouth, creeping toward my lungs. Will swimming be like that? Maybe not, but drowning will.

But "Right!" I say, of course. I hope I don't let Lachlan down. I hope we both don't let Ash down. "If . . . if I don't make it, will you go on and still try to save him?" I ask Lachlan. I bite my lower lip, tense. If I'm gone—with my lens implants, my special undercover assignment—what motivation will he have for saving Ash?

I keep misjudging him. But what do I know of people anyway?

"I won't *let* you not make it," he says with a lighthearted wink. "But if you don't, I'll get your brother for you . . . or die trying."

He makes it sound preposterously melodramatic, but I know he means it.

Lark helps us into the suits, and even before I plunge into the sludge I feel like I'm suffocating. The suit is made of some kind of biofilm that fuses seamlessly wherever the coded edges meet, sealing me inside what feels like a death chamber. When the mask goes on I almost panic. The second my desperate breathing starts to fog up the full-face mask, Lachlan catches one of my hands, Lark the other, like they're in a race to be the first to soothe me. Their competition distracts me enough to make me stop worrying about the suit killing me. I stop hyperventilating and sigh in exasperation. That works, and I find I can breathe tolerably well even inside my latest prison.

"Ready?" Lachlan asks.

"No," I say. "Not at all."

He laughs, thinking I'm joking, and dives in head-first,

certain I'll follow him. That's what happens when you get a reputation for bravery, I guess. Is that how courageous people persevere? They do one brave thing, and have to live up to their reputation ever after? It would be so much easier to be a coward. But harder to live with myself.

Alone, I turn to Lark. Something has been nagging me in the back of my mind. "You told me before you had something to tell me. What is it?" My voice is muffled beneath the mask.

Two lines crease, then quickly smooth between her golden eyebrows. "It's . . . nothing. It can wait." She flashes a brilliant smile and gives me a quick hug. "I'll tell you later. Promise. Don't worry. I'll be looking after you, too."

"What do you mean?"

She hesitates a moment, with a secret little smile. "Why, waiting here of course, to help you if you have to escape this way." She touches my face, but it is remote through the hazmat mask.

Lachlan surfaces in the filth, beckoning me urgently.

Awkwardly, I plunge in after him.

Terrible blackness weighs me down, clings to me with its foulness so that even though I know none of it is touching my skin I feel deeply contaminated.

Then . . . wonderful lightness. I'm clean, pure, in a crystal weightless world. The wastewater pool is huge, but lights set along the walls beam inward, making a star pattern of silvery illumination. Is this swimming, this cool clear hovering that seems to strip all my cares away? I wish I could shrug out of the protective suit and feel the water on my skin.

Then I try to move, and I realize that this is an alien world. Only technology is keeping me alive down here. I have an abstract idea of how to swim, of course. I've seen vids of people swimming. I move my arms a certain way, I kick my legs. In my head, it makes sense.

My first arm stroke sends me spinning sideways. I try to kick, and somersault through the water. Lachlan grabs me and steadies me with one hand on the small of my back, one under my arm. I hold my breath and start to rise upward toward the ceiling of sludge. Lachlan pushes me down, and mimes a proper swimming technique. I try, but end up in a modified crawl, as if I'm scaling a weird kind of malleable wall. But it moves me along—however awkwardly—and we head toward a tunnel.

Once inside I can pull myself along the walls. It's an animalistic kind of four-legged gallop, and would be fun if it wasn't for our destination.

The rebreather built into the mask makes a gentle hum as I breathe. We've been underwater for a while now. What if the equipment fails? Even assuming I could swim, or manage to not suck water up my nose, there's no route to fresh air.

Finally the tunnel opens up. And then *up*.

There's a current here now, with water flowing from all the Center's uses down to the main city system. Luckily the human waste goes through a separate pipe that just opens into the place we entered, so this is just runoff from sinks and such. During the day, Lark told us, the outward flow would be so strong that we couldn't swim against it. At night, though, with a skeleton staff manning the Center, there's little water use, and only a gentle flow for us to swim through.

That's a good sign. Fewer people for us to contend with.

The tunnel narrows, branches, but as instructed we stick to the main one. It finally opens up in a bulb-shaped chamber with a multitude of pipes feeding into it. In the center of that is a hatch.

We've been under a long time. The air I'm breathing seems stale, and I'm starting to feel a strange hypnotic sensation, like my focus is expanding and contracting. Lights dance in front of my eyes. I see the water flowing in front of me . . . but it's different water. That makes no sense. There is the slightly clouded water I'm swimming in (if this strange flailing crawl of mine can be considered swimming), and beyond that—no, on top of that—is another water, more clear, with a different, circular flow.

The edges of my vision dim and all I see is that other water. A light shines through it at an angle, making shadows of the things moving through it. Shapes, the size of my palm, shadows without color or solid form, moving in a unison so precise it must be mechanical. I squint at this vision, confused, trying to see it all more clearly. Is it here? Am I losing my mind?

I pull at Lachlan's arm, distracting him from trying to open the hatch. I point at the shapes, but he doesn't understand. He thinks I'm gesturing to the hatch, and he holds up one finger: he'll have it open in a minute. He can't see what I'm seeing.

He finally gets the hatch open and in the sudden bright overhead light I can see the shapes clearly. They're fish, moving in a tight school, as gaudily colored as inner circle ladies out for a night on the town. I just see them for a flash, and then they're gone, and all I see is Lachlan at the round open hatch.

What is happening to me?

The fresh air will clear my head. I can't wait to tear this rebreather off. I have to suck in every breath as if it is fighting me, and my lungs feel heavy and sore.

But before my head breaches the surface so I can take that yearned-for breath, Lachlan shoves me down again. He pushes up the hatch, kicking hard against the resistance of the water.

He mimes something, and it is a long while before my

fuzzy brain figures out that he's telling me there's someone up there. We can't go out yet.

But we have to! There's something wrong with my rebreather. I'm out of air. Have we been down here an hour? My perception is fuzzy. I don't know what I'm doing. All I know is that I have to breathe and I can't with this thing over my face. I start to claw at it, pulling with desperate brute force at first, then trying to get my fingers between the bonded layers. Somewhere in the back of my mind I know this is a terrible idea, but I can't help myself.

Lachlan tries to stop me, but I fight him as hard as if he's trying to drown me. That's what it feels like. Part of me can see his frantic eyes behind his own mask, but anything that keeps this suffocating film over my face has become the enemy.

Finally I tear it off . . . and as the water hits my face I come to my senses. It's all I can do not to draw in a huge breath. I look through the water, and see a blurry Lachlan inches away. He's doing something . . . ripping off his own mask. He comes closer. I feel his mouth on mine.

He's giving me his air. His last breath. Helping me hold on. I feel a moment of relief, instantly clouded by the twin thoughts that there's no more air after this for me . . . or for Lachlan.

I want to tell him something. Bubbles escape my mouth, and the words are lost to the water.

Then he wrenches the hatch open and shoves me upward. I grab the rim, my head breaches the surface, and I gasp, the first heavenly breath stinging my lungs. I suck in another, and another, before my head clears enough that I remember Lachlan. He went so far back under in his effort to push me to the surface. I start to try to dive under the water to help him—knowing that I'm more likely to drown him than to help him—but without the rebreather I feel like I'm drowning as soon as my face hits the water. I can't do it!

I kneel at the edge and peer over. He used the last of his air, his strength, to save me. I can see him far below the surface, indistinct. Is he moving? Is he trying? He saved me when I was drowning in the nanosand. "Lachlan!" I call in despair, and plunge my hands helplessly into the water. There's nothing I can do. He's just a dim dark shape far beneath the water, sinking deeper every moment.

Suddenly there's another shape there. In a confusion of movement I see a shadow appear, and merge with him. The shapes get bigger—they're coming up! There's someone else down there, pushing Lachlan to the surface!

The second he's close enough I reach down and grab whatever I can reach, his clothes, his hands, his hair, fumbling for anything to hold on to, and pull him up. His rescuer pushes from below, and scrambles out herself, pulling off her rebreather as she stands dripping.

"Lark!" I gasp. "You were supposed to stay behind, stay safe!"

She gives me a soft smile. "Do you really think I'd let you go into danger alone?" I look down at Lachlan, choking up water at our feet, and want to say that I wasn't alone. But I let it go. More quietly, Lark adds, "It's my fault your mother was killed. It's my fault Ash was captured. *I* made the mistake of trusting someone. Now I have to win back *your* trust."

"Oh, Lark," I breathe . . . but there isn't time for more. Lachlan has struggled to his knees. He looks up at Lark, a strange mix of gratitude and hostility in his eyes.

"You're not supposed to be here," he says. I can tell he's deeply embarrassed at having to be rescued. He's always been the fighter, the strong one.

Lark just shrugs. "Well, I am here. Good thing, too."

"You can't come inside with us," he insists. "You don't fit into our plan."

"Luckily, I have my own plan," she says flippantly. There is a row of lockers against the far wall. She takes out a sealed package, tears it open, and slips on a set of pale green coveralls. She hides her lilac hair under a cap and flashes an ID.

"I'll pick up some tools and the things I need in another supply closet, and be waiting for you right outside the holding cells. I won't be able to get any closer than that, but I'll be ready for anything."

"You can't . . ." Lachlan begins, but I cut him off. I know arguing with her is useless at this point. The only thing left to do is make sure she's in a good position. A safe position.

"You can't be so close, or you'll be affected, too. Wait for us near the lobby. We may need your help there." If all goes according to plan, we can make it out without anyone the wiser. I'm hoping not to involve Lark anymore at all. After Lachlan, Ash, and I get out, she can slip out on her own, shed her disguise, and go home. I need her to be safe. I don't think I can go through with all the hard things ahead of me if I can't picture Lark in her bedroom, lying on her mulberry-colored bed, safe and secure.

I latch onto this future, trying not to think about the in-between. After all, we only just made it inside, and we already almost died.

"That's okay," Lark says. "I have a couple of tricks up my sleeve. If you get in trouble, I'll be able to provide a distraction."

I envision her screaming to draw Greenshirt eyes, or even fighting. "Don't draw attention to yourself!" I insist.

She pulls the cap down lower. "No one will even notice me," she says with utter confidence. She looks exactly like an ordinary maintenance worker, so she might be right.

My clothes are dry, thanks to the automatic seal on the exposure suit that bonded to my skin as soon as the mask was breached. Most of my hair is even still dry. When I ripped the mask off, the hood section of the suit bonded instantly to the skin around my hairline. For a second I marvel at the technology humans can create. How did we get to be so powerful, but so destructive? With so much intelligence, couldn't we see the point past which one begets the other?

We dressed for the mission in the typical gray suits of the Center elite. The pants are slim, light steel-colored with the faintest iron-hued pinstripes, the high-necked form-fitting jacket just a shade darker, layered over a black shirt for him, an iridescent silvery mother-of-pearl for me.

I don't know about myself, but he looks the very image of every young Center official I've ever seen on news vids. Except for that scar on his face. That might raise suspicions. That, and the perpetually rakish look in his second-child eyes. He covers them with green-tinted glasses, the kind he says are popular with pretentious young bureaucrats on the rise.

"You have to look more serious," I insist as I tie my own hair into a businesslike knot at the back of my head. The colors Lark added are mostly hidden, and with the severe hairstyle I know I can pass for at least a few years older.

He immediately assumes an intensely bland face. "Better?"

I can't help but chuckle, my default mode around Lachlan no matter how terrible the circumstances. We might have just come close to death, and capture (maybe worse than death) looms ahead of us as a very real possibility. But somehow he can always make me smile. Are other people like that? Somehow, I don't think so. How is it he can always make me happy no matter how bad things get?

I catch Lark watching our interaction, and I bend my

head, flushing. Then I straighten defiantly. What's wrong with having *two* friends? Why can't *two* people make me happy? I had so little for so long. I think I'm entitled to have both Lark and Lachlan without them getting prickly whenever I pay too much attention to either.

But now isn't the time to dwell on that. I steel myself as I've learned to do, and together we head up the long, narrow steps first to the official sub-basements. There, Lark branches off from us, to gather the tools that will be part of her cover, and then wait for us in the main lobby. She blows me a kiss as we separate. I see Lachlan try to hide a scowl. Lachlan and I then go to the data storage floors, and finally to the ground floor, the headquarters of all Center law and security.

We've made it so far without incident. My father's security card buzzes us through every barrier, and the few people we've passed hardly glance at us. Lower down, I think most of the people were just trying to finish jobs that had taken longer than expected, so they could go home. They were maintenance types and lower-level data clerks, who probably wanted nothing to do with what we appeared to be—powerful young officials on the rise. People who could make trouble for them, assign them extra tasks, criticize their work. So they lowered their eyes, pretended we didn't exist, and hoped we showed them the same courtesy.

Here on the ground floor, though, things get harder. Now we have to make sure our story is perfect.

26

WE WENT OVER it as many times as possible before we broke in so I'd know exactly what to do. Lachlan, buoyant with confidence, explained that even though the Center was the most secret and secure place in Eden, it relied far more on technology than on people.

"If your card scans, you're legitimate," he had said. "They trust the EcoPan. If the EcoPan believes we belong here, no one else will question us. Thanks to your father's ID, one of the highest-ranking Center officials is simply making a tour of the facilities, or taking care of secret business. There's no cross-reference, no body scans at this level. They won't analyze me and figure out that I'm thirty pounds lighter and thirty years younger than the owner of the ID."

There was a complex assortment of scans and checks at the main entrances—biometric readings, lens scans, all sorts of detectors—but we had neatly bypassed all of those by going through the sewer. Once a person was in the building they were in the clear. It was assumed that the EcoPan had done its job. Anyone inside was one of the privileged, the elite. So even if our faces are unfamiliar, Lachlan told me, we'll be accepted. They'll think we work another shift, or we're new, or the children of someone so important they don't dare question us. Students who are children of the elite often get internships here, or high-level jobs straight out of school, so no one is surprised if we look a bit young.

"People underestimate the power of expectations," Lachlan whispers to me as we make our way toward the prison section of the security floor. "We don't have to prove we belong here. We simply have to *be* here." In strange circular logic, our presence is proof of our right to be here.

We're climbing the spiral staircase to the second floor. It is a strangely beautiful architectural touch, broad and lovely as a bisected seashell. Strong light streams into the lobby—the only part of the Center most civilians ever see—and everything is white, bright, with blue accents and touches of green, like a seaside. A waterfall feature cascades down from the second floor to the first, right beside the spiral staircase, flowing an unreal shade of aqua. Three tiny cleanbots scurry around the pool at the base, mopping up the few drops of water that splash onto the floor.

So far, so good.

When the spiral turns and lets us into the security section of the Center, all that beachy brightness is stripped away. This place is bare, sere. I'd almost call it gritty if it wasn't so clean. The entire tone has changed, of the building and the people. I glance down to the lobby floor and see an innocuous maintenance worker pushing a wheeled cart full of tools and buckets across the atrium. Only the slight build clues me in to the fact that it is Lark. I wish she'd look up, give me the brief reassurance of her bright gaze. But she's too sensible for that, and I tear my own eyes quickly away.

We pass a check-in desk with little more than a word from Lachlan and a wave-through. Somberly, seriously, we move through corridors that Lachlan mapped out from the Underground's intelligence and water system schematics that Lark provided.

Now we go down a narrow hallway that feeds into a large chamber. I hear the sounds of human misery, subdued but evident. I smell something I can't identify, subtle and sharp, that makes my skin prickle. Maybe it is the smell of fear.

I stop abruptly. There are prison cells lining the walls.

"Remember who you are," Lachlan says under his breath. By which he means, remember who I'm supposed to be. A young psychology student with her Center guide, come to interview the renegade Ash about why he would betray his home, his very species. My knowledge, through my father, of the workings of high-level Center medicine will allow me to answer at least the most basic questions anyone might throw at me.

"I think the *me* I'm pretending to be would still be surprised at this."

I've seen the violent side of Eden, but I haven't seen it institutionalized.

Walls and bars. Through some of them I see fingers straining. For what? For aid, for food, for freedom?

Civics vids always talk about how there's so little crime in Eden. Who would steal, or kill, when to steal is to take food from the entire human species, to kill is to end a statistically staggering percentage of the surviving human population? I suppose there aren't many prisoners in comparison to the entire population of Eden. I can see maybe a hundred cells spread along in diminishing perspective down the long rectangular room. But there are far too many for a society that claims to be a utopia. I wonder how many people, normal people, know about this place?

Two burly guards stand at the entrance. I expected them to be armed, but oddly, they aren't.

"We're here to see prisoner eighty-nine," Lachlan says brusquely, twirling a pen cleverly around his fingers. There's another stuck behind his ear.

"You're not on the list," one of the guards says without moving.

"Request should have been forwarded while we were en route." Lachlan sounds supremely bored, and adds a yawn for good measure. "Overtime for me, firing for my secretary." He shrugs, and gestures to me over his shoulder with his thumb. "I have to shepherd this one around to make the boss happy." He lowers his voice conspiratorially. "Boss's pet." He winks, and I look uncomfortable. Not a hard act under the circumstances.

"Do you need him out of the cell?" the guard asks.

Lachlan looks at me, and I play my part, saying primly, "The psychology of the deranged mind cannot be properly explored through bars." I fiddle with the clipboard in my hands, taking out the attached pen and slipping it back again. "It is important to understand what inspires these societal aberrations so that we can nip such actions in the bud." I hope I sound like a pure academic without any motivations beyond proving myself to my lead professor. I practiced the pedantic tone a lot.

I see Lachlan roll his eyes. "Wants to rehabilitate him, probably."

"Too late for this one," I snap, "but maybe we can help other people before they go astray."

Lachlan clenches his hand and pummels his other palm. "There's only one way to correct people like this," he says. "The fist if you catch them early, and a more terminal solution if the fist doesn't work."

The guard laughs and, recognizing a like-minded man in the young official Lachlan pretends to be, waves us through to another man, who waves a handheld device over us, checking us for weapons. I assumed we'd bring the guns, but Lachlan said no. No weapons are allowed in the secure area, not even for the guards. Lachlan says this will make everything easier. When there are weapons, people die . . . and some of those people might be us.

All we have to do is get Ash out of his cell.

The guard escorts us to a stark room that is bare except for two chairs, a table with built-in hand restraints, and a dark tinted window I can't see through. "Wait here," he says. "I'll bring the prisoner to you."

"Lachlan," I whisper, "there will be someone watching." I tilt my head toward the window. "And if he's handcuffed to the table . . ."

"Shh," he cautions. "It just means we have to act right away." The original plan was to pretend to interrogate him until we were sure the guards were in the right position. I thought I had a few minutes to brace myself, to take a few more deep breaths. I'm not ready for this!

But I have to be.

"We have to do it outside, in the main room," Lachlan says, so we step out of the interview chamber.

"Psst!" I hear from the cell next to the interview room. Lachlan shakes his head. Don't get involved. Focus, he seems to project. But I can't help looking.

It's a small, portly man I don't recognize. He's dressed in a gray prison uniform, and there are marks on the exposed skin of his face and hands that look like burns. He creeps up to me then says the most frightening thing of all. "I know who you are."

My eyes fly open wide in horror. He's speaking in a low voice now, but all he has to do is shout, get a guard's attention, and we're done for. "What do you want?" I hiss.

To my dismay, he starts to blubber. "I'm sorry. I didn't mean to tell them, I swear."

He might know me, but I have no idea who he might be. "Who are you?"

He says a name I don't know. "Clayton Hill." Then he adds, "You look so much like your mother, and your brother. I'm so sorry she was killed. It's all my fault." Tears stream down his pudgy cheeks. "I didn't even hold out very long. I couldn't. They . . . they . . ." He holds up his hands, showing the burn marks. "Then they told me she was killed. That was worse than the torture. She was such a lovely person. Such a big, kind heart."

Can it be? "You're . . . the Center official who was helping her?"

He holds his hands through the bars in supplication now. "Forgive me, please. Forgive me for not being strong enough."

It wasn't Lark. It wasn't her fault. The bitterness that had consumed me at the thought that she, however inadvertently, brought about Mom's death evaporates.

I have to force myself to turn away because the guard is bringing Ash out now. His hands are bound behind his back, his pale, confused face bruised. He's staggering; the guard has to hold him up. Is he drugged? For a second his bleary eyes see nothing. Then he seems to wake up, and in a horrible moment, before I can flash him a warning gesture, before he can figure things out himself, he blurts out, "Rowan? What are you doing here?"

Bikk! The guards flanking Ash look confused. We could probably play it off, say he was drugged, confused, or attempting a ruse, that he's never seen me before. But suspicions once roused are hard to quell, and we only have one chance at this.

We had a plan. Such a good plan. But if there's one thing I've learned in the last few days it's that plans almost always change.

Lachlan lowers his trendy green-tinted specs and looks at me over the rims with his beautiful second-child eyes. "Ready?" he mouths. My hand goes to the pearls at my throat, and I just barely nod.

As if we choreographed the move for weeks instead of talking about it for a scant few hours, Lachlan lunges at Ash's face with the pen he's been twiddling all this time. The guards, probably thinking Lachlan is trying to assassinate their prisoner, reach for the pen . . . but suddenly it isn't a pen anymore.

At the exact same time, my fingers clench around the short strand of pearls and rip them violently away from my throat. I hurl them to the hard floor and they bounce and roll all around the open room that is lined with cells. Some skip into the entranceway, where more guards are waiting. I see uniformed men and women look down at the innocent-looking little pearls . . . until suddenly they're not pearls anymore.

I pull my pen that isn't a pen from my clipboard and press it to my face, where it unrolls itself into a bioadhesive sheet similar to the one in the hazmat suit's mask. It presses itself to my face, sealing in my eyes, nose, and mouth with just a little gap so I can see and don't feel like I'm choking. A chemical reaction will give me air for about ten minutes, which should be enough. Through the slight haze of the protective film I can see that Lachlan has his mask on, too.

Then, with a subtle series of pops, the pearls detonate and release their bursts of toxic gas.

I can feel it on my skin, coldness as sharp as if I'd stepped into a freezer. But the drug itself won't be absorbed through the skin, only through the lungs and eyes. As the guards are beginning to find out.

I remember the smell so well, and I almost wish I could breathe it in one more time. With my new eyes, my new mission, I might never again see that glorious camphor tree that gives the Underground second children hope, happiness . . . and after a little bit of chemical tweaking, an aerosolized plant-based poison capable of taking out a roomful of people.

Nature gives life, and nature gives death. And what are we humans but a part of nature?

It all seems to go perfectly. Lachlan was sure we'd be able to smuggle in the cleverly disguised technology, and he was right. He was certain the camphor-based drug could disable anyone who breathed it in, and he was right. The guards are choking, vomiting, collapsing. Lachlan told me they'll recover, eventually, but looking at how quickly the guards go from health to misery to stillness, I wonder if he just told me that so I wouldn't think about having more deaths on my conscience.

In seconds, every guard in our sight is on the ground. This is our moment. We need to run, now, downstairs and out the front door, just three panicked employees fleeing a terrorist attack. We'll get into the car Lachlan's people will have stolen and left parked outside the Center, so we can get away as quickly as possible. Within an hour, Ash should be in the Underground, safe.

But there was one thing I didn't plan for. Beatings, drugging, stress, terror . . . Ash isn't strong at his best. Now, through the bioadhesive film over his face, I can see the panic in his eyes that heralds one of his attacks. He's starting to wheeze, his breath a muffled whistle behind the mask. He looks at me in apology for one instant . . . and then his knees buckle.

Our plan relied on a quick exit. Now one of us can't run.

Lachlan doesn't hesitate. He strips a jacket from one of the fallen guards and drapes it over Ash, hiding his cuffed hands so that at first glance he looks like a guard, not a prisoner. "Go!" Lachlan shouts, and picks up Ash as if he weighed nothing, slinging him over his shoulders.

We run, out past the fallen guards, to the spiral staircase. The camphor essence makes my exposed skin tingle. Over the railing I can see people on the first floor looking up in alarm.

"Help us!" I shout, my desperate, terrified expression not

an act at all as I gesture wildly behind us. "There's been an attack! They're all dead!"

I barrel down the stairs and toward the front door. There aren't as many people as there would be in the daytime, but there are enough to make a panicked crowd, as most run for the exit and a few head up the stairs toward the chaos.

No one seems to notice me. I must look as alarmed and confused as everyone else. But a few are looking suspiciously at Lachlan as he struggles a little bit behind me with Ash over his shoulder. I see a woman point to him, say something to a nearby man. They look around and the woman beckons urgently to someone I can't see.

Lachlan is slowed by Ash's weight, and only halfway down the stairs. We're far enough apart that anyone seeing us wouldn't think we were together. I want to look at him to call *hurry up!* But I don't dare attract more attention. I keep walking slowly across the wide-open lobby toward the door, moving almost sideways, pretending to look up at the commotion on the second floor like almost everyone else is doing.

Then I see who the woman was beckoning to. A Greenshirt appears, heading toward the couple and at the same time scanning the lobby to see what they're talking about. He has a gun on his belt, but I have no way of knowing if it is the lethal kind.

It doesn't really matter. Killed or stunned, if we're hit, we're done for.

Whatever the people say convinces him. He starts striding across the lobby toward the stairs Lachlan is laboriously trudging down. "Stop right there!" When Lachlan doesn't react, the Greenshirt starts to run straight for the stairs.

I don't know what to do. I take a step toward them, not knowing if I'm going to run to help Lachlan and Ash, or attack the Greenshirt. I hesitate too long. I realize I can't make it to either of them in time. Lachlan is almost at the bottom of the stairs. The Greenshirt is almost on him. His hand goes for his gun.

Then I see the maintenance worker near the pool at the base of the decorative waterfall tumbling from the second to the first floor. She raises her head, meeting my eyes with a quick worried, loving look that somehow reminds me of my mom. My heart seems to dissolve within me, making me weak. I know that look. Mom wore it just before she sacrificed her life for mine.

"No!" I cry out, sure that Lark is going to do something foolishly, fatally, nobly heroic to save us all.

She is. I just underestimate her resourcefulness.

In one swift motion she pulls a heavy wrench from her tool cart and latches it onto a gear in a control panel hidden at the far side of the waterfall. With a grunt of effort, she torques it counterclockwise.

For a sickening second, nothing happens.

Then I hear a rumbling from somewhere over my head. Suddenly the water at the top of the waterfall erupts in a foamy rush, ten times the volume, flooding down in a power-ful arc to the first floor. It sweeps across the lobby in a gushing river, knocking the Greenshirt off his feet and sweeping him ludicrously on his back halfway across the lobby. A dozen other people go down, foundering in the knee-high water. I'm far enough away that the water just splashes my toes.

Lachlan, still on the stairs with Ash, watches in apparent amusement as the Greenshirt floats by. Then he looks at Lark and grins. Her face is hidden by her cap, all but her curling lips. I see her smile back for an instant before she squats down and pretends to be fixing the malfunction instead of acting as a saboteur.

Somehow, that quick interaction between them makes my

heart lighter. We make it to the door before we seem to attract any more notice. Everyone has their hands full with toxic gas and floods. An alarm sounds, but no one seems to know exactly what it is for. I see a guard coming down the stairs. *Bikk!* It's the man who let us in. He's choking, clutching his throat, but still standing. He must have been out of range of the worst of the camphor toxins. He points at us, shouts, but there's too much confusion and no one seems to know what he's saying. He starts to chase us himself, holding tightly to the railing as he staggers down the stairs.

The only thing in our favor now is that the guards on the prison level don't carry weapons. Otherwise he would have shot us already.

Lachlan catches up, but we've lost precious seconds. "Where's the car?" I ask.

It's nowhere to be seen.

And now we have another problem.

"Lachlan, I don't think Ash is breathing!"

I'm not completely sure. It's hard to see at this odd angle, slung over Lachlan's shoulders. But I don't see him breathing, can't see his chest rise and fall. I pull his mask off, my own, too, gasping as we make our way toward the street, searching desperately for the car. Ash's eyes are closed, he's pale. I slap his cheek but there's no response. If he's breathing at all, it is terribly shallow and weak.

"We have to get him to a doctor!" I know Lachlan has connections. He must know a safe place to take Ash. Even Flame might be able to help him. Even . . . "My father can help him!"

"No, we stick to the plan," he gasps. "The Underground."

"But he heeds help! This is all for him."

"They're too close. We have to get underground fast. If we stay on the surface, they'll track the car and catch us."

"If he dies, I won't help you!" I cry, desperate.

Lachlan grinds his teeth but doesn't answer.

We're around the side of the Center now, and there's no one near us. They're all in the front, escaping, milling.

"There it is!" Lachlan shouts, and makes his labored way to the waiting car. I can hear the guard coming after us, but I don't dare spare the extra second to turn around and check how close he is. Lachlan shoves Ash into the car and dives toward the driver's seat. He's expecting me to follow, and flips on the manual override without looking back at me.

He's right. The guard is too close, bearing down on us. If he can't stop the car, he'll call in a description and have all of Eden after us. Ash will never make it to medical help. Not to Lachlan's secret contacts, or Flame, or my father. We need to get Ash away without this guard letting the city know exactly what to look for.

"Are you in?" Lachlan shouts without turning around, gunning the engine.

"Yes!" I call back.

He hears the door slam and jets off.

But I'm not inside.

I'm running at full speed toward the guard. We crash into each other.

He's big, as solid as the trunk of the camphor tree, and any other time I know I would have just bounced off him. But he inhaled at least some of the camphor poison, and he's weak, off-balance. We both go down. For a second he's on top, and he's so heavy I think I don't have a chance. His hands close on my throat, cold from the camphor in the air, and I tuck my chin and push at him in vain. But then he starts coughing so violently that he lets me go, and I manage to shove him off me and get to my feet.

Maybe he'll pass out. Maybe I won't have to hurt one more person.

But the universe isn't that kind. The coughing fit passes. He drags himself weakly to his knees, reaching for me.

"I'm sorry," I whisper, before I kick him in the side of the head. The sound is sickening.

He crumples flat on the ground. I don't know if he's alive or dead. The important thing, I have to tell myself, is that he can't give a description of the car. The little vehicle is long gone. That gives Lachlan a chance to get away. That gives Ash a chance to get medical care.

I've done it. I've saved my brother.

I wonder if Lachlan has even noticed I'm not there yet, or if he's too focused on driving.

I feel strangely free, as if I've done everything that is expected of me and can finally rest. I even feel—and this is something I never expected—almost relieved that Lachlan has driven away, that Lark has by now no doubt found her own stealthy way out, and I'm all alone again. It's normal for me to be alone. The status quo. I always hoped my solitude would end one day, but all this time with people has been draining. Now Lark is gone, and Ash, and Lachlan, and everyone who matters in my life.

I'm alone, and I feel strong.

I'm not alone for long, though. A moment later five or six Greenshirts round the corner, spy me and the fallen guard, and start shooting.

And I, as always, start running.

I hear a rumble, and the world around me seems to shiver. I ignore it. There have been too many strange visions dancing before my eyes lately for me to pay this one any mind at this particular moment. It might be real, it might not. It doesn't matter. Running is the only thing that matters.

27

THERE'S ENOUGH CONFUSION in the Center that I manage to make a quick break and slip into darkness before they can catch me. After that, I make my way quickly toward the outer circles. I don't know how to find the entrance to the Underground, and I'm not sure if I should go there anyway. There's no immediate sign of pursuers, but they'll find me eventually. I can't risk leading them to the hidden second children. I can go to Serpentine, maybe. No, that's been compromised. The soup kitchen? Yes, that's my best bet. If I survive the night I might have a chance of blending in there, and people there have connections to the Underground.

But my hopes of reaching it are slim.

I'll die tonight. Of that, I'm fairly certain. The lull and lack of pursuit at the moment don't deceive me. How many times have I beat the odds racing through Eden? This is the night my luck won't hold. But it's okay, I tell myself. I've saved Ash, so part of me will live on in my brother. And all those second children will live on. Maybe Lachlan won't have me and my lenses anymore, but he's resourceful and dedicated. He'll always find a way to keep the second children alive and safe.

Acceptance of mortality is liberating. I start taking risks.

If I'm doomed, why not save my feet and take an autoloop? I have the eyes for it now. Feeling reckless, I skip down the stairs to a station and let the scanner check my eyes. It blinks, sending me through. Whoever I am now, whoever I'm supposed to be, I must have credits on my account. I'm welcomed.

I smile at the few people riding on the autoloop, looking them boldly in the eye. They seem uncomfortable with my boldness. They never dream that I'm an impostor. I ride all the way to the second outermost circle and exit with a feeling of lightness. Heaviness, worry are for people whose fate is uncertain.

Dawn is coming, lightening the east, and I look around marveling at the beauty that surrounds me. Yes, beauty, though I wouldn't have noticed it in any other state. Last time I was here, fearing for my very life, I saw only squalor and poverty. Now I notice how the rosy new light touches the edges of the buildings, how the quickening breeze stirs up dust in eddies that look like something undersea. Now that I'm resigned to leave it, the world seems lovely. It should make me sad, shouldn't it? Now I'm just glad to have been a part of it. Even a small part, for just a little while.

There's the food pantry, but I see someone who looks suspicious. It's probably just a hungry man waiting for them to serve breakfast, but it could also be a Center official undercover. So I don't even glance at the soup kitchen, but just walk past. He doesn't follow me. Good. Because it's not that I *want* to die or anything. I hope I can get to safety, get back in touch with Lachlan, see my brother again, spend long hours talking to Lark, resume my spying mission. I just hope it in a hopeless kind of way.

I think about doubling back and seeing if I can get into the soup kitchen unobserved after all. It will be full light soon, and I'll lose the advantage the darkness and dim dawn have given me so far. Then I have a better idea. I'll leave Eden entirely. Why not spend the day in the forest of synthetic bean trees? It will be safe and cool. Maybe it will even occur to Lachlan that I'll go there. Maybe he'll come and find me.

I know they're coming before I see or hear them. How? It's like a little switch goes on in my brain. Like I'm seeing the scene from somewhere else, on a datablock screen maybe. Close but far away. I see myself, tiny. I see myself being spotted by a group of Greenshirts turning slowly with their handheld scanners. As if I'm watching from above I see them all focus in my direction and start to move toward me.

It's just a paranoid feeling, I tell myself. How could I see them as if through the eye of a bot or a security camera?

I have to be imagining it . . . but I start to run again anyway. There's the wall of junk, piled high, another wall to keep me in—or out? I recognize the place I managed to crawl through the last time, and I'm on my belly wiggling when the Greenshirts shout.

"She's over here, some place."

"Do you see her?"

"Scanner says a hundred yards or less."

Of course they can scan me now. I have lenses, real lenses that link to the EcoPan. They don't know I'm Rowan, but they must have scanned me at the Center, and now it is a relatively simple matter to have the cameras and bots that all connect to the EcoPan look for me. In becoming a first child, I've lost my anonymity.

"There she is!" one of them calls out just before my legs wiggle all the way into the dense pile of refuse. I move as quickly as I can, but I must take a slightly different route and I'm blocked in. I double back, but they've started to crawl after me.

I hear a hum, and think it must be in my head, another

weird symptom. Are my lenses humming now, as well as giving me visions?

For long moments more I crawl through the twisted junk, the refuse of civilization. I can hear clattering behind me, but I still have hope. They might get lost in the labyrinth of garbage. They might get trapped.

But then, so might I. I've lost all sense of direction. Right now I'm just crawling away from the sounds of pursuit. That seems like the best bet right now.

Then I hear more sounds, rattling from all around me. I'm surrounded? But how?

Finally I see an opening ahead, and I wiggle toward it. If I can get out ahead of them and run . . .

Then the ground begins to shift under me. There's no ignoring it, no denying it. The entire Earth heaves up like it is breathing a huge sigh of exasperation at the humans crawling across it. That first movement is almost gentle.

It is the last gentle thing for a very long time.

With a violent, jarring punch the entire Earth seems to throw me upward against the trash, then throw me down again. Things start to collapse on my head.

From the shouts and agonized wails behind me, I can tell the pursuing Greenshirts aren't so lucky. One cry is abruptly cut off. Someone shouts for someone named Wolf and gets no answer.

Piteously, one calls for his mother.

I get half of my body out of the wall of trash, and then another mighty heave of the Earth lifts me, and everything, up high and brings us crashing down again. I hear a terrible creak above me and drag myself forward, not even daring to look up. There's a deafening crash, and a huge beam shifts and pins my leg.

I scream, my cries of pain joining those of the surviving Greenshirts. At first I'm sure my leg must be broken, even severed, it hurts so much. But as I pull, I realize it's just painfully trapped at the thigh. Not that that's much better. If the Greenshirts don't find me, I'll die a slow death of dehydration . . .

My head is clear of the tangle. The beanstalk forest is just in front of me, the massive tree-like constructs moving gently in the wind.

No, not the wind. Some of the giant bean trees are shifting from the roots up. I watch as the ground buckles, liquifies around a clump of them nearest to me. Then I see in horror what is happening. In slow motion, three of the mechanical behemoths begin to tilt. Slowly, with a grinding, creaking sound, they topple. . . right toward me.

I scream again, begging for help I know will never come, and pull with all my strength, but my leg remains wedged under the beam. With my lips curled back in a primal snarl of fear, and rage against my coming end, I watch the three bean trees gain momentum as they crash toward me. Two of them cross, bouncing and sliding off each other, sending the massive trunks in two different directions. But the third is listing directly toward me.

I want to meet my fate directly, with strength or at the very least with anger, but to my shame I cover my head at the last second. The booming crash deafens me, the sound alone so painful I almost think I've been crushed. Instead the weight miraculously lifts from my leg and I instinctively squirm free of the tangle. Only when I've crawled breathlessly away do I see that the bean tree fell at just the right angle to seesaw the crushing beam off of my leg.

But it isn't over yet. Not by a long shot. Trees are falling all around me. I drag myself to my feet and try to run, but the ground buckles under me, falling away from my feet, and I have to crawl.

The Earth is spitting the artificial trees out, tearing the

fake things from her breast and casting them on the ground. Under the ground there are cables and wires, all useless now in the face of the Earth's own awesome force. Spellbound, on my knees like a supplicant, I watch them fall.

All around me they crash, closer and closer as I desperately try to find my balance on the shifting ground. I try to tuck my feet under me and jump away, but the Earth seems to have turned liquid, as bad as the nanosand in the desert. I flop and flail helplessly, trying to get away as the huge twisted trunk crashes toward me, but I can't maneuver. I curl my body, and throw my arms over my head. I expected to die tonight, but not like this.

I feel the whoosh of air, hear a crash so loud I can't hear anything else for a few minutes, as the tree snags on another tree's vine and lands just a few feet to my side. Another miss! I use the monstrous leaves to pull myself out of the heaving, devouring Earth and on top of the stalk. The shaking has lessened, but the ground around me is like a sea and the trees keep falling. I run, slipping and sliding on the broad gnarled trunks, dodging other beanstalks as they fall.

When the heat of the desert smacks me in the face, I turn behind me, and find a ruin. At least half of the synthetic beanstalks are down. I don't even want to think what this will mean for Eden. The algae spires and the photosynthetic material impregnated in all the buildings make oxygen, too, but is it enough? Without these beanstalks will Eden suffocate?

I see movement on the far side of the massive deadfall of collapsed bean trees. Two of the Greenshirts made it through the wall and are picking their way over the tangle of trunks and vines. I don't know whether to be relieved or disappointed. I think of the man crying out for his mother, and want to run to the survivors, to see if they're okay, if I can help rescue their comrades.

But I don't. Because the world doesn't work like that, and people don't think like that. We're not altruistic. Humans fight and kill and follow orders, and the only way to survive is to be like everyone else, only worse. They don't ask for help, or see if I'm okay. We don't find common ground in the face of this catastrophic earthquake. We just keep fighting, running, hurting, killing.

They open fire at me, and I run into the desert. There's nowhere else to go.

It's as awful as I remember. The heat smacks me like an explosion. Each breath scorches my lungs, but I keep going because the Greenshirts keep shooting. Why do they care about duty at a moment like this, with the ground trembling beneath our feet? Or are they so persistent because they blame me for their comrades' deaths? But they don't have to chase me, shoot at me. It's not *me* making them do it. Don't they realize they could just stop?

But *I* can't. I have to keep running out into this brutal oven while they do their best to kill me for reasons none of us fully understand.

And the nanosand is coming.

Now that I know what to look for I can see it. It shimmers just a little, setting it apart from the matte dun color of the rest of the sand. There's a patch behind me, and one to my left. Maybe another ahead of me, I can't quite tell. They're moving at the pace of a brisk walk, swimming through the sea of sand directly toward me. The quaking has stopped for the moment, and I can move faster than the nanosand pools for now. But there are more now, two coming from the right, and I know however fast I'm traveling now the heat will make me slow down soon. They'll surround me, swallow me down.

My skin is scorched pink, so hot I don't even sweat. I stumble to one knee but scramble up again right away. For a moment I look at the two Greenshirts standing on the edge of the desert. They don't dare follow me. Smart men.

What if I just walk toward them? Will they shoot me the moment I'm in range? Will they talk to me about how ridiculous it is that we three of the few surviving humans on the planet want to kill each other? The nanosand slithers inexorably closer.

Uncertain, I raise my hand to the tiny distant figures standing on the edge of the ruined beanstalk forest. I see one of them start to raise a hand, too. To wave, to beckon me in? Or to shoot at me again?

Before I can decide, the Earth decides for me. I hear a terrible grinding, cracking, exploding sound, and in the most powerful tremor of all the ground rises at least ten feet, throwing me down on my belly. From my new high vantage point I think I see the Earth begin to smile, a fierce grin of jagged, rocky teeth. Another vision from my lenses? No, the Earth really is splitting, opening up in a fissure fifty feet wide. As I watch, it stretches from the desert toward Eden, traveling like an arrow toward the Center. I see a brilliant green flash at the heart of Eden, so bright it burns an afterimage on my retinas.

And then, from one blink to another, the world changes.

As if by magic all the heat is sucked out of the air. The glaring white light dims to pinkish morning sunshine, rosy and comforting. As the ground shivers and grows still again, I see the merciless desert change to a mere strip of sand. It's cool beneath my hands. I look down at my palms, scorched and blistered from touching the sand just a moment ago. A soft wind begins to blow from out beyond the desert, cooling my skin.

I look around me. The shimmering nanosand is gone.

I smell something, sharp and strange and compelling, carried on the fresh breeze. It reminds me a little bit of the camphor tree, wild and peaceful all at once. I turn toward the scent, eager. In this sudden calm, the terror of the earthquake, of my escape and pursuit, are forgotten.

On the far horizon, where before I only saw the shimmer of rising desert heat, I see a smudge of green.

I take a step toward it. Another.

Then I'm running, not away from something for the first time in forever, but toward something. Some spark, some nerve hidden deep within me hopes—no, knows—what it is. But my conscious mind doesn't get that far. I only know I have to get to it.

I hear indistinct shouting behind me. The two surviving Greenshirts are coming after me, moving swiftly now that the sand is solid, the heat gone, the land still, and the air gentle. I don't care. I have to get to the horizon. Something primitive and atavistic in me has taken over.

The very sand beneath my feet changes. It's no longer thick, rolling dunes of desert, but a sprinkling of sand over something else. I kick at the sand as I run. Earth! Black, rich dirt, of the kind no one in Eden has ever seen. Wild dirt. Laughing as I run, I want to roll in it, rub it on my arms, taste it.

But ahead of me the green smudge is resolving itself into something wonderful.

How long do I run? A mile, two miles, over land that until recently was desert. But I see now it was a fake desert, false like so many things in Eden. Where the breeze blows sand away I see the grates of what can only be heaters, now cool and dead. They must have been elevating the temperature, creating a desert environment where none existed.

To keep humans from venturing out into the dead, barren land, I would have guessed once. To keep us safe from the poisons we put into our own world.

That was before I saw the forest.

It makes a mockery of the fake beanstalk woods. When

I first saw them, I thought they were glorious, because I had no grounds for comparison. Even the camphor, huge and lovely and unbelievable as it may be, is sad compared to what I'm looking at right now. The camphor is a tree out of place, trapped as I was trapped my whole life. They've done wonders keeping it alive, thriving even, but how can a tree be a proper tree imprisoned underground?

I'm standing in grass, as high as my knees, shot through with flowers and scratchy seed heads. There's a low buzzing sound, and I think another tremor is starting, but no, it is only a bee flying sleepily from flower to flower.

Beyond the little field of grass the forest springs up abruptly, thick and dark. Birds flit through the boughs. There's a movement to one side. An animal, as tall as I am, slenderly made and elegant, steps carefully on small sharp hooves, testing the air with its black nose. Antlers branch from its brow. It smells me, but doesn't seem to see me. I'm perfectly still, and it can't have ever seen my kind in all its lifetime.

Everything I've read about, seen illustrated in datablocks, animated in vids . . . it exists, right before my eyes. This isn't another vision. It's not a trick.

The trick was keeping it from us.

Has the world been healed all this time? Why didn't they tell us? Do they even know?

I want Lachlan to see this, and Lark. And oh, my mother! What I wouldn't give to have her standing beside me gazing at what we all thought was lost. How many times Ash went to the temple to repent, on behalf of mankind, for the terrible things we did to the planet, the animals, the very dirt itself. How guilty we all felt that we'd destroyed our home, killed almost every living thing but us. I want the people I love to be here with me, knowing they can let that guilt blow away in the tender breeze.

Maybe we hurt the world. Maybe we even killed it.

But it's back to life now.

I sigh, and at the sound the deer tosses its magnificent rack, stares at me a long moment with one prancing hoof raised, then turns and, with a bunching of muscles, springs away. I feel a pang of regret when it is gone. But it doesn't matter. The world is here, and it's not dead!

I smile, and the smile turns into a laugh. Giddy, I turn to look for the Greenshirts. They're still far behind me, but they must see it. I wave, laughing like a maniac. Wait until they're close! Wait until they see! Nothing else will matter to them. Wait until the citizens of Eden see. Rich and poor alike. Politics, poverty, second children—it will fade into nothing once people know that the world has been reborn.

"Look!" I cry joyfully to the Greenshirts. "Can you believe it? Look at it!" I run toward them. I want to embrace them, to dance with them. They are sharing this incredible discovery, enemies no more.

I move lightly over the grass, then the sand, back into the artificial desert. "Come see!" I call to them.

Then the air around me smacks me from all angles with a *whoosh*, and I'm enveloped by killing heat, blinded by white light. I can see the heat rising from the almost-hidden grates. Whatever the earthquake broke, it's been reactivated.

It doesn't matter. The Greenshirts will join me out here. We'll manage to get back somehow, to tell everyone the miraculous news. The Center officials will shut down this burning hot wall-without-walls that has kept us clueless about the outside world for so long. We'll start anew in the world.

In this beautiful green world of birds and deer and trees and rich fertile Earth behind me.

I turn . . . and the forest is gone.

All I see is the shimmering silvery wave of heat rising from the desert sand.

The cry that escapes my lips has no words, only raw, wrenching pain.

Gone.

Was it there?

Yes. Yes! I know it. I saw it, smelled it, felt it beneath my feet. It was real.

It *is* real.

I try to run to the place where it was, but I'm hit by a wall of heat so intense I can't cross it. When I try to put my hand through, my fingertips come back blistered.

The Greenshirts know. They've seen it. We can go back to the Center and . . .

They tackle me from behind, putting their combined weight on me, pressing my face into the burning sand so that I can't breathe, can't see. I try to shout at them, beg them for help, tell them that the wonderful wooded living world we found is more important than punishing a second child. But my words are choked in the sand.

One of them hits me in the back of the head, and a second later everything goes black.

But in that second I realize the truth. The Center knows about this. They've been deliberately keeping everyone in Eden from knowing that the Earth healed itself long ago. Maybe it was never even really destroyed in the first place. Now, for reasons unknown, they are keeping every human left on Earth trapped in a giant cage.

I WAKE IN cool comfort. I'm lying on a bed, dressed in something light and clean. The torturous desert is gone. I open my eyes to gray walls. To a door with a small barred window.

A face looks through the bars. It's a woman, with a cap of dark curling hair and comforting brown eyes. She smiles at me.

"Good. Our friend is awake at last."

"Where am I?" My voice is hoarse, my throat scratchy and dry.

"Someplace safe," she says.

Am I in the Underground? I sniff, but detect no sharp, cool camphor smell.

"The forest," I begin, but she shushes me.

"There's time enough for that later, during your session." Session? "You should eat something first." She opens a slit at the base of the door and slides a tray inside.

"Where am I?" I ask again. When she doesn't answer, I pull myself awkwardly to my feet, only now noticing that my ankles are chained together. My wrists, too.

"You're in the Center prison, Rowan. But only for a little while." Her voice is soft and hypnotically soothing. "We have a place for you. A safe place where you can be made whole again. We know you've had a great many troubles in your life. You've been kept from your proper place as a first child. But now—after a little treatment—you can rejoin society and take your proper place in Eden."

She tilts her head to the side, the bars slashing her face with diagonal shadows. "We're so happy to have you back, Rowan. Don't worry. We'll make you well in no time. Before you know it, your delusions will be gone."

"I don't understand," I say. How long have I been unconscious? My brain feels fuzzy, my eyes blurry with their new lenses.

"We know that you are the firstborn, that your brother took your rightful place. You were lied to all your life. We know you were tortured by members of a dangerous rebel movement, brainwashed into helping them, drugged, convinced of impossible things. You've been raving for days. Things about underground trees, and worse."

"Worse?" I ask.

She laughs softly. "Don't be embarrassed. It's not your fault. They gave you some strange psychotropic drug. You must have inhaled it. We could smell it on your skin for days, no matter how much we scrubbed you. You kept talking about a forest out past the desert. Bees and birds and animals. You described it so clearly. The hallucination was totally real to you. Do you remember? But you're much better now. A few more sessions and the horrible memory of your ill treatment will fade away."

No. It isn't true. The people of the Underground didn't torture me. Well, they did, but it wasn't like that. Was it? My memory feels shaky. Brainwashed? No, Lachlan just talked to me, explained things to me. Drugged? I remember the sharp, sweet smell of the camphor tree. Lachlan said the camphor essence could be turned into poison. Was I drugged?

No! I know what's real, and what isn't. This woman, with her soft, persuasive voice and calming demeanor, is lying.

"The Earth isn't dead," I say firmly, approaching the barred door.

"Now, Rowan, listen to reason . . ."

"The Earth isn't dead!" I shout as loudly as I can. "I've seen it—the forest, the animals! It's just beyond the desert!" I lunge for the bars, grabbing them, rattling them with all my strength. "The desert is fake. It's all lies—lies!" My voice has risen to a shrill pitch I don't even recognize. The words seem to be ripped from my raw throat. "We have to get out of here!" I rave. "We have to go to the forest! It's alive! The world is alive! It's Eden that's dead!"

The woman shakes her head sadly. "I thought you were closer to being healed." She shrugs. "That's okay. We have all the time in the world."

She turns and walks away. Through the bars I can see the prison we rescued Ash from . . . how long ago? Long walls of barred cells.

I put my mouth to the bars. "Do you hear me?" I kick the polished silver food tray aside and pound on the walls until my skin tears and bleeds. "They're lying to you! They're lying to us all!"

But no one answers me. No one at all.

Later—a minute, an hour, I don't know—I fall to my knees, my voice gone. The silver tray is at my side, the food spilled over the bare floor. I bow my head in despair . . . and catch a glimpse of my reflection in the shiny tray. As I bend, the pink quartz necklace slips out of my shirt and dances from its cord.

I pick up the tray and look at my face. At my unfamiliar eyes.

I stare at myself. The eyes are gray and flat, almost the same steely silver of the tray. They're not my eyes. I'm not myself.

But I fight the despondency that washes over me. I won't let them win. I'll escape, I'll tell all of Eden about the forest. Whatever they do to me, whatever these "sessions" entail, I won't let them force me to forget. I'll hold on to the truth, and somehow, someday, share it.

Hold on to yourself, I tell my reflection as I grasp my precious crystal from the Underground. *Even if your eyes aren't your own, you're still Rowan inside, no matter what they do to you. Hold on to the truth—to Lachlan, and Lark, to the Underground and the camphor tree and the forest.*

I make a pact with myself. Every day, I will look at my reflection. I will memorize myself, remember myself, and everything I've learned. The Center can't take that away from me.

I stare at myself now. Aloud, in the barest whisper that's left of my voice, I declare to my reflection, "I see you, Rowan."

And from somewhere else, not quite inside of me, I hear another voice, cold and tinny and mechanical, say, "And I see you, too, Rowan."

ACKNOWLEDGMENTS

THANK YOU TO my readers for always being the best friends I could ever ask for. Thank you, Laura Sullivan, for helping me uncover the world of Eden and making my vision come to life. Thank you, Rakesh Satyal, for challenging me and correcting all of my mistakes. Thank you to everyone at UTA and Addition for always supporting me and helping me achieve my dreams. Thank you, Whitney, for always sparking my imagination. And thank you to my boyfriend, Daniel— I'd be forever lost without your constant love and support. I love you always.

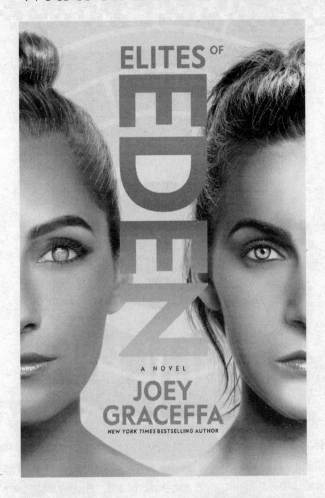